DEFIANT SURRENDER

A Medieval Time Travel Romance

TAMARA GILL

Defiant Surrender
A Medieval Time Travel Romance
Copyright 2013 by Tamara Gill
Cover Art by Wicked Smart Designs

ISBN-13: 978-0-6484133-5-6
ISBN-10: 0-6484133-5-7

DEDICATION

This book is dedicated to all the mudlarks of this world, past and present.

PROLOGUE

England 1078 - Cumberland

Vanessa cuddled her babe close, the little girl's cry torn away by the raging wind. The air bit into her skin to the point of pain. Still, she waited. Would not leave until her lover's warming strength enclosed them both and gave them sanctuary.

She struggled to her feet as a door hidden within the stone walls of the gatehouse opened. A door she'd used often. The person she waited for and longed to see stepped forward. Wrapped in a fur cloak, he looked warm and well fed. His attractive visage with the short beard along his jaw heated her blood and inspired the desire to run her hands against his hard flesh.

"Why did you summon me, Vanessa?"

She started at the harshness of his words and looked into unforgiving eyes that were nothing like she remembered. His voice resonated with loathing and distaste, a tone he had never used before with her. Such severity was normally directed toward his wife or serfs. Never her.

"My lord, I have birthed our daughter. Look." She pulled the shawl away and smiled at the babe as love blossomed within her. "She is yours."

He cast their child a cursory glance before his eyes, vacant of warmth or interest, met hers again.

"What of it?"

"I had thought—" Vanessa's words trailed off. Her lover had become a stranger. She willed him to look at her as he once did, like a man in love who cared for her well-being and happiness. After all the months she had spent in his bed, had acquiesced to his every need it was not possible he could now feel...nothing! Panic tore through her breast when she realized the truth.

Vanessa pulled forth all the dignity she could muster, before lifting her chin as scornful eyes scrutinized her dirty gown and unwashed hair.

"What of it?" he asked again.

The cold penetrated Vanessa's thin shawl, but it was not the elements this night that made her shiver. His lordship's voice, emotionless and hard, chilled her blood and all hope dissipated.

"You had said, my lord—"

"What, woman?" he bellowed. "That I would take care of you?" His Lordship sneered. "Why, that babe is probably not even mine."

Vanessa gasped.

"You are a fool if you think I'll acknowledge your child as my blood. I have a wife, and a legitimate babe on the way to secure my wealth and family line. I've no need for a bastard. Off with you, woman! Do not let your shadow darken my lands again."

Dread crashed over her like a fallen tree. Vanessa's arms tightened with fear and the baby mewed in protest. She eased her hold and stepped forward.

"But, my lord, where will we go? I have nothing. My family are not even from these parts." She grabbed at his arm, stumbling when he wrenched it away. "Anthony," she pleaded, "you must help me!" Tears welled at such harsh treatment. Vanessa shook her head. Her heart refused to acknowledge his callous, cold manner, though her mind reeled. He no longer loved her, nor even cared.

She had been used as a temporary bedmate for a peer of the realm.

His hawk-like features revealed no trace of sympathy as he reached into his pocket, pulling out some coins, and throwing them at her feet. The hem of his fur cloak slapped her leg as he turned and ordered the door bolted. The sound of the lock putting paid to her services.

Vanessa bent down, picked up the minuscule amount of coin and stared, stunned, at the cold stone structure. With the wooden door now firmly shut in her face, there was little choice but to place the meager amount into her pocket. She swallowed threatening tears as the taunting sound of the guard's laughter echoed behind the oak. Distant flickering lights paved her way toward the village and she wrapped the shawl tighter around them both and walked away.

She needed to get back to London. Could only pray her family would welcome her, with a bastard child in tow.

She turned and looked back toward Aimecourt Castle. Anger coursed through her like a burning flame, evaporating any love she once felt for his lordship.

No man treated Vanessa Boulogne in such a way. The Baron of Aimecourt would be the first and last man, she silently vowed, to treat her like a piece of meat to be tossed to the wolves once his own gut was gorged and his hunger quelled.

No, Anthony Vincent would rue the day he had used

her so. Chin high and back steely straight, Vanessa walked into the night shadows and an unknown future, promising revenge.

Aimecourt and its grand baron would pay.

CHAPTER 1

Present Day – London

M addie St. Clair looked up at the ominous clouds that rolled overhead and shivered into her £9.00 Marks and Spencer jacket, a bargain from last year's sales, as she continued her weekly scavenger hunt.

Her breath created steam patterns in the freezing temperatures as her gaze lowered to the sandy soil beneath her feet. It had been a slow day so far. A couple of coins—late twentieth century, unless she counted the numerous beer cans she had found. At that moment, her trusty second-hand metal detector beeped. Maddie started at the high-pitched sound, and, kneeling down, started to dig.

She grasped her small gardening shovel and searched through the soil, her hand protesting the work on such a cold day. No matter how much she hated being out in the freezing elements, she loved this part of her hobby the most. Being a proud member of the Society of Thames Mudlarks, a group of enthusiasts lucky enough to hold a permit to search the banks of the ancient waterway for lost treasures, brought a smile to her face and excitement to her soul.

Today might be slow, but plenty of memorable days kept her coming back for more. Ones with her parents who had dragged their reluctant nine-year-old along with them one day and given her a spade. Maddie hadn't missed a weekend since and her heart pinched knowing her father would have loved being out here with her if he could.

"Maddie, hurry up. You've been at it for hours."

Maddie looked up at her sneezing friend, Jackie, who sported the most ridiculous beanie ever made and chuckled.

"I won't be long now, I promise. Why don't you go wait in the car? I just want to finish this search. I think there's something here," she yelled back over the wind.

"Okay, but not too much longer. I'm frozen."

Maddie returned her attention to the small hole, and gave thanks to a loyal friend, one who braved the English winter just to spend a Sunday afternoon together. Sort of.

"There you are..." A small rectangular box pulled free from the dark, sludge-like mud. Water rose up within the hole and Maddie, using the little puddle, scraped the mud away as carefully as possible. Excitement thrummed in her blood when the small article revealed itself to be pewter.

She stood and placed the treasured item inside her provisions box. Back at the hole, she ran the metal detector over the surrounding area once again. Then, satisfied she had all there was and being too cold to continue anyway, she made her way to the ladder. She climbed the stairs, soon to be submerged in water, and headed toward her clapped-out Nissan and suffering friend.

"So, what did you find today? Anything worth the frostbite I have on my fingers?"

Maddie laughed but turned her attention to the traffic

as she pulled the car out of the parking lot. "I think I did. I found a little case I believe to be pewter. I'll try to open it when we get home and see if anything's inside."

"Do you think it's worth any money?" Jackie asked.

"To me it's priceless. It's old and has some sort of insignia on the lid. When I get home I'll clean it up and take a closer look," she said.

"Are you not going to come out with us then?" Jackie turned toward her, disappointment etched on her face.

Maddie watched the road and tried to think of a way to answer that would let her friend down nicely. There was no way she'd attend tonight's dinner if she could help it. Just the thought of eating food in close proximity with her ex made her stomach turn.

"You promised, Maddie. You can't keep hiding yourself away."

Maddie's attempt at a smile failed. "I'm not hiding. I just don't want to go. I'm cold and all I want to do is snuggle up at my desk and study what I found today." She clasped her frustrated friend's hand and squeezed it. "You'll have fun. All our friends will be there. You don't need me. We'll go out another night."

"It's because of Scott, isn't it? You can't let his presence always deter you. You know he thrives on your absence, thinks it gives him free rein to dish you." Jackie paused. "God, I hate that man."

Maddie nodded knowing full well how nasty Scott could be toward people he no longer liked or cared about. "Well, if he does, I'm sure you'll stand up for me."

"It's been six months. You need to let what happened between you two go. He's not worth it."

She drove on in silence toward Greenwich. The memory of walking into her shop after a day at the Thames and finding her fiancée going at it with her friend,

7

Fiona, on her store counter had nearly undone her. She had stood there, still and unseen for what seemed forever, listening to the grunts and groans of the two people she trusted most. Neither had noticed her, not until she'd dumped her bag on the counter next to their naked bottoms.

Scott had moved out the same night and she hadn't spoken to either of them since. Nor would she. If her friends were true friends, they would take it in turns inviting either she or Scott to different outings. But gradually over the last few months, she most commonly was the one who didn't receive the invite.

Maddie looked at her loyal friend, her only one, really. "I'll try to make an effort soon. I promise." She smiled. "It was bad enough walking in on them, Jackie. I don't want their relationship thrown in my face. And you know Scott will."

Jackie sighed. "I know. I understand. Perhaps we could go out later in the week. We could try The Vanbrugh? I've heard it's really lovely."

"Yeah, that sounds great."

Maddie pulled up beside her store just as darkness fell.

"Well, I'm going up to get ready. I don't need to ask where you're going," Jackie said as she made her way inside.

Maddie smiled and upon entering her home, flicked on the main lights to her shop and checked all was as it should be. The smell of polishing oils permeated the air; cabinets overflowing with antique linens, cutlery, and silverware twinkled in the dim security lights. Her lips quirked and a quiet satisfaction settled over her like a balm knowing this wonderful store was hers. All amassed by sheer hard work and a determination to make something of herself and her life.

She flicked the shop lights off and walked up the short corridor to her workroom, automatically collecting along the way everything she needed for cleaning up her newest find. Her fingers tingled with excitement, impatient to discover what lay beneath the Thames filth.

She turned on her work lamp and inspected her find. Using a special solution, she cleared away the muddy debris to reveal a small intact box that resembled a medieval ring case.

No bigger than her palm, rectangular with a flat lid that sat, when closed, within the main body of the box. A design, Maddie assumed to be a coat of arms or family emblem, was etched on its surface. A single dragon sat proudly on what appeared to be a hill, with a flower she could not make out, beneath its paw. With a fingernail, she tried the clasp and stared in amazement when the lid popped open with ease.

How could a box, perhaps hundreds of years old, buried in water and sludge, open without a hint of trouble? Nerves fluttered in her stomach. It should not.

"What on earth..." she said as the item within was revealed.

"What?"

Maddie screamed and snapped the lid shut, only just managing not to drop the case. "What are you doing, Jackie? You scared the...you scared me."

Jackie laughed and peered over her shoulder. "Can I borrow your black cocktail dress tonight? I can't find mine."

Maddie shook her head and turned her attention back to the case. "Well, if you washed your clothes once in a while you wouldn't have to ask to borrow mine. But yes, you may."

"So, what did you find?"

"The case has something inside." Maddie opened the lid for the second time and felt her jaw drop.

"It's a wedding band," Jackie stated, awe tinging her tone.

"Yeah," Maddie said. "And looking as new as the day it was made." It lay on a bed of crimson velvet, not at all marked by the passing of time. Her fingers itched to examine the small pewter ring, and after some deliberation, she clasped the cold metal and wondered about the person who'd last held it as she did now.

"Didn't you say the ring was old? Why does it look so new?"

Maddie studied the smooth, polished metal. "I have no idea." They both paused, peering at the ring more closely.

"Look Jackie, it has diamonds embedded in the band." Maddie sat back. "Oh, how beautiful."

Jackie clasped her shoulder. "It *is* beautiful. I'm glad you found it and not some other treasure hunter." Her friend swung away and headed for the door. "I'm off to change or I'll be late. Don't spend all night at your desk. And don't forget to eat."

Maddie waved goodbye over her head and continued to study the ring. The craftsmanship was superb for such an old jewel. Twisting the ring between her fingers, she noticed the Old English inscription on the inner band. Maddie sent up a silent thank you to her father, an English teacher who'd tutored her on ancient scripts, both reading and speaking them aloud.

Willelm ○ Madaline. A sigh escaped at the sweet gesture while her finger traced the circle between the two names. They must have loved one another a great deal. But how strangely coincidental that the name inscribed was the same as her own. She shook her head, dismissing the bizarre chance.

MADDIE RUBBED HER THROBBING TEMPLES, HER EYES HEAVY and stinging after staring at the computer screen all night. She checked the setting on the humidity chamber and placed the ring and case inside. The jewel was old, far older than she first thought if the inscription was anything to go by. Buried as it had been for years, she didn't want it to start deteriorating in the open air. Especially as she was required to forward it on to the Museum of London after her own research was complete. It wouldn't do at all for her to ruin the ring due to a lapse in concentration or care.

Some hours later, she was downstairs again, in front of the glass cabinet, warm milk in hand, and staring at the blasted ring. Maddie shook her head. Why was she so tempted to hold it? It wasn't like the ring was the most extravagant ring she'd ever found, or the most valuable. But, like Frodo in Lord of the Rings, it pulled at her.

Maddie sighed and finished her drink, then collected the scattered dishes from the previous day littering her wooden counter space. She loaded them into her second-hand dishwasher and headed back to bed.

Sleep didn't happen. Instead, she watched the tree outside cast moving shadows across her bedroom walls.

"This is impossible." She couldn't remember the last time she had been so obsessed with anything. Maybe the excitement of the day was getting to her. The knowledge that, come tomorrow she would be able to search out her treasure's origins and perhaps put a year to its creation. She shut her eyes and willed herself to sleep.

"Damn it!" She thumped her bed and threw back her quilts. Her inability to leave the ring alone was ridiculous.

Moments later she stood staring into the glass humidifying cabinet in her workroom. Maddie flicked the latch and with trembling fingers picked up the small jewel.

What was it about this ring that drew her so? As a historian, she believed items of historical value were for all to look upon and wonder about. Jewels like this ring should never be worn, but admired from afar. Keepsakes of the past, they deserved protection and love from a distance, preferably behind museum glass.

So, what was wrong with her? Why was she about to defy all of her strict rules?

"This is sacrilege," she muttered, placing the band at the tip of her finger. It slid on, a perfect fit. Her heart sped up as if recognising an absent friend, long forgotten and thought lost.

"Yah...Yah..." Maddie jumped, hearing a yell, a distinct male voice that seemed to come from nowhere. She froze as the room started to disintegrate and melt around her. An image started to form, one her mind couldn't seem to comprehend because it didn't resemble her workroom at all. She swallowed and tried to calm the panic taking flight inside her mind.

"This isn't good," she said, before she landed with a thump, on coarse wooden planks.

CHAPTER 2

"Oh, m'lady!"

Maddie's heart thundered with lingering panic. At the question from an unfamiliar voice, she looked up and blinked. Where the hell was she? She sat up and swayed as a bout of dizziness took over. Strong feminine hands clasped her shoulders, lifting her to sit on soft cushions that did nothing to stop the jarring of the vehicle. Maddie rubbed her head, looked around, and baulked.

It was a carriage of some sort, with neither glass windows nor suspension if her bottom knew anything about such things. Her eyes widened with shock as she took in her surroundings. The woman who'd helped her was dressed in what...some sort of woollen gown with a cloak?

Maddie took a reluctant peek at her own clothes and grasped her chest in horror. Gone were her comfortable cotton pyjamas sporting red hearts. Instead, an outfit from a long ago past met her eyes: a chemise of some sort overlaid with a beautifully woven woollen gown.

The sort of clothes one saw in museums and costume books.

She swallowed the panic rising in her throat, and strove for calm. The dress, of light blue wool, was overlaid with a cloak, similar to the stranger's, but a darker shade.

This couldn't possibly be happening. She could not be sitting in a carriage, clothed in medieval fashion. Her temples started to ache, reaching up she rubbed beside her eyes only to find a veil either side of her face and a metal crown holding it in place.

Maddie jerked her hand away, unwilling to venture further, scared as to what else she would find.

"I'm dreadfully sorry," Maddie said, taking a deep calming breath. "But can you tell me who you are and where I am?" Not that she wanted to hear the answer, knowing somehow it wouldn't be to her liking.

The woman paled and Maddie instinctively reached out a hand to console her, not sure why such a question would cause alarm.

"Hwæt lá!"

Maddie jerked as the words, spoken in Old English, hit her.

"M'lady, are you...well? I know you hit your head when you toppled from your seat but I did not think the knock was as severe as this. Do you not remember me or what you are doing today?"

She struggled to fit the antique words to their modern equivalents. She frowned and looked out the window, only to find her worst nightmare was true. Determined to contradict the horror, she poked her head further out the window, only to glimpse four cantering horses dragging the uncomfortable carriage along a muddy track. A clod of mud flew up from under racing hooves and struck her cheek. Maddie gasped, and pulled back inside the rickety carriage and wiped the dirty piece of god-knows-what from her face with shaking fingers.

"Please don't tell me there are horses attached to this vehicle. If you do I...I think I'm going to pass out." Her breath notched and held, on the verge of hyperventilating. She spoke in modern English, too alarmed to try to pull the correct ancient vocabulary to mind. "What if they bolt or overturn us? Please have them stopped so I can get out."

"Lady Madeline, no such thing will occur. You have travelled such ways numerous times. Please, try to calm yourself." The woman's brow puckered in distress. "My concern is more for your lack of memory. Do you not recall your plans for today or what you have done over days past?" the woman asked in a solicitous voice.

With white knuckles, Maddie held the seat with both hands. She hated horses. They were large, big hoofed beasts that couldn't be trusted. When she turned twelve, her parents had thought to give her riding lessons. Something all city girls surely wanted to do they'd said, but not this one—ever! Not only was she bucked off on her first lesson, but then the monster-like animal had tried to run her down. Maddie had refused to return, and had never been near a horse since. And now, after all the years of careful avoidance, she'd landed in a blooming carriage at the mercy of not just one, but four. It was enough to make her cry. And she never cried.

"What?" Maddie asked in the same language the lady used, if a little hesitantly.

"Do you recall, Your Ladyship, what you have done over the last week or what your plans are for today?"

Her Ladyship? Why was the woman calling her Her Ladyship? And how could she answer such a question without sounding ridiculous? She supposed she could describe how she opened her store every day, gossiped and chatted with the butcher across the street and looked for historical artifacts in the Thames, all in the twenty-first century... She rubbed her throbbing temple. This was all so wrong. How was she in a damn carriage when she should be home in bed! She was obviously going crazy, cuckoo from working around and breathing in turpentine and methylated spirits all day.

Maddie took a calming breath and looked down at her hand. The ring she had put on only minutes ago was gone. She frowned, at a loss as to where it would be. Could it have fallen off?

She leant forward to look on the floor and suffered an instant bout of vertigo. Not all the floorboards meshed and the road beneath the carriage zoomed past. Maddie swallowed the nausea that rose in her throat, sitting back she closed her eyes and willed herself anywhere but here. Wherever here was. A strangled moan escaped her tightly closed lips.

"Can you tell me what it is I'm supposed to be doing today, Mrs....?" Maddie asked, not sure how to address the middle-aged woman who sported a look of horror on her weathered face?

"Lady Madeline, you are to marry today. We are headed to the church anon," she said, her hands clenching and unclenching in her lap. "What should we do, m'lady, for I believe you have lost your memory? I will strangle that cursed driver when I get my hands on him. I told him to be wary of the roads for there are many ruts and stones." The woman paused, and her bosom heaved taking a much needed breath. "M'lady, will you continue with the wedding as planned? Or shall I notify our driver to return us home to Aimecourt?"

Maddie's heart stopped at the word wedding. Was this some sort of sick joke or ridiculous dream? If so, neither one was amusing. She pinched herself trying to wake up, then absently rubbed the painful welt on her arm. What was she to do?

"What did you say your name was? I missed it with all this noise." Not to mention the screaming panic in my head.

The woman gasped, her eyes flaring with a mixture of fear and puzzlement. "I am Mistress May Rhode," she replied, hesitantly. "I have been in your family's service since your birth, m'lady. I am your personal maid and companion."

"And I am...?" Maddie asked.

"Oh, my dear!" Mistress Rhode cried, her voice wavering in panic. "You are the Lady Madeline Vincent, daughter of the deceased Baron of Aimecourt."

Maddie started at the little tidbit. A baron's daughter.

"And I live...?" she pressed, not happy with any of the answers so far.

"At Aimecourt Castle, of course, in Cumberland."

Cumberland? Could the maid mean Cumbria? If so, at least it meant she was still in the UK, despite Mistress Rhode's slight foreign accent.

"I'm sorry to be a nuisance, but who is it I'm supposed to marry today, Mistress Rhode?"

"Lord William Dowell, Baron of Kingston. His property abuts your own, Your Ladyship. Your parents arranged the marriage many years ago. I should imagine they thought to strengthen their forces in such hard and trying times."

Maddie tore her attention from the land outside and met Mistress Rhode's gaze. "What do you mean by that? Is the country at war or on the brink of one? Am I in danger?"

"Nay, child, and you're quite safe. But as you well

know, life is hard in these unforgiving times." Mistress Rhode looked away, a frown upon her brow.

"What is the date today?" Maddie waited anxiously to hear the answer, and at the sound of the woman's uneasy laugh, trepidation settled in her stomach like a rock.

"Why, it's the twenty-first day of September, my dear."

Relief made her shoulders sag. The day at least was the same, as she knew it. But what year did the woman think it was? From looking at their gowns, Maddie was certain the era was before indoor plumbing and central heating.

"And the year, Mistress Rhode?" she pressed.

"It's the year of our Lord, eleven-hundred and two, m'lady."

"What!" 1102! Was the woman mad? Maddie shook her head denying such a thing was possible. "Who is the current monarch of England?"

"Good King Henry, m'lady."

"No," she muttered. "That cannot be right." Obviously, she was having a very bad dream, and any moment now she would wake up. Come on Maddie, she chanted...bloody well wake up. Now!

She didn't. "I can't be here," she whispered, squeezing her eyes closed in denial.

"M'lady, are you saying you do not wish to proceed with the marriage?"

Maddie met the woman's confused if not slightly scared eyes and nodded. "That's exactly what I'm saying. I'm from the year 2011, I can't be in 1102, it's not possible."

"You are not from the year 2011, m'lady," the maid said, impatience tinging her tone. "You were born in 1078 at Aimecourt Castle."

Maddie's mind froze and struggled to think. What was she to do?

"What is your decision, m'lady? Shall you continue with the marriage as arranged?"

Today could not be her wedding day. Maddie laughed, the sound far from humorous. This was absurd.

"We shall go to the church, but only to cancel the marriage. I don't wish to be rude to the man waiting there, but I'll not be joined with him today or any day." And obviously, she would wake up very soon, not a little bit relieved and able to laugh about this ridiculously detailed nightmare she was currently living.

"I'm sure you will regain your memory anon, m'lady. 'Twas after all, a small rut, and not much damage done, I'm certain." The woman fiddled with her rosary. "'Tis right you should speak to the Baron of Kingston of your decision. I would hate to keep his lordship waiting."

Maddie flicked a glance at the woman. "What do you know of this man, Mistress Rhode? Have we met before? Are we acquainted? Are we friends?" Maddie's heart dropped as her supposed maid cringed before hastily masking her features. She tamped down the panic demanding to burst free. Had she been about to marry a raving medieval lunatic and the maid was playing coy? Please, please, please don't be the case. For if he were mad, her coming meeting with him could prove difficult.

"Some say he is a respectable, strong man of many riches. You, m'lady, have never met him. Your parents and his were...acquaintances, close land holders for many a year."

Some say, what did the rest say? And why did her maid pause over her answer?

"This Baron of Kingston guy, how old is he?"

"I believe his lordship is nine and twenty."

Both Maddie's neatly plucked brows shot up. So her dreamed up betrothed was only five years older than herself. Did that make her an old maid in this time? Twenty-four was a fair age, she would assume in medieval England. She shifted in her seat; the woollen dress she'd acquired somewhere between here and reality prickling against skin used to cotton and fabric softener.

"Ah, here we are, m'lady. We have arrived."

Pulled from her thoughts, Maddie looked out the carriage window and gazed upon what would seem to be a church.

"Isn't there a town that goes with this church?" she asked.

Mistress Rhode cast her a puzzled frown. "No m'lady, this is the Baron of Kingston's chapel. He wished it to be built here. It acts as an outpost, I believe, a lookout if you will, against any impending attacks."

"What, do you mean attacks? Like war parties?" Fear crept up Maddie's spine as the woman spoke with conviction.

"Yes, m'lady. Now, come along."

The church, built of stone and rectangular in design, looked plain and oddly unused. The roof with a mix of wood and thatch looked badly in need of replacement. Maddie stepped out of the carriage and instantly cool sludge surrounded her slippered foot, her embroidered gown lying on top of the muddy puddle.

She rolled her eyes. Great, what else could this dream throw at her?

Inside the church, Maddie was surprised to find it vacant of guests. Was she so sad, she couldn't even dream up a few relatives to invite? A man dressed in a brown, rough-sewn cloak, bowed and greeted her by her title. Was this her fiancé? He seemed a lot older than twenty-nine.

"I'm sorry, sir, but there will be no ceremony today,"

Maddie said, looking to her maid who stood in the doorway wringing her hands.

"Bring her forward."

Maddie spun about at the deep commanding voice and looked toward the altar. Ah, so this was her fiancé. "My lord, let me apologize for the confusion, but you must understand I cannot marry you."

"Bring her forward."

Maddie frowned at the hardened tone, then gasped as the man who greeted her clasped her arm in a punishing brace. "No! I will not marry him," she yelled, struggling against her captors hold. Oh my gosh, they are going to make me marry this man!

Maddie yelled for Mistress Rhode, and, looking over her shoulder noted a knight pinning her maid's arms behind her back and pressing a blade to her chest. Maddie dug in her heels and fought against the cloaked man dragging her toward her groom. She screamed for her conscience to wake up and get her out of here, it had always worked before.

Not today.

Her mud-soaked slippers scraped against the wooden floor as her captor thumped down the exposed wood, her weight no impediment to him. The nauseating smell of burnt incense instead of the nice vanilla candles she was used to back home made her queasy stomach roll.

Maddie took a deep breath, refusing to panic. Not yet, at least. But the continued lack of tenderness in her supposed groom's hard-featured face didn't sit easy in her mind. If this *were* her imagination, surely her dreamed up fiancé would gaze down the aisle, filled with pride, love and if she was really lucky, perhaps a hint of lust.

She craned another look over her shoulder, seeking out

someone who might help. She whimpered when the grip on her arm tightened, hauling her more roughly forward.

As they approached the Baron of Kingston, her captor shoved her and she fell, her hands stinging when they hit the rough wooden boards. The baron wore weird leather shoes and a hose that seemed to be held up with ribbon crisscrossing up his legs. Lying at his feet, the man seemed powerful and very, very tall. Annoyance jabbed at her conscience at her fiancé's ability to refuse to acknowledge her. Or help her to get up.

Nerves soon replaced her annoyance. This all seemed so real and lifelike. Doubt that it was all a dream started to form and take hold. Maddie stood and squared her shoulders, refusing to cower before this man, a dreamed up figment of her imagination. He couldn't hurt her. Only her mind could, if she let it.

"I'm not going to marry you." A blade appeared in his large hand, his fingers idly twisting the knife. Sunlight filtering through the church window flickered off the weapon. Maddie swallowed and stilled. Her eyes focused on the silent threat. Jaw clamped, she waited, trying to ignore her maid's echoing whimpers, which did nothing to quieten the fear clawing her stomach.

"You will, my lady, as it pleases our sovereign you do so. So, unless you wish to end up dead, say your vows and let us be done with it."

Maddie bit back what she thought he and his sovereign could do with the decree and turned beseechingly toward the watching priest. The elderly man wiped sweat from his brow and started the ceremony.

Maddie's eyes widened at the priest's lack of help. Surely a man of the cloth would aid a defenceless woman. With no help from the Almighty's servant, she turned on her heel and walked away. Not two steps down the aisle and her arm was wrenched behind her back. Fear unlike any she had ever known denied air into her lungs when cold, whispering words sounded beside her ear. "'Twould be wise you turn about, my lady, and marry me. Unless the prick of my blade is what you wish to feel."

Her gaze flicked to her whimpering maid and the fight to argue left her. She had no desire to die. And if this did turn out to be a dream, come tomorrow morning a good strong coffee would set any residual nerves to rest over the nightmare.

"M'lady, do as he says. I beg you."

At the elderly woman's plea, Maddie nodded. "Release me, you medieval oaf, and I'll marry you. But if you stick that bloody knife anywhere near me again, I'll stick you with mine." Not that she had one, but he didn't need to know that.

"So we have an agreement, Lady Madeline?"

She glared. "Yes." For the moment.

Maddie studied her groom as much as possible without being obvious. Senses she hadn't experienced for an age ran along her skin and came alive. He had sinfully long eyelashes that shielded eyes the color of chocolate. Light-brown locks sat loose on well-proportioned shoulders. Maddie looked down to the wooden floor, not at all happy with her turn of mind. The last person she would consider attractive was the ogre beside her.

And yet she couldn't deny his envelope of flesh was appealing.

Unable to stop herself, she peeked up at him again. Heat washed across her cheeks when his cold stare met hers. Instinctively she knew she was in trouble. His eyes narrowed, distaste and annoyance crossed his features, before he blinked and was once again looking at the priest, all emotion now wiped from his face.

She had to get away, and if sensing her imminent bolt, a large, warm hand clasped strong around her wrist. He squeezed, hurting her, silently communicating for her to keep quiet, before placing both their hands onto the Bible. Maddie looked up at the priest in disbelief, shocked and fearing for her future, however long it was to be with this man. What was his problem? And what was hers? How could she dream up fiancés who hated her?

The service ended as quickly as it began. Within minutes, she found herself escorted, or perhaps a better word was dragged, outside toward her carriage. His hand around her arm held firm, his fingers a mere squeeze away from painful. Maddie yanked free from his grasp, absently rubbing bruised flesh as she scanned her surroundings. She stopped as the sight of endless fields, free from housing or motorways met her view. She inwardly smiled, unaware she had it in her to imagine such picturesque countryside.

"You will travel back to my holdings immediately, my lady, within your own carriage. I will join you there at my convenience."

Maddie turned her attention back to her husband. His deep, commanding voice sent tingles to dance over her skin and she didn't dare argue with him. Even the way he looked at her wasn't pleasant. And if she wasn't mistaken, the situation he now found himself in was not to his liking. Well, at least they agreed on that score.

Lost in her musings, she watched him move to open the carriage door. In the afternoon light, away from the dimness of the church, he seemed larger than she first thought. Tight, fitted hose outlined the strong, lean-muscled legs. A blue tunic covered his broad chest; a mantle tied by a cord held the outer garment to his body.

He towered over her, strong, domineering, not to mention very good-looking. And, perhaps worst of all, he was now her husband. By the laws of this time, he had control over her. Absolutely.

She swallowed, a peculiar nervous feeling settling in her stomach. It would all be okay. By tomorrow she'd wake and all this would be a dream. Better to play along with his orders than make trouble she didn't want to face.

"Is there a reason your vehicle can't also carry your new bride, my lord?" Maddie stepped back and into her maid when his cold look answered her question. This was her dream. Her dream, in which men were supposed to do what she decided, not think for themselves. Why was he staring at her? She raised her brows, not knowing where to look, uncomfortable under his harsh, penetrating inspection.

"I do not choose to spend time with you, Lady Madeline. Sharing a carriage with you is beyond my tolerance. 'Tis necessary to be clear. As a man of honesty, I must disoblige you of any notion this will be a marriage of the truest kind. Not only will we not share the marriage bed very often, we will live in separate quarters. Our marriage might strengthen this area of the kingdom, enabling us to be powerful allies against attacks from the north or the coast, but that is where our common bond ends."

Maddie beat down the urge to argue. Caution warned her that this man would not take kindly to a twenty-first century set down. Jaw clenched, she stepped up into her carriage, refusing the hand he offered.

How dare he try to be civil after what he just said? She flicked a glance to her maid, whose eyes were as round as saucers, having heard every word. Oddly embarrassed by his treatment, Maddie looked away. She hadn't done anything wrong after all, other than dream him up. What was his problem?

The carriage lurched forward, and he thankfully disappeared from view. She didn't need to look to know his face still held the same scowl of a minute before.

Bastard!

CHAPTER 3

"The Baron of Kingston lives in a castle!" Maddie shut her mouth with a snap. "Who are you people?"

Her maid looked up from her needlework and frowned. "Where else should the baron live, m'lady? Of course, Aimecourt is much grander than the half-completed Kingston Castle, but 'tis here we will be for a time. You will grow accustomed to your new role as his wife."

Set on a small rise, the castle was surrounded by a moat, the waters calm and slow-flowing. Wood and stone made up the outer defensive walls. People, or serfs, Maddie supposed, were working to remove what must be the original wooden fort, replacing it with stone.

The inner defensive structure was already complete. It stood high and dominant behind this new partition, giving the castle a strong defensive position against attack. They entered through a gatehouse, the horses' steps hollow as they trotted over the wooden drawbridge. Soldiers with hard, non-welcoming faces stood watching the cavalcade of horses and carts pull up within the inner bailey.

Maddie took in what was to be her home with a

mixture of fear and excitement. Had she somehow cheated time and landed in 1102? The thought of seeing a working medieval community was at least one positive. With a little difficulty she opened the carriage door and stepped down. People bustled about, carrying out their chores within the small village. Children's laughter rang out as they splashed each other from the communal well. The smell of baking bread had her stomach grumbling. She turned and looked at the keep. Rectangular in shape, several stories high, and with square towers on each corner, it looked cold and foreboding. Suited the baron's temperament perfectly.

Her maid bustled around, giving orders about their belongings.

Maddie wondered what these people would think of their baron's new wife. Her husband had all but shouted his lack of esteem for the Lady Madeline. Would they follow his lead? Surprisingly most didn't even bother to look at her or acknowledge the new visitors within their home. A shiver of unease rippled through her and Maddie wondered what sort of man she'd married. What sort of life were she about to begin—if all this was in fact true and not a dream.

"M'lady, this way."

Maddie took a step and tripped on her gown. With an oath, she clasped the bulky material and walked toward her maid.

"Mistress Rhode, the baron is a tyrant isn't he?"

"Shush, m'lady. You should not say such things?"

"Well, he pulled a knife on me when I refused to marry him. And no one here seems overly friendly, beside the children that run free." Maddie paused at the doorway of the keep, then entered. The dark grey stone enclosed her. Cold moisture seemed to seep from the walls, chilling her already freezing skin. "By the way, do any of those children own shoes?"

"I do not know, m'lady. Do you wish me to find out?"

Maddie nodded.

"This way to the Great Hall, m'lady. Tomorrow I will show you around your new home. 'Tis growing too late to do so today, and you will need your rest."

A crunch underfoot had Maddie looking down only to gaze in amazement at the neatly laid rushes beneath her slippers. The scents of lavender and rosemary floated up with every step and then they entered the hall.

Armour lined the walls of the massive room, and hanging tapestries imbued the room with a sense of warmth. Trestle tables clean and bare, sat before a dais that ran the length of the far wall, with a large well-stoked fire behind it.

However, it was the white flag hanging above the hearth that caught her eye. Maddie clasped a table for support on seeing the design sewn upon it: an emerald dragon sitting atop a green hill, a flower that resembled the yarrow, held beneath its paw.

"Mistress Rhode, what is that?" Maddie asked, gesturing toward the flag.

Mistress Rhode looked up to where Maddie pointed. "That, m'lady, is the Kingston coat of arms."

Maddie clasped her finger, feeling for a ring that was no longer there. Was it possible the ring belonged to her new husband? His name was William and the coat of arms matched the one on the ring case. She shook her head. Not possible. Whoever owned the ring had loved his wife. And this William did not love this Madeline, which was well and truly proven by his treatment of her. Had the ring somehow thrown her into another's life?

Which left her wondering what she looked like. Her

hands lifted to her face. Familiar lines, eyebrows and nose met her fingers and she relaxed a little.

"Are you pained, m'lady? You look troubled. Is there aught I can do for you?"

Maddie looked over to Mistress Rhode and smiled. "I would like a mirror please."

"Mirror?" her maid asked, looking at her as if she'd sprouted two heads.

What did they call them in this time? "A looking glass perhaps, all I want to do is look at myself somehow," she answered.

"Follow me, m'lady. I'm sure your room has all you ask for." Mistress Rhode clucked her tongue, Maddie assumed, at her strange behaviour.

But unless her room held a magic porthole that could take her home, wake her up somehow miraculously removed from this time, it seemed unlikely.

They followed a Kingston maid, and Maddie proceeded up a steep spiralling staircase, running her hand along the wall to help keep her balance. Two floors passed by as they climbed higher into the keep, before the maid veered onto a landing of clean stone flooring bare of rushes.

Through narrow glassless windows, the last of the day's rays knifed into the corridor, and torches, already alight, burned in the poorly ventilated space. Maddie blinked several times as the smoke started to sting. The local maid curtsied and gestured to a bedchamber. Thanking the girl, Maddie watched in amazement when she scuttled off as if the devil himself was after her.

Maddie stepped into her room that was rectangular, large and oddly welcoming. A mammoth bed made from chunky dark wood sat against a wall opposite the fire. The air was surprisingly warm, despite lack of carpets or central heating. She looked around searching for any modern convenience. Surely, in a dream one would think to include a flushing toilet and running hot water. She ran a finger over an earthenware jug and bowl—apparently not. She sighed as she looked out a glassless window over the land that stretched beyond, looking awfully barren of roads or farm houses.

Dusk was upon them and she welcomed the night. Surely upon waking tomorrow all of this would be a bad memory. It had to be, she mentally screamed. Nothing else was an option, period!

"M'lady, all looks in order here. I shall return with your supper. It has been a long day. With some rest, I'm sure you will be put to rights."

Maddie turned to her maid. "Thank you, Mistress Rhode, for all your help. I'm sorry to have been such a nuisance today."

The woman frowned, "I do not..."

Maddie waved her away. "Don't worry about it, Mistress Rhode. I'm sure a meal and sleep will fix me up as good as new, just as you said."

"Well, then, m'lady, I shall return anon."

"Oh, by the way, where is the mirror?"

Her maid turned, and gestured toward a corner, "On the trunk, m'lady."

Maddie walked over to the large wooden chest and stared at a bowl of water. "There's no mirror here."

Her maid suppressed a chuckle. "It's a special water bowl, m'lady. If you look into it you will see your reflection."

"I have to look into water to see myself?"

"Yes, m'lady."

As if doing such a thing was normal and commonplace, Maddie looked down at the bowl as her maid shut the door behind her.

This was ridiculous! But there was her face, plain as day—and it was her face, just as it had looked in her own time.

৩৩৩

MADDIE SETTLED DOWN FOR THE NIGHT AFTER A surprisingly tasty meal of beef stew and vegetables, accompanied by cheese and bread. If she ignored the vile tasting wine she could not possibly finish, dinner was nice. Lying on her bed, she watched the tapestry sway from the draught the window allowed in. Her cheek lay upon the soft woollen underlay, and she absently rubbed her face against it as she listened to the noises coming from the great hall below. The sound carried up the outer wall as clear as day.

Rowdy masculine laughter and feminine giggles met her ears. The sounds of shifting furniture and then goodwill banter followed, as music from the baron's minstrels began.

However, as the noise increased she couldn't help wondering what they were doing down there. Having a party? A wedding reception without the bride? Maddie rolled onto her back and stared up at the ceiling and counted the boards along the roof. Did they never sleep, these people? And by God, could the women sound any needier or more annoying? Moreover, was her husband sampling those ridiculous females, whose voices grated on her nerves?

A female laugh and the muffled chuckle of a man caught her attention, as they stepped past her door and Maddie sat up. Who were they? She clutched the sheet high against her chest and listened. No one had introduced her to anyone when she arrived. In fact, her absent husband hadn't even thought to have her introduced to the servants. Weren't husbands of this era supposed to do that, so the wife could start to carry out their duties? Mistress Rhode never mentioned any sisters of the baron, or brothers, for that matter, who may be married and housing a wife in this castle. So who was it out there?

The feminine laugh came again followed by a deep throaty voice, one Maddie intuitively knew. She didn't stop to think before the decision to find out for sure overtook common sense. Anger coursed through her. How dare William sound so...so...? She didn't know what. But whatever it was, it was definitely the opposite of what he felt when around his wife.

Maddie pushed the blankets away and sprang from the bed, sucking in a breath when her bare feet met the cold stone floor. She crept to the door and inched it open to peek out into the corridor. Her eyes widened as she watched the Baron of Kingston, aka her husband, hold a blonde goddess up against the wall, his hands somewhere under her dress.

The woman moaned then ripped open her gown, exposing breast and stomach to her husband's heated gaze. Maddie's face burned in mortification. Holy shit, what type of man had she married? Only four hours wed and he was already cheating on her? A record, even for her.

Maddie silently shut the door and crossed back to her bed, shaking her head in wonder and a little disappointment. She obviously had one warped mind to dream up this type of situation for herself. Hopefully in the morning, she would wake up, cozy under her goose-down quilt and on her Sealy mattress.

"Oh, for crying out loud," she yelled, when the feminine throaty moan from the hall increased. "Get a room for God's sake." Maddie sighed in thanks as a door shut further down the hall, taking the horrendous sound with it. Rolling over she willed herself to fall asleep, out of this nightmare and away from him. Please, God, she prayed, before I'm tempted to kick him in the balls, like I did the last bastard who cheated on me.

UPON AWAKENING, ONE THING BECAME CLEAR. SHE WAS STILL in the twelfth century. Maddie absently stroked the fur blankets keeping her warm, before throwing them off in disgust. How was it possible that she hadn't woken up, back at home, above her little shop and busy street? Her heart jumped into her throat when a knock sounded on her door, only to relax when Mistress Rhode entered with steaming water.

"Ah, m'lady, you are awake. Naught was amiss through the night I trust?"

"No," she sighed, the sound a gloomy whinge; such dejection tended to happen, especially when one's heart was set on awakening in the twenty-first century, not the twelfth.

"Are you well, m'lady?"

Maddie smiled at her maid's genuine concern. "What nationality are you, Mistress Rhode?" she asked jumping out of bed.

"Naught would please me more to answer your query, m'lady. Nationality you say. Pray explain what such a word means."

Maddie washed her hands in the warm scented water and not able to find a hairbrush, started to comb her hair with her hand. "Race, population, people that sort of thing. My family, for instance, are French. But what is yours?"

"I am of Welsh blood, m'lady."

"Are there any wise women among your people, Mistress Rhode, any healers?" Maddie's hands tightened around the linen square she was clasping and hoped for good news.

"Yes, m'lady, my mother in fact. But we do not call her such names as 'wise woman,' lest it be misconstrued. She is but a common healer."

Maddie walked over to the bed and sat on the edge. What she'd been hoping for was to find someone who could help her get home; who may have some idea how all this happened. Wise women tended to be cluey with that sort of thing, magic, curses, spells—time travel. She shuddered.

"Lady Madeline, you still seem ailed. If there is aught I can do to ease your distress, you have only to ask."

Maddie looked over to her worried maid, and thought it better, for now, not to reveal more facts of her true life. A life a long way away from here. Instead, she turned her mind to finding out about the mystery woman who had graced the halls last night.

"Does the baron have a mistress under this roof?" The blood drained from her maid's face before it bloomed red enough to rival a darkest ruby. Maddie clamped her mouth shut, and waited for a reply.

"I believe his lordship houses his distant relative, the Lady Veronica de Walter, under this roof. I do not know the nature of their association, m'lady."

She didn't believe that answer for a second. After what she'd witnessed last night, Maddie hoped they were very distant relatives. She sighed but decided not to push the matter. There were other, more important, things to find out anyway.

"So, you said yesterday, I'm the late Baron of Aimecourt's daughter. Do I have any living relations, siblings that sort of thing?" Did she hope for any? A single child in the twenty-first century, would discovering a family in this time lessen the shock and horror of being stuck in medieval England? No. Not a chance in hell.

Mistress Rhode fluttered about, in an almost nervous fashion. "I cannot believe you do not remember still, m'lady. To answer your questions, you are in fact an only child, my dear. You currently hold all properties your father acquired during his lifetime in trust for any future children you may have." Mistress Rhode finished making the bed before moving over to a wooden chest from which she pulled clean clothing. "You do have an aunt who lives in London. Your father was not fond of her."

Mistress Rhode paused. "What I'm about to declare is far from proper, but I believe you must know, since you knew these facts before hitting your head yesterday. The lands and monies you inherited upon the death of your parents were not part of the dowry paid. A sum I am not privy to was presented to Baron Kingston upon your marriage. Although it is most unusual, your father arranged for you yourself to control the holdings of your family's land. Your husband may guide you if you allow. But you, m'lady, have final say in everything concerning your former home."

Maddie gasped. She was...rich? Now that could buffer this era somewhat. But still, being married to a man who not only hated her for some unknown reason, but seemed to sleep around was not ideal. In vain, she rubbed her temples to dispel the tension.

"How much do I own, Mistress Rhode?"

"Your father was the king's closest confidant, m'lady, your holding is prosperous, the biggest in Northern England. Your army is great, three-fold larger than your new husband's."

Maddie sat and took all this in. All these facts were well worth knowing and could be useful if her husband continued to be difficult. "Did the baron marry me because of my wealth? From what you said yesterday, this union was arranged years ago. Is he poor, Mistress Rhode?" Surely not, this castle, although sparsely furnished seemed well-maintained by a horde of servants. Not to mention the armed men who patrolled the grounds, and the village people living within its walls. No, a baron with no financial resources couldn't possibly keep up such a farce for long.

"Not that I'm aware, m'lady. But what I do know is, the dowry paid has allowed his lordship to increase his might and rebuild areas of Kingston Castle not previously achievable," she replied. "Now is the red mantle to your liking, Lady Madeline, or would you prefer the green?"

Maddie let her maid fuss over her while she turned her thoughts to the days ahead and the one thought most prominent in her mind, the coming confrontation with her husband, about his high-handed, roguish ways. She sighed in resignation. It wouldn't be a pleasant conversation.

Maddie sat alone at breakfast within the great hall two days later, eating porridge with a dash of honey. It seemed a normal enough breakfast, if you could ignore the armoured knights standing guard not ten feet away. No matter what she did, she couldn't get used to the sight of them. It didn't help they wore tight fitting hose and tunics that gaped, exposing hard, masculine bodies. Maddie looked down at her food, her cheeks burning and wondered how many times she'd blushed since being here. Too many times to count.

To keep herself occupied, Maddie toured the keep, surrounding buildings and visited the village stalls. The people living within these grand walls were friendly and accommodating, and she'd enjoyed her time with them.

Come each morning, she'd hoped to miraculously arrive back in the twenty-first century. But it hadn't happened, and over the past days, Maddie accepted that fate had, in fact, sent her flying through time, and plonked her in the twelfth century.

And being here, living in this society brought home the fact, she could very well be stuck in 1102, forever. It wasn't feasible to believe this type of life was a farce her friends had organised to tease her with. So it must be true. The constant use of words such as naught, anon, comely, and wench, no matter how amusing, hammered home the era she now lived in, and Maddie wondered how she'd manage.

She was dressed today in a purple woollen gown, with a white chemise underneath to eliminate the annoying itch of the rough wool. With some debate, Maddie was saved the embarrassment of plaiting her hair like a child and instead had tied it back using a piece of ribbon she had found. It didn't matter what she looked like, anyway, so long as she was comfortable. She bit into some bread and welcomed how her breakfast settled her nervous stomach.

Over the past days whenever she thought of meeting her husband again, her stomach somersaulted not knowing how it would turn out. Who knew what her life would be like when he decided to take an interest in her.

A servant stopped at her side and topped up her goblet

of mead. Maddie eyed the beverage with abhorrence then turned at the sound of someone entering the hall. She looked up, surprised to see the woman who'd slept with the baron walk toward the dais. The supposed distant cousin who was staying for a time.

Dressed in a grey chemise, with an overlying red gown, the lady walked toward the table with all the precision and grace of a woman of high birth. Long, golden blonde hair hung loose, highlighting fair skin and perfect angelic features.

Maddie shifted on her seat, feeling like an adolescent surrounded by beautiful teenage girls again. She smiled in a gesture of friendship—better that than enemies—and soon realized her mistake when the woman scowled and ignored her.

The woman cast dismissing sneers at everyone then settled herself at the dais like a regal queen. Distaste and loathing overtook Maddie's nerves. The woman certainly thought a lot of herself and very little of anyone else. At the sound of brisk footsteps, Maddie looked away and met the scowling glare of her husband.

He strode toward the dais, barking out orders as he went. The distaste he felt for his wife obvious in the way he looked at her. Maddie frowned and wondered why. Their families had been neighbours for many years. One would assume there would be some sort of amity. His eyes sought his mistress and yet his features remained cold and blank. Odd.

Maddie gulped down the mead and cringed. So, she'd married a cheating arse who had the audacity to have his mistress live under the same roof as his wife.

Well, she wouldn't put up with it. She may be twenty-first century born, but even she knew such an arrangement in this time was not acceptable.

"Lady Madeline, allow me to introduce you to your guest, Lady Veronica de Walter."

Maddie looked over to the baron, surprised he was lowering himself to speak to her. He sat down on a large ornate chair and summoned a servant.

"My guest? How do you figure that?" Maddie took another sip of her drink as all the warmth seemed to seep from the room. A shiver ran down her spine at the notice-able silence that settled over the hall and the knowledge that all eyes were now watching...them.

"You mock, wife?" Menace laced his cool tone.

Maddie beat back the urge to run like hell. He was her husband and be damned she'd cower to him. No matter the century. "Not mock. I'm just confused. Am I to welcome this lady to our home as a guest of mine? I've never met this woman before in my life."

"You know her now."

Maddie swallowed the porridge past the lump of fear in her throat. "Yes, I suppose I do. But I can't help thinking I've seen her before."

With you, up against the wall in the hall outside my bedroom.

"You have not," he said with a dismissing tone.

The baron took in his lover and his hard, cold features softened a little. Fear knotted Maddie's stomach, threat-ening to bring up her food. This man was in love and not with his wife. Oh gosh, where did that leave the Lady Madeline...leave her?

"Lady Veronica is a guest here, Madeline. I expect you to treat Her Ladyship with all due respect. Do I make myself clear."

"Perfectly," Maddie said, looking for a napkin and, not finding one, wiping her hands on the tablecloth. She cleared her throat. "May I have a word with you in your study after your meal, my lord?"

"My study?" he asked, a confused line to his brow.

"Ahh..." she stumbled, stuck for inspiration, and with no idea what to call the room.

"I will join you in the solar shortly," he said.

The scrape of her chair was loud in the quiet hall. Maddie walked from the room, but not before seeing Lady Veronica place her hand on the baron's lap. Did the woman have no respect for his wife? Not that Maddie cared what they did together, but had he married the real Lady Madeline surely she would have. She walked into a corridor that ran parallel to the hall and stopped, unsure as to where the solar was. With the aid of a servant, she entered a small box-shaped, sparsely furnished room.

And readied herself for the coming confrontation with the mighty Baron of Kingston.

"DARLING, MUST YOU GO TO HER. YOU PROMISED ME A ride after breakfast, and I hoped you had not meant on horseback."

Lord William glared at his vexing wife's retreating back then turned to face his distant cousin. Veronica could be a teasing little minx when she wanted, and normally he would never delay such an appointment. However, Lady Madeline, no matter his thoughts of her, was now his wife, and deal with her he would. Never had he known a more forward-speaking woman. But she would learn to curb her sharp tongue.

Aimecourt may be held in her delicate little hands in trust for their children. She may be far wealthier than he.

But as his wife, she would learn to live under his rule or suffer the consequences.

"I shan't be long. I'll walk you to the stables after morning prayer," he said, ignoring her pout and settling down to finish his meal.

෯෯

WILLIAM STRODE INTO THE SOLAR AND NODDED TO A SERF to close the door. "You wished to see me, Lady Madeline?" he said, in a tone of bored negligence before seating himself behind his desk.

"Yes, I did."

William watched as she smoothed her skirts with trembling fingers. She lifted her jaw and met his gaze, her apparent nervousness not strong enough to curb whatever it was she wished to speak to him about.

"Firstly, I would like to know why I am being forced to live under a roof with my husband's mistress."

William raised his brow, surprised by her question. "Our stewards settled our marriage contract last fall. 'Tis too late now to change your decree, m'lady." Her defiant little chin rose and an odd twinge twisted his gut.

"Refresh my memory, if you will."

Not interested in going over their marriage contracts again William inwardly groaned. "Aimecourt would be held in trust for our future children. I would look past your indiscretions after the birth of a son, as would you, me. Have—"

"You would allow your wife to sleep with other men after she bears you a male child?" Madeline asked, interrupting.

William frowned. "'Twas what was agreed. Have you changed your mind?"

Madeline stood and started to pace the floor. The gown swished about her legs showing a lithesome and well-proportioned body with curves in all the right places.

She stopped and turned to face him. "I don't want to sleep with anyone else."

Blood pounded to his groin at her declaration. "Am I to take it you wish to sleep with me?" And sleep with her he would, should she wish to. It had been many months since he'd had a woman warm his bed. Why he had remained faithful to his future wife he couldn't fathom. He supposed seeing his own father's faithfulness to his mother and their happy union had something to do with it.

"No!"

William chuckled at the vehemence behind her reply. "Do not fret, my dear. I do not care to share your bed today or any day soon." His words not true. With her long brown tresses tied neatly with a ribbon, he could picture her on his bed, hair cascading over his furs. Over him...

He cleared his throat. "Do not tell me you went ahead with the marriage with the thought of changing our agreement?"

His wife came and sat before him on a stool and frowned. "No. But neither will I have your lover thrown in my face."

"The king decreed our marriage. Our arrangement will suit you well enough in time. 'Tis nothing either of us can do to change our lives." Nor did he like having to remind the woman she'd agreed to all his commands. Was the woman daft? Never in living memory had a fever of the mind cursed the Vincent blood. Or so he thought.

"Why did the king decree a marriage between us when it is clear you loathe me?"

William stood, walked to the narrow window and looked onto the bailey. He'd married a crazy woman. Lady

43

Madeline knew the history between the two families. "Does a sickness of mind run through your family, my lady?"

"What?" she asked, looking at him as if he'd grown two heads.

"Well," he said, sitting back down. "You know the reason why and yet you ask. To find you're afflicted would at least explain the callous actions of your father. I always believed he was mad."

His wife shook her head. "I'm not mad."

"Good, for I'd hate to have to send you away." The blood drained from her face and a twinge of guilt nipped his gut. He watched her chew her full bottom lip, making it red. They were delectable lips, full and pouty. Supple.

"Where would you send me?"

William noted her concern and clenched his jaw against the unwelcome feelings she evoked. "To a convent." With his reply, her dull brown eyes sparked to life like embers in a fire.

"I'd die first before I'd allow you to do that," she said.

William stifled a laugh. "Our bargain stands, m'lady."

She stood and started to pace again. "My room, if you hadn't realized, is on the same floor as your lover's. And, two nights ago, you should remember, it being our wedding night, I had the dubious delight of seeing you two within the passage."

"What I do, and where I do it, is my business, Lady Madeline. 'Twould be wise to remember that." William knew he should explain that he was merely putting Lady Veronica to bed. His cousin, ever since he had stopped sleeping with her months before, had become a little forward of manner, and—if truth be told—a little scandalous. Madeline obviously thought he was bedding her and for now that would suit his plans. Until he figured out how to handle his attractive and strong willed wife, keeping her at a distance would suit him very well.

"Remember such things. How about you remember the vows you took not days ago. Or do you not respect the church's word as you should?"

His fist slammed down on the wooden table. "Those vows were only spoken because I did not have the authority to cancel our marriage arrangement. Only the church has such a right. And your parents made sure before their untimely deaths that their wishes and the king's could not be overturned."

"Did you not want to marry Lady Madeline, then?" she asked him, clearly shocked by the venom in his tone. He paused and wondered why she would refer to herself in such a way. William tore his gaze away from her bodice that rose and fell with swiftness of breath.

"No I did not." Not that he wouldn't bed the wench now that she was before him married or no. The delectable, outspoken minx she was turning out to be could prove a worthy bedmate and lifelong partner. William stepped back and ran his fingers through his hair, surprised by his own thoughts.

Lady Madeline was a Vincent. To think in such a way brought shame on him and his family. He would never touch the Baron of Aimecourt's daughter unless under duress of duty.

"Good, then," she replied, her eyes throwing sharp little daggers at him. "Because I wouldn't want to sleep with you either."

"Then we are in agreement." William stood to go and stepped around the desk.

"I haven't finished," she said.

William stopped. "No? Pray, what else is there left to

45

say?" He sat on the desk, deliberately close so as to make her uncomfortable. She squirmed away.

"I want to return to Aimecourt."

"Out of the question!"

You cannot stop me."

He smirked. "I believe I can."

"Until this arrangement, as you call it, ceases, I refuse to live here with an adulterer," she said, scowling at him.

"Adulterer?"

"Yes, an adulterer, a cheating arse if you prefer." Maddie glared at him. "If this is the life you have planned with such precision with the Lady Madeline, then I want a divorce. This is no life, for either person."

"Why do you keep talking as if you're not involved in this union?"

He leaned toward her, and traced the neckline of her gown. Goosebumps followed his touch as he skimmed over the tops of her breasts before she slapped his hand away.

"Who do you think you are? Some sort of sheik with dozens of lovers all clutching at your legs for sex?" Madeline glared at him. "I'm not one of them, so keep your hands to yourself."

He laughed and held his hands up in defeat. "Forgive me, my lady. I will endeavor not to offend again."

His new wife walked toward the hearth and stared at the fire. "Can you not see a marriage, no matter how advantageous, is doomed if the couple do not care for the union. I don't want to argue with you about your way of life. We do not care for each other, so what a wasted future it would be if we kept to the current course."

William joined her. "If I take you to my bed, Lady Madeline, not even the church or the king's influence could save you then."

"You would take me by force?" She fumbled at the mantle. "Are you serious?"

William felt a wave of lust crash over him, then subside at the thought of bedding her. "It's my right as a husband to consummate the marriage, Lady Madeline."

"How dare you throw the law of the church in my face?" She narrowed her eyes and crossed her arms over her chest. "I want you to agree to some *new* rules."

"*New* rules?" he said, crossing his own arms.

"First, I don't want your philandering thrown in my face. Second," she said, ticking off her fingers. "I don't appreciate your mistress being rude and ignoring me. And thirdly, I request a guard."

William grasped her arm and turned her toward him. "Have you been threatened? Why do you need a knight?" More than a little surprised at the strength of his reaction to her statement.

Madeline wiggled out of his hold. "Some of the men who walk the outer perimeter walls scare me. They're not like my knights."

"I will assign my first knight, Sir Alex, to your side." William yelled for a serf and ordered a missive for Sir Alex to join him in the bailey immediately.

Madeline shrugged. "Perhaps I could bring my own men here, or return home like I suggested earlier."

"I thought my answer was clear on that score."

"I have a larger garrison than you and my men are used to me. They would be more than willing to look after me here."

William stared at her a moment, a muscle on his temple twitched, ticking the seconds passing by. "My knight will be more than adequate protection. And *again*, you will remain at Kingston until I decide otherwise."

"Are you keeping me here like some sort of prisoner?

47

Am I not more powerful than you due to my father's obscene wealth? And since you said yourself my parents had the ear of the king, wouldn't it be assumed that I would also?"

"Are you threatening me? 'Twould be unwise to make an enemy of me, Madeline." William gritted his teeth as he waited for her reply.

"It would be unwise to make one of me, William!" she retorted.

"The arrangement under this roof will remain, and so will you," he said, stealing another look at her breasts when they shook with the fervor of her tone.

"Stop doing that."

"What?" he asked with mock innocence.

"Looking at my breasts."

He smirked. He had to admit, though her temperament was not to his liking, she certainly had other qualities he found appealing.

"I will respect your wishes, in regards to Lady Veronica and grant you a guard, Madeline. But do not cross me and leave Kingston. 'Twould be an error to do so. Have I made myself clear?"

"Perfectly," she said.

Without another word, he turned on his heel and left the room.

Maddie sat down and massaged her temples. What a mess. Looking down at her hand, she ran a finger over the spot the wedding band should be. If only she could find that ring again, it would surely return her home. But such a thing would be more than likely impossible. It was probably lying in the mud somewhere between Aimecourt and the church, thanks to the anything but solid carriage floor. It may have, for all she knew, disappeared into space as she flew through time.

She adjusted the cushion behind her back and sighed. What was it she didn't know about these two families she was now a part of? Since it looked like she wasn't going anywhere, no doubt she had plenty of time to find out.

CHAPTER 4

As the days turned into weeks, Maddie kept mostly to herself. She strolled around the battlements of the keep and inner defensive wall; both locations gave ample views over the surrounding area. She walked daily in the magnificent forest that lay before the castle walls and welcomed the dense woodland to hide her from scrutiny for a time.

With the warnings still ringing in her ears over rogue Scottish raiders in the area, Maddie thought it best not to venture too far away. The sentries had ceased looking at her with distrust and hate. She could only surmise it was due to the fact she now had a guard, who would keep a close eye on the woman from Aimecourt. And, in a time fraught with danger and uncertainty, she had slowly started to feel safe.

Helped by the fact Maddie liked her guard, Sir Alex Bourke. It had taken her some weeks, but with a little coaxing, the knight had opened up enough to be a friend and confidant. Her designated shadow hailed from the southern areas of England. Her husband's first knight since the day William had claimed the title of baron. A quiet man, he seemed to take his duties as protector very seriously. She often wondered what would happen to him if something did befall her. Would he really risk his own life to save hers? Something inside told her he would. Although, the way her husband continued to treat her, it was obvious should harm befall her, Lord William would probably award the knight some sort of medal for his lapse in protection.

Maddie's urge to return to Aimecourt increased with every passing day. Mostly, due to the sheer need to look for the missing ring. As no rings were exchanged through the wedding ceremony, her hope of getting it back that way was lost. It only left the road that lay between Aimecourt and the church. Perhaps it was there. Unfortunately, her husband had decided to be an arse and not allow her freedom to leave. However, a small measure of hope had sparked since that first denial. Apparently, "her people" held an annual festival celebrating the winter solstice. Or so Mistress Rhode had informed her. This year the festival would include the celebration of her marriage and a welcome to Lord William.

The letters from her steward told her of her people's excitement over the daylong celebration. All the details were planned with the utmost care and proceeding in a timely manner. He had explained in an almost sycophantic detail her people's eagerness to see Lady Madeline again, and her esteemed husband, the baron.

Maddie rolled her eyes, irked that they thought her husband noble and worthy. The Baron of Kingston was neither of those things. For all she knew, her husband and his mistress could be lying along a road somewhere, dead.

Six weeks he'd been gone and without a word of good-bye. Who left an estate without a single word? Obviously his "greatness" did. The castle staff had begun to silence their conversations whenever she entered a room. She loathed the pity she saw in their eyes, although the conde-scension of others was worse. Maddie was not oblivious to what they whispered behind her back. That the baron had taken flight with his lover, escape his only course. The marriage bed with the Lady Madeline too abhorrent for any man to stomach.

Maddie again wished she knew more about the real Lady Madeline. From what she could gather, the woman was the opposite to her own character in every way. Was this why William would not offer her the hand of friend-ship? Because he still thought her the same as the old Madeline? Or what he had heard of the old Madeline, since he had never met the girl prior to their wedding.

After their little tête-à-tête within the solar that one morning, he had disappeared off the face of the earth. The reprieve had not dampened her temper. She wasn't finished with him quite yet. His dismissal of her and his disappearing act burrowed into her skin like a thistle. It festered, made her temper worse with every day that passed.

It was silly really, because as soon as she had the chance, she'd be out of here, gone. However, as a woman, she could not help but be slighted, hurt, by his callous manner toward her. It made her feel sorry for other women in this time who suffered the same fate.

She stood next to a boulder and watched the waters of a local river flow away. The dormant landscape, under the sprinkling of snow, glittered in the soft sunshine and she couldn't help but admit that being stuck in this time did have some positives. The air was fresh and the seasons more pronounced. Animal meat tasted more delicious and the butter their cook made was to die for. If only she had fresh water or a beautiful aged wine, her stomach at least would have been content. She picked up a flat stone, threw it, and skimmed it across the water. She watched as a startled bird flew out of the reeds on the opposite bank.

"A strange ability for a lady born to privilege," Sir Alex said, his face passive.

Maddie smiled. At least with her knight she had one friend in medieval England. "I learnt as a child, Sir Alex. My dad taught me."

Sir Alex frowned. "Did you always address your father as dad?" the word sounded foreign and awkward on his tongue. "It seems most strange, Lady Madeline."

"Would it make you feel better if I said father instead of dad?" She laughed at his perplexed gaze. "Is it so strange for you? What did you call your father?" He looked at her with a small smile on his lips.

"I used to call him Papa."

"And you mock me, Sir Alex, shame on you. For if anyone deserves to be teased, it is not I." She grinned. "You were obviously very close to your papa."

He nodded. "Yes, I was."

Maddie dusted down her dress as she walked up the river's bank and stopped at the edge of the forest. "Shall we return, Sir Alex? The day grows late and chilly, and Mistress Rhode said she had a surprise for me when I returned."

"Of course, Lady Madeline. Whatever you wish."

They walked for a time in silence before Maddie asked, "Are your parents still alive, Sir Alex?"

Pain crossed his visage before he masked his emotions.

"I lost both my parents some years ago. Mother at my birth, my father not long before my tenth year to a winter chill."

Maddie touched the knight's arm in support. "I'm sorry for your loss." They walked on. "It's not easy being alone."

"The Baron of Aimecourt was a hard man, and yet his daughter loved him still."

Maddie looked about the forest and wondered over Sir Alex's words that were neither a question nor statement. "What do you know of my father?"

Sir Alex adjusted his scabbard and Maddie's throat closed at the size of the knife held in the leather sheath.

"I never met the baron."

Maddie started over Sir Alex's curt reply. Had her medieval father been a tyrant and she the only one who didn't know it? They walked into the shadow of the castle and Maddie pulled her shawl closer to her body as a shiver ran over her skin. She looked up at the looming edifice and her steps faltered at the sight of the man who stood there.

The Lord William watched like a falcon over the surrounding land; a bird of prey out for its next meal. She steeled her resolve to be unpleasant. What did he expect? For her to be home, meek and mild awaiting his grand arrival? She thought not.

Why he'd even look for her made no sense. If he thought to worry about her now, it was a bit late. Weeks without a word proved how much he cared for the Lady Madeline's welfare and his home. If he tried to act the caring husband now, she'd probably feel more inclined to slap his face.

WILLIAM PACED THE BATTLEMENTS LIKE A CAGED ANIMAL, only to stop every now and then to look out to the forest beyond. What was wrong with him? Kicking his heels atop the mammoth walls for the past hour was not what he would deem normal behaviour. It was damn time his wife returned. He did not want to have to send for her. In his current state of mind, he would not wish that upon his worst enemy.

Having arrived back at Kingston Castle in the early morn, he had proceeded to his apartments without notifying his wife of his return. Later, when he looked out over the inner bailey and watched Lady Veronica practice archery in the ward, he'd summoned Lady Madeline. Why he had done so he couldn't fathom. Perhaps to see her again, if only to push her away.

Minutes passed before a servant, game enough for the task, had informed him of her walk with Sir Alex.

His jaw clenched. Why should that bother him? Too angry to dwell on that thought now, he set the question aside for later evaluation. What were they up to all that time in woodland? He would string them both up if he even heard a whisper of infidelity.

He studied them as they walked back; their mutual ease with each other almost palpable. Her laughter rang out, echoed off the wall and his temper notched. Over the many weeks away, had his wife and trusted knight become passionate toward one another?

His eyes met hers and held. He glared at the unfaithful wench until she passed beneath the gatehouse. Her gaze, short as it was, mocked him, spoke of a woman who cared naught for him and his rule. He gritted his teeth, rankled by the realization.

William strode down the steps and fought an inner

conflict. It was beside the point that he could not stand the woman. Or the name she once harboured. She was his wife now and never would be another's. 'Twould be unwise for her to attempt to sleep with any man other than himself. And if she did, she would pay for her disloyalty with her life.

Had he been wrong in assigning Sir Alex to her side? Known to act the scoundrel at times, surely his vassal would not dare lay a finger upon his delicate skinned wife. He frowned. Thoughts such as these had plagued him for weeks. Since the day he'd argued with her in the solar, he had thought of little else. Her eyes sparkled bright in anger. The colour upon her cheeks had made her more beautiful than he cared to know. She haunted and pleased him at the same time. There were not many who would stand up to such a man as he. Except for his wife...Madeline.

In the hopes that distance may lessen the pleasant thoughts of Lady Madeline writhing under him, he had taken Lady Veronica to her brother's home in Cheshire. Days of hunting and nights filled with hearty meals and talk of King Henry's exploits had not helped. Madeline had haunted his dreams even there. It was no secret that Lady Veronica, for many months, no longer held the allure she once did. In fact, his distant cousin had become a nuisance more than anything else, and she would soon need to leave Kingston. Her time as his guest had come to an end.

Before his departure, Madeline seemed to be everywhere. If not checking the welfare of his serfs, she was sitting at the dais taking a meal, talking amicably with other guests, or in her room...only a door away. He had started to feel desperate and in need of seeing her. To be near her presence, like a fish in need of water. A man consumed with noting every little act and gesture his wife performed.

His fists clenched. Damn the woman. It had become an absurd situation he could not allow to continue. So he had done the only thing he could. He had fled.

Like a coward.

William climbed down the last of the steps and awaited them within the courtyard. His fisted his hands as his wife walked alongside Sir Alex, comfortable and, if her smile was any indication, happy. What was she about looking at another man such?

"Sir Alex, thank you for your escort. You may go," he said, glaring at his wife. Her eyes flashed at his harsh words. William welcomed her fear. She ought to be scared of his temper, especially if he found any wrongdoing on her behalf. His nose flared, his teeth ached from his clenched jaw. How dare she mock his command and ogle his head knight, *adoringly*, still.

He mentally swore. If Madeline thought to act the common whore, she would pay dearly for it, with her life. Or perhaps under him in his bed. Either option would not be pleasant. Well, on reflection, maybe one would be, for him at least.

"Yes, my lord," Sir Alex replied, a calm indifference to his words, before he walked away.

MADDIE LOOKED OVER TO HER HUSBAND AND RAISED HER brow. So she had infuriated him. Well, good, he deserved it. With him regularly looking at Lady Veronica as if she was the only women on the planet, he deserved a little pay back. Not that her revenge would involve sleeping with his men, she was no whore. Nor was she stupid enough to lose her head in this time.

She took a calming breath as he stood before her, brooding and still. Nerves skittered across her skin. What was going through his mind? Whatever it was it did not bode well for her. She lifted her chin, told herself that the man before her, for all his muscles and temper, was still only human. Not some super power who could wipe her out. Or, perhaps he could, but not without a bloody good fight beforehand.

"What is it you wish to speak to me about, Lord William?" she asked, watched as a perplexed frown marked his brow. She wondered if he did in fact have anything to discuss, or if he had now forgotten it. She raised her brows questioningly, annoyed to be confronted by him and in such a public place.

Lord William's gaze stole to her lips and she just stopped herself from taking a step back. She would not fear him. His eyes darkened with an unknown emotion as if he fought some inner battle she neither understood nor wanted to.

"We leave two days hence for Aimecourt. Only a day's ride from here, we should make the journey safely in daylight. I've taken the liberty of informing your maid to pack. We shall be gone some weeks."

Maddie's annoyance instantly disappeared. They were going home. Well, her apparent home in medieval England, in any case. Would the ring be there, by any chance? She could only look and hope for the best. The thought of removing herself from this time, sent a burst of energised happiness throughout her body. She smiled up at him with the thought that the twenty-first century may be only days away. It was enough to extinguish all irritation at her husband.

William grunted. "I see this pleases the Lady Madeline."

If possible, Maddie felt her smile widen. "It does, my lord, very much so." As silence ensued, Maddie looked at William only to see his gaze taking in her form. She cleared her throat to gain his attention and inwardly laughed as he masked his features to one of cool indifference.

"It is only fair your people have the opportunity to see you and your new husband. I will, of course, be bringing Lady Veronica. She will act as your companion."

Maddie lost all enthusiasm for the trip. She narrowed her eyes and bit back a horde of curses she longed to fling at him. How dare he.

"I do not think so, my lord." Her voice was hard, unmovable. "I will not allow that woman to enter my house. Unless you want to sleep with her outside the castle walls? She'd be more comfortable left here."

"Do not presume to tell me what to do, Lady Madeline. I am your husband and what I say is law."

Maddie held her ground and refused to give in. As the silence stretched, William shifted his stance and placed a hand upon his sword belt.

"She is not welcome in my home, nor will you be, shall you think to bring her," Maddie said unsympathetically. "You may be baron and lord of the manor here, but Aimecourt is my home. You may get away with such activities under this roof, but I will die before I lower myself to allow such under my own."

Her words snapped his temper. Grabbing her arm, William dragged her toward a woodshed beside the gatehouse. He ignored her shocked gasp and attempts to dislodge his grip as he led her inside, away from inquisitive eyes. Away from help.

"I could have you whipped for speaking to me in such a way. Cease this jealousy over Lady Veronica and accept the situation."

Maddie puffed out a breath of temper. How dare he think her envious of him and that slut? She couldn't hate him more than she did at this moment. "I accept it here, my lord. But do not think to bring her with us. Don't—" she squeaked as his mouth came down, demanding and intent against her own. It quelled her outburst and she stilled. What the hell was he doing? As reality asserted itself, she bit his lip—hard.

He wrenched away, his hand against his mouth, his eyes astonished. A tiny spot of blood marked his lip. Maddie flicked her hair behind her shoulder and turned to leave. At the door, she paused to look back at him. Still and watchful, his eyes burned with fury at her rebuff. She took in all his form, and then allowed her distaste of him to settle on her features.

"Don't think to control me, Lord William. I may be your wife and I may be a woman, but I'd die before I would allow my people to see your degrading treatment of me. They will never see their Lady allow her husband's whore to sleep with him under her own roof. Now if you don't mind, I'm going to pack. And if I see you at the carriage in two days, then that is fine. But if you think you cannot spend a month at least without Lady Veronica, I suggest you stay exactly where you are."

She walked out and hurried to the security of the castle. She looked toward the smithy and noticed Sir Alex watching her. She ignored his worried countenance and proceeded into the Great Hall. It seemed to take forever to make her way to her room. With shaking fingers, Maddie shut her door and turned the massive key in the lock.

Slumping against the wood, she sighed in relief before she touched her lips.

When he'd kissed her, with such demanding softness, had she not been so angry with his obnoxious audacity, she would have unravelled like a ball of wool. She would have kissed him back and enjoyed every second of it. Her stomach fluttered as the memory of his tongue sliding into her mouth raced through her mind.

Holy mother of Christ, after everything he had done; ignored her, cheated on her, and frustrated her, she was in lust with him. She closed her eyes in self-disgust, thumped the door behind her. How could a twenty-first century woman fall so low? But fall she had, for the worst kind of fiend alive.

⚜

LATER THAT EVENING, MADDIE SAT ALONE IN HER ROOM. Her hand idly twisted the rosary beads Mistress Rhode had given her the day before. She wondered how she would go about hiding her mixed emotions from William. God forbid he try to touch her again, she may not have the sense next time to push him away. And why, when she made him so obviously angry, would he kiss her? She shook her head as she stared out over the darkened land beyond her windows. A group of outlying cottages the only shadows that marred the hills, dimly lit by the scatter of stars appearing in the night sky. As an all too familiar knock sounded on her door, Maddie turned and watched Mistress Rhode bustle into the room. Flushed, she fluttered over to her in excited haste.

"M'lady, there you are. I have been searching everywhere for you, the baron wishes to see you."

"I've already had the pleasure."

61

"You have?"

"Yes...he happened upon me as I came back from my daily walk to the river," she replied, half-smiling as her maid visibly relaxed at the news. Her jaw clenched in annoyance. How dare the man frighten people? It was pathetic that they ran themselves ragged just to please His Lordship.

"So, m'lady, did His Lordship tell you of the new bathing quarters in the castle? This is my surprise for you."

Maddie stood at the mention of bathing and cleanliness, not something she'd seen a lot of in this time. "He never mentioned a bathroom."

"Over the past months the floor beneath this one has been having some improvements. The new bath chamber is now ready for use, m'lady."

"Can I see it?"

"'Twould be my pleasure. Follow me, if you please," Mistress Rhode said opening the door for her.

Moments later, Maddie entered a room, no doubt once a bedchamber, now decked out as a medieval bathroom. A maid busily stoked a fire, pots of boiling water bubbled over the large hearth. A round wooden tub lined in cloth, sat in the centre of the room. Soaps that smelt of lavender lay within a bowl. Cloths and towels, neatly folded on a wooden shelf, sat ready for use. Despite the lack of running hot water and a flushable toilet, the room was lovely. Maddie took in the room before she noted a door beside the window.

"Where does that door lead to, Mistress Rhode?" she asked, sure no balconies joined this side of the keep. Her room, directly above, would have revealed this.

"That, m'lady," her maid said in enthusiasm, "is the new garderobe."

"Garderobe?"

"Come, m'lady. It is most visionary."

Maddie walked across the room and stepped into the wooden structure, which seemed to protrude from the castle wall. She looked down a circular hole and into the flowing moat below.

"Is this the toilet then?"

"I do not understand toilet, m'lady. But this is the garderobe, where you may do your...private business."

Maddie stemmed a laugh. "So they built this wooden structure onto the wall just so a toilet could be housed within the keep?"

"Garderobe, yes, m'lady."

"What's the little pot for, the one on the shelf in there?" she asked, picking up the container before putting it back in haste. Her eyes watered from the foul stench.

"Lady Madeline, you know urine is saved for dyeing of cloth."

"You use urine to dye our clothes?"

"M'lady, you know of this way. You have used it yourself." Her maid smiled.

"I would not put my hand into my own urine, let alone someone else's."

"I'm sure, once your memory returns, you will remember all of your life as it was before. Do not trouble yourself, m'lady, it may only lengthen the time before your memory does come back."

Maddie nodded, not sure she wanted to remember her previous life, especially if it had her remembering working with urine to dye clothes. She looked down at the gown she wore, and wondered whose pee had been used on the fabric. She lifted her arm and smelt her sleeve, thankful the only smell that met her senses was one of clean, washed cloth.

She looked over at her maid, who seemed to be chuckling silently. Maddie laughed.

Two days later, Maddie sat comfortably—well, as comfortably as one could in a medieval carriage with no glass windows or suspension. She bit back a smile and refused to gloat over her triumph. Her husband had in fact met her at the carriage this morning, and alone at that. She couldn't help but think she had won a battle against His Lordship this day.

They travelled for most of the day and were due to arrive at Aimecourt within the hour. Or so her bad tempered spouse had uttered while glowering across at her. Other than those few words, William hadn't spoken at all. Not that she minded. It saved her from having to argue with the ancient he-man.

She'd enjoyed the day immensely even with the shocking conveyance and her "delightful" travelling companion. They had stopped for lunch and had partaken of an impromptu picnic. Sir Alex was a welcome friend after being stuck with William. They had companionably eaten bread, cheese, and a tart wine. She had almost dozed as she listened to him speak of his own home south of London and the woman he hoped to make his own.

Sir Alex spoke with such love and wistfulness over his betrothed that Maddie could almost be jealous of the lucky woman who would marry him. William had sat away from them, brooding and quiet while they talked. His eyes had burned a path across to them, until, unable to stand it any longer, she had looked away. Maddie wondered if William was a little jealous. It would serve him right if he was.

"Aimecourt is just ahead, Lady Madeline."

Pulled from her musings, she looked out the carriage window as they reached the peak of a hill, allowing her apparent ancestral home to come into view. The foundations sat on the edge of the valley before them; the castle itself sat above a monstrous amount of stone. The fortress was magnificent. Bordered on three sides by ocean, it looked to sit on an island. The gatehouse, situated over an ocean moat that filled with seawater, its only entrance.

An impossible building to take during battle; no wonder Lord William wouldn't grant an annulment. Who in their right mind would give up ownership of such a place? It reminded her of Tintagel Castle which she had once toured while in Cornwall.

"You are looking at your home, Lady Madeline, like you have never seen it before. Have you missed it so much that you cannot keep from gazing upon its grandeur?"

She ignored his sarcastic tone and looked back toward the castle.

"I'd be lying if I said I am not looking forward to being home. Do you not miss your own when away, my lord?" she asked, a double entendre to her question. She had not been thinking of Aimecourt or Kingston Castle at all, but her own home in Greenwich, which seemed a million life times away at present.

"It is only a stone building. I travel a great deal, Lady Madeline; it is easy to forget where home is," he said, before looking away.

Maddie kept her eyes on his and watched as he squirmed at the lie he just told. For all his words that his home meant nothing, the beading of sweat atop his brow and his inability to look at her told another truth. His home was run with dedication. Not a thing was left untended, including those who worked his lands. No, William did not fool her; he loved his home and his lands.

Took pride in them. Even if he did disappear for weeks on end.

"You are very different from what I'd been told of you, Lady Madeline."

Maddie looked back from the view of passing fields and working serfs to her husband. "Oh, how so?" She refused to fidget as his dark, hooded gaze studied her profile.

"I find it strange that Lady Veronica has more grace and finesse than you, when you were brought up in and around privileges rivalling those of the king."

Maddie frowned. "Are you calling me common?"

"Well, Aimecourt is a thriving stronghold so I rank you more than common. And you seem to have wits, since your holdings strength and production have only increased since your father's death. However," he paused, "I believe when your father had you undergo tutelage in the arts of being a lady, he allowed the standard to slip."

"And you my lord, to point out my flaws, were never raised as a gentlemen."

A heavy silence ensued. Maddie glared, before she turned away. What an obnoxious arse.

THE CARRIAGE CROSSED A WOODEN DRAWBRIDGE, WHICH spanned a deep ravine. They passed through the gate-house and stopped within the outer bailey. With the help of Lord William, Maddie disembarked, pulling her hand free of his clasp the moment her feet touched the ground. Why, whenever she inadvertently touched him, did nerves assail her? At shouts and commands behind her, she turned and watched, entranced as the draw-bridge closed, isolating them within the walls. People were everywhere; it was a complete working village on top of a rock.

The carriages moved on to be unloaded and a moment later, Mistress Rhode joined her before accompanying her inside. Since her husband had thought to take himself off elsewhere, Maddie pretended indifference and proceeded indoors to inspect her property.

It only now dawned upon her that she knew no one, nor did she know her way around the massive edifice. As she walked into the Great Hall, she stopped, stunned, in front of two life-sized paintings of people she recognized. Without the period clothing, she could have been looking at her mum and dad, exactly as she had seen them last. Before a drunk driver took them away from her at seventeen, and her dreams along with them.

She slumped into a large chair and tried to make sense of it all. A gust of heat from the roaring fire nearby heated her cheeks as her mind fought with the possibilities. What was happening? Was all this some sort of reincarnated life? Everyone here certainly saw her as the Lady Madeline. So she must look like her. And the people in the painting were most assuredly her parents. So maybe somehow people were not only reborn over and over again, but continued to have the same family repeatedly?

No, that couldn't be right.

"Some refreshments are being brought in, Lady Madeline," said Mistress Rhode as she lowered herself onto a wooden chair next to the hearth and held her hands to the flames. "Does your home seem familiar to you, my dear? If you have not recovered your memory by spring, I will consult my mother. She normally passes through this area during that time of year. She may know if there is anything to be done. Is that agreeable to you, m'lady?"

Maddie smiled over to her, and nodded.

"That's fine, Mistress Rhode, do as you will, but I believe nothing can be done. I have no memory of this home or the land surrounding it. I only remember my life before, and that existence did not occur in 1102."

She paused as she sipped the fruity mead handed to her by a servant. Thanking the maid, Maddie frowned when the girl appeared stunned by the gesture before scuttling off. Why did people keep running away from her like that?

"One thing I will admit to, Mistress Rhode, is the couple before us in that painting are indeed my parents. Their clothing may be unfamiliar to me, but otherwise they are most definitely a familiar pair."

"Lady Madeline," her maid gasped, "Do you still think yourself from the future? Surely not. I'm sure given time, your memory will return and all this worry will be for naught."

"I'm sorry, but you're wrong. I'm not sure what the other Lady Madeline was like, but surely you must see how different we are. My actions, my speech. Your Lady Madeline was a powerful baron's daughter. A lady of the first water. I'm," she said, clasping her hand to her heart, "the only daughter of a teacher and a housewife. I went to a public school, wore hand-me-down clothes and now run an antique store for a living. I have no social graces, and I do not remember anyone or anything here at Aimecourt, or at Kingston castle for that matter."

Mistress Rhode pursed her lips. "It is true, m'lady, that you hit your head. Perhaps worse than I first thought. But you are the Lady Madeline in features. There is perhaps," she frowned, "a certain coarseness now about your manner of speech and graces that had never been there before. But that is nothing that cannot be fixed."

Maddie nibbled on a portion of bread and sipped her mead. "What was the Lady Madeline you knew like?"

Mistress Rhode sighed and sat back within her chair. "A tyrant, just as her father was. The property was always to be hers, or any sons she may have. Lady Madeline's tutelage was thorough and hard. Your former self would never have said thank you to a mere vassal for anything. So it does not surprise me, m'lady, if your people are a little in awe and wary of you."

Maddie nodded, understanding now what William had meant by his dig at her in the carriage. It also explained why whenever she used her manners people looked at her as if they were waiting for another person to appear.

"Perhaps something did happen in that carriage, that neither you nor I can explain, Lady Madeline. But you are a kind and considerate woman. Whilst Lady Madeline of old, the woman I had protected all of those years past, was mean, uncharitable, and hard." Mistress Rhode paused, her attention fixed on the flames as she spoke. "I had at times even felt sorry for Lord William. I knew Lady Madeline would not make an easy wife." She chuckled. "It seems even the new one will not."

Maddie's smile fell short as she sat forward. "This time in history scares me, Mistress Rhode. I haven't had the Lady Madeline of old's upbringing, nor do I know what I'm doing. I'm lost."

"I will admit, m'lady, that you are changed, but not for the worse. You may lack some of the social graces appropriate to your status, but that is easy to overcome." Her maid leant forward and clasped her hand. "You must promise me not to speak of your concerns or former life with anyone other than myself. It reeks of witchcraft, and if you are in fact from the future, you know what happens to such unfortunates."

Maddie's stomach knotted. "I understand. But you will promise to ask your mother, when you see her, what could be done to return me home?" Maddie asked.

"Of course, my dear," she replied, smiling.

They sat in silence and watched as their trunks were carted through the hall toward the winding stone staircase.

"Mistress Rhode, while I'm here, there is something I must find, or at least try to find. You see, the day I returned to 1102, I had found an ancient ring, buried on the shore of the Thames River in London. It was a wedding ring of sorts, one made of pewter with an inscription inside. When I placed the ring on my finger, the next thing I was conscious of was sitting on the carriage floor talking to you. I am hopeful that...that if I find this ring, I will find a way back home."

Her maid frowned and held her response as the food platter was placed before them. "We shall look for the ring anon, child. Never fear, all will be well in time. But I pray your mind is confused as I would not want to lose you."

Maddie clasped her maid's hand, oddly touched by the sincerity in her words. "Nor do I wish to lose you, Mistress Rhode. Thank you for being my friend."

☙❧

NEITHER SAW NOR HEARD THE WOMAN WHO HAD LISTENED to their damning conversation. The maid, dressed in nondescript clothes, smiled, a malicious tilt to her thin lips. The information would be quite useful to Her Ladyship and could possibly afford her a valuable trinket or gold coin once repeated. She allowed the shadows to close over her as she stepped out of the castle and headed toward the hidden exit near the guard's gate.

She smiled as her mind filled with all the pretty things

she could buy. How Her Ladyship would be pleased once she heard of the Lady Madeline's strange musings and dilemma. She snorted, all of it was codswallop, the Lady Madeline's mind was addled by a knock, and that was all. But she'd enjoy seeing the lady hang or burn for witchcraft, she knew where her loyalty lay and it was not at Aimecourt.

CHAPTER 5

I t wasn't until the evening meal that Maddie saw William again. Earlier in the day, he had moved into her father's bedchamber. A room joined to hers by an interlocking door. Upon entering her bedroom, Maddie's first action was to lock that connecting door. After their kiss in the woodshed, she would take no further chances with the man.

Tonight Maddie was dressed in a silver-threaded gown, with sleeves almost the same length as the dress itself. Blue and purple thread was skilfully stitched around the plunging neckline and ends of her sleeves. The hem of the gown was adorned with beautiful hand stitching. She couldn't help but love the dress. It was surely the most gorgeous thing she had ever worn.

"Do not forget your rosary, m'lady."

Maddie frowned and turned back from the door. Walked to her trunk and snatched up the beaded necklace made of ribbon. "Do I have to wear it all the time?" she asked, placing it over her head.

"Lady Madeline was a devout Catholic. 'Twould be

wise, I believe, to continue her religious beliefs," Mistress Rhode said.

"So I have to attend church every Sunday?"

Her maid smiled then bent to stoke the fire. "Nay child, not every Sunday."

Maddie sighed in relief. "Thank God."

"You must attend mass at dawn, followed by your prayers. Then mid-morning prayers before your midday meal. Evening prayer is held before supper in the hall. Followed by your bedtime prayers."

Maddie laughed. "You're joking, right? I have to pray four times a day!" She shook her head in disbelief. "Mistress Rhode, I'm not even christened."

"Well, consider yourself so now, m'lady. Now, you had best leave, supper is about to be served."

Oh gosh, and Maddie thought the mirror water bowl was ridiculous.

Maddie basked in the warmth that seeped into her bones from the well-stoked fire situated behind the raised dais she now sat at. She watched, seated like a queen over the absurd proceedings in the hall. The pomp and ceremony almost made her laugh. Really, it was too much for her common soul. Her husband had no such reactions; he was completely in his element. She peeked at his handsome features and strong jaw, which tonight sported a five o'clock shadow. His hair was newly cut to the cropped style the Normans favoured. William fit the part of medieval lord to a tee, strong, hard and unforgivably handsome. He spoke with authority and power to his knights and their ladies seated at the table.

The meal was delicious. Almost every bird in existence

was served: pheasant, chicken, duck, and turkey adorned the table along with fruits and cheeses and the ever-present mead. Maddie had grown accustomed to the beverage. Although she preferred it made with hops, which was much more palatable as the end-product tasted like beer.

She studied the hall, and noted the knights who she presumed to be her own. Although they ate and spoke to everyone, their reserved interactions with her husband's men were obvious. An air of unease floated in the air and Maddie, not for the first time, wondered why.

"Are you enjoying yourself, Lady Madeline?"

Maddie looked to William and tried to form a smile, the gesture a half-hearted effort. "Of course, my lord, why wouldn't I? I am home, back within the bosom of my own people. How could I not be content?"

"Is that how you inform me you are not content at Kingston, my dear?"

"Please do not call me by such endearments, I do believe their falseness will make me vomit," she said, thanking a servant as they handed her some bread, before looking back at her incredulous husband.

"Pray tell me, Lord William, how do you like my home? Is it everything promised upon marriage to a rich man's daughter?"

"No, I find not only the home but its occupants lack taste and refinement."

"Well, that is a shame. If you dislike it so much, maybe you should leave and return to Lady Veronica, who no doubt misses you greatly. Ah, but..." she said, tapping her finger against her lip, "alas, perhaps not. She's undoubtedly otherwise occupied bedding every other male within your walls while you're away. You know what they say, when the cat is away the mice—"

"You are lucky, Lady Madeline, that no one can hear

your vulgar words. You may be a powerful baron's daughter but you mouth is unusually common."

"I resent that greatly, my lord. In fact, you have insulted me. Please do not speak to me again—ever," she said, looking him dead in the eye and not sounding at all wounded by his words. It really was quite entertaining vexing the man. She supposed she could push him too far one day and end up dead. But better dead than caught for life in this forsaken time. She chewed her food and wondered if that was how she could return home? If something were to happen to her here would she then be catapulted back through time? Maddie pursed her lips as the thought took hold. Her now bristling husband beside her, completely forgotten.

"When we return to our quarters tonight, I would like a word with you, Lady Madeline. So you will unlock the connecting door and allow me entry. Do not fear that I will ravish you, my mind's repulsed at the thought of such an activity."

Maddie inclined her head in what she hoped was a regal gesture, while her knees trembled beneath the table. She didn't want him in her room, or anywhere near her for that matter. Somehow, he brought out the worst in her, always caused her to bristle. Too male, too controlling and the masculine pride was suffocating in the extreme. And, over the days and weeks since their marriage, she had poked fun and distaste at his every word or gesture. Perhaps he was not always so vile, but as he allowed his mistress to reside with them, it was too much for her twenty-first century pride to allow. It didn't matter that she wasn't staying, it was wrong of him to impose such behaviours on whoever he married.

"As you wish, my lord."

"I do," he said, before he turned and summoned a servant for more wine.

Maddie finished her meal, stood and withdrew from the room. She ignored the startled faces of her people when she pushed back her own chair. While she was able, she would do that herself, no matter what anyone else thought. She walked upstairs, and allowed the argument with William to recede in her mind. Mistress Rhode had promised her earlier today that she could take a bath in her room after supper. Maddie had thought to use the communal bathing chamber, but then changed her mind. At least in her room she could lock her doors and take as long as she'd like.

A little later, she sank within the warm scented water and sighed in pleasure. The tub was round, not overly large but big enough to submerge herself, if she bent her knees. Mistress Rhode had insisted on washing her hair before Maddie convinced her she could well and truly dry and dress herself, and dismissed her dear maid for the night.

Maddie relaxed back in the bath, with her knees and shoulders the only parts uncovered by water. Sleep beckoned with the help of the lavender scent that wafted from the water. All too soon, the water cooled and Maddie stirred to get out. As she reached for her towel, she cringed when her hands met nothing but wood. She swore and looked for the elusive linen before seeing it lying on her bed.

Nothing else for it, she stood and allowed the excess water to run from her skin. Just as she stepped upon the bear skin rug, she gasped as her door flew open and her husband burst in. They stood rooted on the spot; Maddie from incredulity and William, it seemed, from sheer shock. Maddie refused to panic; instead, she walked as casually as she could, under the circumstances, to the bed and grabbed her towel. She shook it out, before folding it around her body and facing him.

"If you do not mind, my lord, I would prefer no one else to see my state of undress."

"Why did you not leave the connecting door unlocked...wife?"

She sighed at his menacing tone. "It was an honest mistake. I merely forgot." She walked over to the fire for warmth, unwilling to dress with him in her room.

"Now that you are here, Lord William, what was it you wanted to discuss?"

"Is that all the excuse I'm to hear? A mere mistake?" He laughed, the sound mocking as he joined her at the hearth. "Come, my lady, do you deny this plan to entrap me with your charms?"

Maddie frowned and looked up at him as she dried her hair. "Entrap you? Ahh," she smiled. "You think highly of yourself, Lord William. You think I left the main passageway door unlocked so you would storm in without knocking and find me unclothed and in a bath. Come now, we are married and I am not ashamed of my body, but even I wouldn't stoop to sleep with you. As far as I'm concerned we are married in name only, you take your pleasure elsewhere and no doubt, eventually, so will I. And I can guarantee you, my lord, it will never be with you."

A chill ran down her spine as the last of her words left her lips. William's face mottled in anger. The change in his mannerisms gave her an overwhelming urge to run. She swallowed her panic as he closed the space between them in lightning speed and pulled her hard against his muscled chest. She froze then gasped as his hands ripped the towel from her body, leaving her as bare as the day she was born. *Oh crap, I'm in trouble now.*

His long woollen tunic couldn't mask the hardness that

sat against her stomach. Her chest flattened against his, and she struggled for air. His large, strong hands flexed against her flesh as they roamed over her body and slid down her back to clasp her buttocks. The stubble on his jaw rubbed against her cheek as he bent down to her neck. She heard the intake of breath, as he smelled her skin. Even she could smell the floral aroma, left from the bath. Maddie shivered, hoping the action was repulsion, but knowing in a small part of her mind that it was in pleasure.

"I could take you, Lady Madeline. Conquer you so you could never speak to me with such hate and abhorrence again. I could make you want only me."

She swallowed as her nipples hardened to tight little peaks. Why was his tunic open? Please God, say she hadn't done that herself. The coarse black hair tickled her skin and she shivered. Her mouth dried as his hands travelled further between the valley of her thighs. Hot wetness pooled at her core. Maddie fought her desire, hated her reaction to him. His warm breath hitched as he kissed her shoulder. His tongue ran up the length of her neck and caused the most delicious sensations, all of which she tried to ignore.

He pulled back, his gaze searching, but for what, Maddie didn't know. She looked at him, unsure of his next move, but secretly hoping he would not stop. She should stop him, should not allow him to seduce her. But as his lips, soft and beckoning, settled over hers, all such thoughts disappeared.

She moaned when their lips met. Fire ran down her spine, igniting a wild need within. She allowed his tongue to caress hers until she all but clung to him in need. She could feel his hardened penis strain against his clothing. She wanted him. Wanted desperately for release. Wanted to be filled over and over again by this man.

He nibbled her bottom lip. Maddie opened her eyes and caught his wicked, heated gaze. She clasped his jaw, and pulled him back to kiss her, needing to feel his tongue and lips demand her own. She purred when he pulled her against his engorged member, his mouth suckling her bottom lip in a beckoning manner. Her breath caught in her throat, and William swallowed her moan as his fingers teased the moist apex between her legs. Maddie shuddered.

How was it possible the man in her arms, the same one who irritated, argued and hated her, could conjure such wants and needs from her body?

His hand clasped the hair at the nape of her neck in an almost punishing hold, and his kiss turned savage. She whimpered and wrapped her leg around his waist, opening to more of his touch. His chest was hard, all heaving muscle that moved beneath her palm. A man who fought battles to the death and lived in an unforgiving time only made him more desirable. Maddie fumbled with the knot on Williams hose and shivered when his manhood sprung free.

Her desire for him consumed her and she rubbed against his ample sex seeking release. A fire burned within her soul; a blaze that only William could extinguish. Never had Maddie acted with such wantonness before, but never had she felt such need in her life either. It was a sobering thought.

William tore away from the kiss and pushed her aside. Maddie stumbled before she righted herself and watched as he stormed from her room. Shocked, she stood still for a moment then without conscious thought threw on her silver surcoat and ran after him. He couldn't just do that to her, and then leave with no explanation.

She stepped off the stone stairs in the great hall and

caught sight of him heading toward the entrance doors leading to the keep. She hastened to follow him then stopped when she reached the front steps of the castle.

A pain she shouldn't feel ran through her, paralysing everything but her vision. She watched incredulous, as the man who, not minutes before had been kissing her, about to make love to her, walked into a cottage behind a young woman. Nausea settled in her stomach. How could she have let him hold and kiss her body as she had? How could she have acted with such stupidity? Maddie wanted to wash away the filth of his touch. At that moment, she could almost feel sorry for Lady Veronica.

First thing tomorrow, the search for her ring would start in earnest and William could go to hell. Shutting the castle doors, she walked back to her room with renewed vigour and relief. Glad she hadn't slept with a man who tumbled any woman who stepped before him.

Back in her room, Maddie clasped the rosary around her neck and looked out the window to the heavens above. The stars bright beyond imagining above the medieval world she now lived in. "Please God, get me home," she said and willed the Almighty to listen to her first ever prayer.

❦

MADELINE'S BODY—BREASTS FULL AND HIGH, SMALL delicate waist, hips that flared at just the right angle, long lean legs that went on forever—invited worship. William's jaw clenched as he fought his body's desire. He reminded himself yet again, to breathe as he tried to calm his over-whelmed senses. Holy mother of God! He swore into the darkened hall as he made his way outside. What had he done? The night's cooling air did little to fight the overwhelming urge to return to her room. To take her.

He would not give her what she wanted. Christ, what he wanted. His body roared in protest at denied release. William could not, would not, have *her*. He breathed hard, his resolve almost crumbling as he remembered her naked flushed flesh and willing mind.

But Lady Madeline Vincent was the devil's spawn. Her father hailed from such origins, after all. His wife by decree, one he abhorred, was not only smart, intelligent and maddening, but also more passionate than he had ever imagined possible of a woman. He clenched his jaw with the realization that from this day on he'd only crave his wife.

Self-disgust clawed at his flesh. He was a fool, and yet, he couldn't understand why Madeline had looked wounded when he'd left. If she hated him so much she should not have allowed such liberties. But she had...

He would not sleep in his chamber tonight. Staying there would almost certainly see him end up in her bed. Instead, William walked out into the bailey and strode down toward his knights' barracks. A hard bed away from Madeline would be the safest place this nightfall.

A comely serving wench crossed his path and with a beckoning glance William's resolve to sleep alone deserted him. No matter what his past promises or current thoughts were, he would at least put himself out of pain. He followed the wench into her cottage, and shut the door on his conscience.

THE MORNING BROUGHT A HEADACHE, WHICH MADDIE thought would surely split her head in two. Just to roll over in bed made her brain shudder and pound inside her skull. She rubbed her temples and squinted as Mistress Rhode pulled the tapestry away from the window to allow the bright morning light to enter. The cool air swept into her chamber and she shivered from the temperature drop. Maddie pulled a pillow over her head in the hope it would ease the pain.

"M'lady, are you ailed this morn?"

Maddie winced as the lid of her clothes chest slammed down somewhere near the hearth. "Yes, I am. In fact, I think I'm dying." She heard her maid *tsk tsk* before the straw bed dipped, and the pillow was pulled from her head. Mistress Rhode placed a comforting hand upon her brow.

"You do not feel warm, m'lady. Is it your stomach that gives you pain?"

"No," Maddie said, sitting up. "I have a headache, nothing more."

Mistress Rhode stood and walked to the door. "I shall make up a tisane for you. I shan't be long."

Maddie closed her eyes in bliss as the quiet enveloped her once more. The only sound was that of the ocean and its waves as they crashed against the craggy, jagged rocks below. It lulled her to the verge of sleep before she started at her maid's return.

"Here we are then, m'lady. Now, it may not be to your taste, but it will rid you of your ailment."

She took the cup and stared with trepidation at the soup-like mixture. She smelled the drink and looked back at her maid who stood ready, it seemed, to pour it down her throat.

"It smells," she said.

"Would you rather it smell like mead or wine; a nectar, which fools you into thinking it will leave you feeling well until the next day, after you have drunk too much? You are correct, m'lady, it does smell. But it will rid you of the headache your sweet, nice tasting drink has given you."

Chastised, Maddie took a swallow and sat up coughing. "What on earth is in this?" she gasped, as she tried to catch her breath.

"An assortment of ingredients my mother always uses. Cabbage, iris, a small dose of comfrey."

"And you believe this will help me?"

Her maid turned away to stoke the fire, a grin upon her lips. "It will, m'lady. Never fear. Now drink!"

Maddie blocked her nose and drank down, or ate down, the remainder of the broth. It left her unsure whether her queasy stomach was from the hangover or the medicinal drink. She looked out the window from her bed. The day seemed to be clear, despite the late snow that had started to fall over the last week. The chill air raised goose bumps on her arms.

"You will need a mantle today, m'lady, it is quite cool out. Is the green gown to your liking?"

Maddie turned around, and nodded at the dress her maid held up for inspection. "That's fine. Whatever you think is best," she said, ignoring Mistress Rhode's worried frown. She jumped from the bed, and swore as the cold stone met her feet.

"You missed mass this morn, m'lady."

Maddie washed as best she could in the small bowl of tepid water. She sat down on a stool beside the fire and tried to warm herself. "I'm sorry, Mistress Rhode. I'll go tomorrow. Please make sure I'm woken in time."

Her maid helped her into her gown, the warm wool taking some of the chill from her bones. "'Tis a good idea, m'lady. There has been talk among the servants of your noticeable absence."

Maddie stood and tied her mantle in place. "What sort of talk?"

"Naught to concern yourself with, m'lady, as all will be well by day's end. You will attend mass on the morrow and perhaps ensure at each meal today prayers are held?"

Maddie met her maids pointed stare with one of her own. "Okay, as long as I don't have to say anything." Religion was not her strong point.

Mistress Rhode smiled. "Aye, m'lady. Of course."

IN THE HOPE FOOD WOULD MAKE HER SEEDINESS SOMEWHAT better, Maddie walked into the Great Hall for breakfast. She would also ensure, from now on, her consumption of medieval alcohol was monitored. Not so much to avoid the inevitable headache, but rather to escape having to drink another vile-tasting tisane again. Seated at the head of the table she nibbled some bread, and drank water she had requested to be boiled daily for drinking purposes. There was no way she could continue to drink all this wine. Maddie reached for some meat to add to her plate just as William strode into the hall. Her bad mood took a turn for the worst when she noted William wearing the same clothing as the night before. Not that such a thing should surprise her after where he had gone last night. But in a small part of her mind she had hoped her eyes had deceived her. That William wasn't as bad as he acted.

A muscle twitched in his jaw when he noticed her scrutiny of him and Maddie inwardly smiled at his unease. He bellowed to a servant for some breakfast and sat beside her. Maddie shook her head at her husband's high and mighty manner toward her people. She remembered his purposeful stride into the serving woman's home and her annoyance turned to anger. She chose to ignore his good-morning welcome, and continued to eat.

"You cannot even acknowledge your husband, m'lady? It shows very poor taste and breeding to allow your feelings to be so open and yourself to be so free to ridicule."

"I have nothing to say to you, my lord. In fact, I would think it wise for you to leave my home and lands and never return. I plan to write to King Henry, requesting he support my request for an annulment. I have no wish to be married to you."

"You didn't seem to want to be rid of me last night, ma chère?"

Maddie met his gaze. "Save it for the wenches you bed, husband, your endearments hold no sway with me."

He stilled. Maddie could almost hear his teeth grind as he clenched his jaw and picked up his mead.

"And what, pray, do you mean by that?"

Maddie smiled and leant toward him. Placed her hand upon his thigh and smirked as his muscles tightened under her grasp. Men, she thought, were so easy to manipulate; this one easier than most.

"Only that, my esteemed Lord. I know where you went last night. And it wasn't the knights' barracks."

"You followed me?" he asked in the softest tone that sounded anything but sweet.

"Yes," she replied, with a patronizing smile.

"Well," he said. "She was more comely than you, m'lady. And wenches who fit that description are few."

Maddie watched him as she nibbled on her breakfast. Should she be insulted or flattered by that? God, he could be such an arse at times.

"Well," she replied, "I hope she was worth it. No doubt after your pleasure, you will be in a more cooperative mood today and therefore will not yell at the servants."

"I did not yell at my page."

"Yes, you did, my lord."

"Is that all you are angry at? Not that I bedded another woman, but that I yelled at your vassals?"

Maddie laughed then sobered just as quickly. "You think I would be jealous, husband?" She willed herself to forget how pliant and eager she'd been in his arms. Delicious heat spread to her core, but she pushed it away, would not allow such emotion toward this man. She strove not to blush when his eyes darkened and settled on her lips. Maddie refused to give him the satisfaction of her shame.

"I believe you try to fool everyone." His whispered words were like a caress.

"What does that mean?"

William chuckled but there was no humour in the sound. "Your paleness this morn is answer enough. I believe you are sickened that I did not consummate our marriage last eve. I believe your sickly appearance is proof of this."

Maddie wiped the square linen napkin across her mouth. "You're a fool, my lord. I am pale this morning because I have a headache from too much alcohol last night."

"Drowning your sorrows over my departure. I do not doubt it," he said. "You would not be the first wench to be left so."

"Dream on, William. I drowned myself in drink because I allowed a reprobate such as you to touch me. It will not happen again. Now, if you'll excuse me, I promised to help set up some of the activities for the festival tomorrow. Have a good day, *husband*."

CHAPTER 6

W illiam sat and watched as Madeline walked, tall and proud, from the hall, her maid following at her heels. He ran a hand over his jaw, the stubble prickling his palm. What was he doing saying things he did not mean? He was not a spiteful man and yet around Madeline he could not help but be unkind. It was not her fault they married. His anger should be directed at their respective parents, not at her. He took a swig from his goblet, and wondered how she could be so indifferent to him, especially after her reaction to his kisses last eve.

His annoyance was more at himself than Madeline. He would not have treated Lady Veronica in such a derogatory manner and yet he had done so with his wife. For God's teeth, he silently muttered. It was one thing to have a mistress of whom a wife was aware. But it was quite another to leave a woman one was about to thoroughly bed and seek the first wench who crossed his path.

His body hardened as the memory of them, locked together in Madeline's room, assailed him. He thought of that kiss; its strength and intensity had near unmanned him. William slammed his mug of wine down on the dais then cursed when the red beverage spattered his hand.

He never wanted Lady Madeline for a wife. So why, with every accursed hour of the day, did he lust after her skirts. Anyone who looked past his belt would see the evidence of such a statement. But he wondered: how was it she could be so full of fire and welcome his advances only to be cold and distant hours later? He looked up as Fiona, the wench from last night, moved past the trestle tables. She displayed ample flesh to full advantage as she bent and served the morning meal.

He clenched his jaw as he looked at his food. For the first time in his life, he had not been able to bed a woman, though not for lack of trying. Not being able to perform was an unwelcome experience. Somewhere between Madeline's room and the wench's bed, his conscience had won control of his base emotions and needs. He'd known if he had slept with the servant, it would have been the ultimate betrayal of Madeline. A betrayal she would never be able to forgive. She would be lost to him. Ever since he kissed her in the woodshed, something in him had changed. 'Twould seem he had a problem.

He stabbed forcefully into his food, leftover stew from the previous evening meal. William wondered what it was about his enemy's daughter—his wife—that attracted him so much. Like flowers that followed the sun's path through the day, so did his attention on Madeline. Next, he would be spouting poetry to the delectable woman like some lovelorn court bard.

Although he cursed to admit it, he constantly looked for her. He checked with Sir Alex or his steward that she was safe and being well cared for at all times. His wife, with her easy manners and delightful charm, wooed everyone she met. It was no surprise even his soldiers at Kingston

Castle had succumbed to her charms and now worshipped wherever she walked. She was a natural-born leader, one everyone wanted to know, and one from whom everyone sought advice.

Although not once had she sought *his* counsel on any matter pertaining to her ancestral home. Madeline certainly seemed able to get along well enough, when away from him. It was only when they were together that their joint animosity came to the fore, livid as ever. His, from the sheer frustration of her not needing him, and because he did not know what he wanted any longer. And hers, it seemed, because she could not stand him, no matter what her kisses told.

He pushed his plate away, having no taste for the fare before him. He sighed, tired from his constant thoughts and the strained conversations with Madeline. A half smile lifted his lips as he remembered some past disagreements. Fire and ice described his wife. Strong and demanding, just like her deceased father. And he could not but be proud of how she stood up for herself with him. In fact, she was the first ever to have done so. He looked across the hall and noticed Sir Alex stride out into the courtyard. William stood and followed him, not for the first time wondering if there was something between his wife and most trusted knight. His hand fisted at his side, his other clasped the hilt of his sword. Did they dare?

MADDIE PLACED A BUCKET OF WATER ON TOP OF THE village well, and laughed with the other ladies who helped fill the barrels for the apple bobbing contest to be held tomorrow. The men were busy measuring where the archery contest would take place. Maddie had suggested a small area, which sat at the end of the outer bailey's wall. There were still small drifts of late snow on some of the shaded areas within the walls but here was clear and green. A large pile of wood was stacked together with rushes, signalling the location of the bonfire for the night's dancing and celebrations. Hessian bags for the children's jump race lay folded, checked and ready, along with rope for the adults' competitions. The people seemed carefree and happy, welcoming and loyal. An overwhelming sense of belonging and companionship filled her.

"M'lady, ye should not be out here, helping us as ye are. As much as we're grateful and all, it isn't fittin'."

Maddie laughed as she picked up her third bucket. "Its fine, Annie, I don't mind. Besides the festivities are in celebration of my marriage to Lord William. And, in any case, there is so much to be done; I couldn't in all good conscience leave it to everyone else."

"Well, we're happy to have your help, Lady Madeline. And so glad you're home amongst us as well," Beth replied, while she scooped some snow into her hand and flicked Annie with it. "Even if Annie here thinks otherwise."

Maddie watched as an affronted Annie placed her bucket on the ground, and threw her own handful of snow against Beth. "I didn't mean no disrespect to Lady Madeline," she replied. Beth gasped when the cold snow hit her directly in the face.

Madeline smiled at the girls' good-humoured banter. "No offense taken, Annie, and thank you, Beth," she said as she made her own snow pile on top of the stone well.

The women paused and watched her. "What's that ye doing, m'lady?"

"Just this." Maddie hurled the snow at the two women who were becoming her friends. She laughed at their shocked faces, which soon turned to smiles as they hurried to procure their own snow missiles to hurl.

It became an all-out snow fight from that point onwards. The snow soon turned to icy water and in their haste to pelt each other, they slipped on the muddy ground. Tears from laughter streamed down Maddie's face and her gown was soon covered in muck. As another bucket of freezing water landed on her head, Maddie's hair came loose and fell down her back. She gasped for breath as icy water dripped down her back. She pushed her hair from her face and noticed her companions had halted their mirth. A prickling of unease tingled up her spine and Maddie looked over her shoulder and met the unamused gaze of William.

He stood silent, his eyes wide in shock. Sir Alex, who stood beside him, wore the same expression. Maddie turned back to her friends and smiled. "You had better go change, girls. I will see you tomorrow."

"Yes, m'lady," they said in unison and scuttled off to their homes.

Maddie walked up to her husband and curtseyed before proceeding indoors.

Minutes later, Mistress Rhode set about helping her to change; a task that was quite difficult thanks to the woollen dress under her surcoat, which was heavy with water and clung to her like a second skin. Maddie stood in front of the fire and rubbed her arms to beat the chill from her flesh. She inwardly groaned as her bedroom door opened and slammed against the wall.

"Leave us!"

Maddie frowned at William before looking at her maid who seemed undecided as to whether she should obey his command. "You may leave, Mistress Rhode. Thank you."

William kicked the door shut as the maid left.

Maddie glanced at him briefly. The man obviously didn't know the meaning of fun. "What is it, my lord?" she asked, her words, like her skin, far from warm.

"What in God's country were you doing? What has possessed you to act in such a low and undignified manner?"

Maddie watched the flames lick at the wood and beat down a sigh of annoyance. "I do not think that interacting with people is degrading in any way. You may be the son of a rich man and they are not, but that is the only thing different between you. They are human, are they not, even with their low birth, as you would call it?"

"You forget, Madeline, you are also the daughter of a rich man. And from what I've heard of you, you would have thought the same as I on the matter not two months ago."

Maddie looked at him, exasperated. He was annoyed because she had lowered herself. Not that she may catch a cold and get sick. But because her status as a baron's wife had been tarnished. Well, she'd had fun for the first time since being thrown into the twelfth century and she would be damned if she'd apologize for it.

"Yes, I do believe I've changed from what I was, and if I'm not mistaken, for the better. Now, if there is nothing else, I would like to finish dressing before I head back outside to finish my tasks," she paused. "With my lowly, common servants."

She peeked at him and wondered what he was thinking. William stood near the door, his hand clasped tight on the latch. Did he want to leave, or had she ignited a passion within him he refused to acknowledge? Poor man, for he'd get no response from her. If her temper did fan his desire, he would be in a pickle. A devil sat on her shoulder and egged her to test the theory. She ran her fingers through her hair, enjoying the warmth of the fire at her back and his eyes burned a path between them.

And Maddie had her answer.

Silence ensued and she wondered what he would try, or worse, do. His gaze feasted on her breasts, barely covered by the fine chemise she wore. She pulled her shawl over her shoulders and glowered at him. The man was dangerous, and she was well on the way to being in trouble.

William stormed from the room and she slumped into a chair, thankful for the reprieve. But a little part of her felt bereft that he would not reach out the hand of friendship or that she could not control her temper whenever around him.

They seemed destined to be enemies forever.

MEWLING FOOL, THERE WAS SOMETHING WRONG WITH HIM. 'Twas not like him to be like this. He needed Madeline like he needed warmth on the coldest winter night. William reached the hall, and continued outside, wondering why the one woman who vexed and irritated him with every word she uttered had become the one woman he looked and listened for at every moment. She had looked so delightfully young and carefree as she participated in that absurd water fight with the village women. He had savoured every moment of her joy, before his being there was noticed and halted the game.

He summoned his horse from the stables and galloped from the compound. He needed to clear his head. Needed to decide what he would do. After what he had put his wife through these past months, could he make this marriage work? A marriage he was once determined to shatter in any way he could, except legally. And would, or more to the point, *could* Madeline forgive him his actions and come to care for him? Was that what plagued him? That he now cared for her, and she did not reciprocate the feeling?

William swore aloud as the horse's hooves ate up the miles beneath him. What was he thinking? He detested himself for the feelings she evoked. He'd sworn to always hate any blood of the Vincent's. He could not be attracted to her.

William clenched his jaw and ignored the slice of pain as a tree branch whipped across his cheek. He would not give in to a man's weakness for female flesh. There were plenty of other comely wenches to bed and they would have to suffice until he could get *her* out of his blood. He would not fall for his own wife! Stalwart in his determination, he spurred his steed even faster along the snow-covered track.

THE WINTER SOLSTICE FESTIVAL WAS IN FULL SWING BY noon the following day. The weather had continued to be clement for the event. The castle cook had outdone herself with the prizes to be given out for the events planned. Toffee apples were also a hit and Maddie smiled as every child was given one, just for being there.

As lady of the manor, Maddie presented the winning prize in the archery contest. Much to her horror, the winner was her husband, who demanded a kiss from his wife. She was ashamed now to admit that she was still recovering from it. Maddie had walked up to William, about to bestow a sweet kiss upon his cheek when he took control of the contact altogether. Careless of their public display, he pulled her up against him, ran his hands through her hair and kissed her. Hard. Their breath mingled and when his tongue sought hers, she'd melted like the snow does in sunlight.

Maddie took a cooling sip of her mead, her face uncomfortably warm when she remembered the loud catcalls from the villagers. It seemed whenever William became passionate he forgot his hatred of her. And vice versa. He had treated her, since then, with all the cordiality expected from a husband. It had made her not only nervous, but put her on her guard.

She stood next to Beth and Annie and laughed as the men attempted to grasp bobbing apples with their teeth. The water in the wooden tubs had frozen at the top overnight, and was bitterly cold. Sir Alex, who agreed to help her, bestowed the winning prize upon the town smithy before summoning the women to try their luck.

Maddie pulled her hair back into a ponytail and fastened it with a ribbon. She walked toward the barrels and ignored the gasps of delight and shock, which ran through the crowd at her participation in the game.

"M'lady, are you entering this competition?" Sir Alex asked, an amused twist to his lips.

"Absolutely; I didn't fill all these barrels yesterday for nothing. Now hurry along and start us off. I have a contest to win."

"Oh no you don't, m'lady. I've won these past years at such competitions. I'll be not letting the title go without a fight."

Maddie smiled over at Becky, the village healer and nodded. "I wouldn't expect anything less. Good luck to you." The crowd applauded and Maddie caught William smiling at her good-natured banter. Her breath caught in her lungs, as his face softened by the gesture. Hell, he was handsome when relaxed and carefree like this. Her stomach flip-flopped when he grinned at her and she severed the exchange. Nerves fluttered in her stomach and she couldn't tell if they were due to the contest or her husband.

"Ready, ladies? Go," Sir Alex said.

Maddie dived into the water and madly tried to bite an apple. She had always enjoyed this game, even when she came away with the appearance of a drowned rat. Having played numerous times as a child, she had a trick or two up her sleeve. The apple brushed her lips; she pushed it toward the edge, held it there and bit. She inwardly laughed as she jumped up with it firmly between her teeth.

Maddie spied Becky's husband who stood watching and noted his crestfallen visage at her victory. She realized at once how important such a small win was to some people. Determined to be a good sport, she bit through the fruit and allowed it to fall back into the water. She chewed and watched as Becky stood up proud and tall with her own apple between her teeth. Maddie clapped and shrugged in mock disappointment.

"I congratulate Becky, who seems to be the reigning champ one more year." Maddie picked up the prize and handed it to her. "Congratulations, Becky. Perhaps next year, with some practice, I may beat you yet."

Becky, whooping her glee, walked toward the surrounding crowd to bask in her winner's glow. Maddie walked back to her barrel, picked up her apple floating on top and proceeded to eat it.

"You lost on purpose, Madeline," William said, the warmth of his gaze warming her skin.

She laughed. "Of course not, why would I do such a thing? Becky won fair and square, you saw for yourself."

"Nay, I disagree. But I understand your reasoning. It was very kind of you."

Maddie looked at William and could almost forget

what a tyrant he'd been to her. The way he had treated her today, as a woman cared for—not loathed—made it awfully hard to be uncivil.

"Well, I can have toffee apples anytime I like, can't I. And Becky wouldn't be the only person here fighting for such a delicacy. It would've been wrong of me, even if my desire to win is so very great and hard to ignore."

"Do you always strive so?" he asked.

Maddie frowned and wondered if she was inclined to win at all cost. She supposed, up to her parent's death, she'd most definitely been competitive. She had striven to fulfil every last wish or dream her parents had ever held for her. Her antique shop in Greenwich was proof of that; her mother had always wanted to open one with her daughter. And eventually Maddie had done so, but without her dear parent to cut the blue ribbon. And now here she was in medieval England, competing against village women for apples and another woman of a different nature for her husband.

She looked away, startled by such a notion. Was she jealous of Lady Veronica having William's love just because she didn't? And having thought such a thing, did she want it? William was the most difficult, highhanded Neanderthal she had ever known. His kisses may have made her toes curl, but he frustrated her too much for such a delightful exchange to sway her. No, she silently swore, there was no way, no matter how he smiled at her with his full, devil-may-care mouth, was she going to fall for such charms.

She'd sworn to herself never to be fooled by looks or sweet words. Both were gestures known to hide lies. And William's past actions had hurt too much for her to forgive and start over. Men of such caliber weren't to be trusted. She'd learnt her mistake by her unfaithful ex. Maddie wouldn't be duped a second time. And in any case, she wasn't staying—that point, most of all, was foremost. She may be competitive, but not so much that she would stoop to win the love of a husband already bestowing his favours elsewhere.

"I believe I may be slightly inclined so, my lord. But there are worse traits a person can have." She looked into his eyes, murky and swirling with...with... Maddie swallowed. "For instance, I can think of one such trait."

"Oh, and what would that be, may I ask?" His voice deep and husky reverberated down her spine. She strove not to blush from the all-consuming earth-shattering look he gave her. Why did he have to look at her like that?

"I would think the need to have a mistress who lives under the same roof as a wife as one," she said, surprised her voice held steady. She watched as his face turned thunderous, the heated look of a second ago quickly dissipating. She almost regretted having to fight with him, especially when they were being civil to one another. But some things in life were just so, and that was the end of it. If he thought to make it into her bed, he had another thing coming. Either that, or William was out to make her a fool; nothing would surprise her when it came to this man.

Over the past weeks, she had watched, and had noticed his moods often swung in extremes. So much so, the staff didn't know how to proceed with him or go about asking for direction. Well, either way, she wasn't going to be fooled by a handsome face that camouflaged the harsh man with no conscience beneath. Maddie summoned Mistress Rhode and watched as William stormed across the bailey toward the castle gates before disappearing around the stone wall.

"Oh dear, m'lady, I do believe His Lordship is quite out of temper."

Guilt pricked at her conscience. Had she pushed him too far? Was she being catty for no good reason? And could William be trying to change? This day was her people's chance to celebrate their chatelaine's wedding, and now the happy couple were no longer even together, or on speaking terms for that matter. Maddie looked about and realized some villagers, by their interested stares, may have heard their argument.

She swore before setting out after him. If she had done one thing today, it should have been to let sleeping dogs lie. She chastised herself for being weak, allowing the guilt to rise up within her. Was he up to something? More than likely. It was his fault she didn't trust a thing he said or did. She swore again as she walked in the direction he had taken. She hated eating humble pie. Damn the man.

She stopped at the gatehouse and asked a sentry where his lordship had passed. The knight pointed and Maddie walked over the drawbridge to see William seated on some outlying boulders staring into open fields before him. He tensed the moment he became aware of her. She sat next to him and looked out over the land, some parts still covered with snow.

"'Twould be wise to leave, wife."

"I'm sorry," she said. "I should not have said what I did, especially today. We need to keep, at least in public, a display of decorum and liking for one another. Even if false," Maddie added as an afterthought. "Please come back before talk of our public rift dampens everyone's enjoyment."

WILLIAM TURNED AND LOOKED AT MADELINE, FLUSHED AND as pretty as ever. He wondered if her rosy cheeks stemmed from the embarrassment of her apology to him, or the cold. More than likely, the latter.

True, he would not deny his anger at her at this moment. But God's teeth, it did not lessen his attraction to his wife. If anything, it increased it in some way. William ran his hand through his hair to distract himself from reaching out and touching her. She sat beside him, a delicious morsel of everything he desired in a woman. She could be light-hearted and cold-hearted in turn, usually the latter when around him. Even so, he wanted to smash the icy feelings. He wanted her to laugh, engage, and talk with him as she did with all the others who lived within the walls of their strongholds. In truth, she drove him to distraction. Yet he did not want it to be *her* who evoked these unwanted and unknown feelings within. Why could it not be the Lady Veronica who inspired such emotions?

William didn't reply; instead, he stood and pulled her to stand, before placing her hand upon his arm and proceeding back toward the castle. Neither spoke as they walked the short distance. William was thankful for the silence. The Lady Madeline was turning out to be more than a dangerous foe. He rubbed his temple as a headache set in.

HOURS LATER, MADDIE SAT WITH A GOBLET OF ALE between her hands and watched, delighted, as the dancing commenced around the bonfire. Some of the knights and their ladies who attended the feast attempted to dance the intricate steps the folk music required. They could dance in stately procession in the Great Hall but their attempts to out-dance the common villagers on the green were in vain. Annie and Beth, who were both well on the way to being intoxicated, partied hard. Maddie laughed at some of the antics of people who had imbibed too freely of the mead, ale, and wine.

Sir Alex, for instance, was flirting outrageously with Fiona, a servant from the castle. Maddie inwardly frowned as she watched the pair, their heads close in conversation. She wondered what his betrothed would think of him right at this moment.

The woman was a light skirt and well on the way to ruining herself completely, if not already. She had slept with William—her husband after all. Her eyes narrowed at the thought.

"Dance with me, Madeline?"

Maddie looked at Lord William, who sat beside her on the trestle seat. Firelight played across his face, accentuating the hard angles of his features. He really was gorgeous. She wondered how to answer. After their earlier fight, the day had progressed wonderfully; it was a miracle, really. Especially when she considered that previously the two of them could hardly last five minutes in each other's company without jumping down one another's throats. She would love to dance, but if he expected her to dance like a noble lady he'd be sorely disappointed. And more than likely extremely embarrassed by the end of it. She wondered how to go about refusing him, without causing offence.

"My father thought I did not require such delicate teachings, my lord. I'm afraid that unless you want your toes trodden on, you will have to be content with other partners." Maddie stilled as he took her hand and her heart stopped as his lips skimmed the sensitive skin on her inner wrist. Sexual need thrummed between them and Maddie bit her lip wondering where it came from. They were so close his breath fanned the skin on her cheek. Not to mention, William smelt divine, like leather and the lavender soap he favoured. A shiver ran down her spine. Her husband was very good with the act of seduction.

"Dance with me, ma chère."

Her resolve to deny him drowned in the intensity and heat of his dark hooded orbs. His lips were only a slight lean away and she swayed toward him. She wanted to take all that he offered, taste him again and see where the kiss would lead. He, too, moved and time seemed to still.

A ruckus around the fire startled her and Maddie jumped back, knocking her drink over as she did so. Her cheeks flamed.

"Very well, my lord, if you insist. But I warn you, I really do not know how to dance," she said, standing quickly to hide her embarrassment.

William smiled and stood. He captured her around the waist and his fingers flexed, kneaded her body as they walked out to other dancers. She bit her lip knowing he'd seen through her bravado. The imprint of his hand left a flame in its wake and her skin burned from the contact. Maddie smelled the alcohol on his breath as they swung into the music. Was his politeness toward her today due to his inebriation? Why did she hope this was not the case?

"'Tis no concern. I'll teach you how to move."

His whispered words floated against her ear before his lips grazed the sensitive skin beneath her lobes. Maddie swallowed her shock as the dance separated them and she moved on to her next partner. Even with them dancing with others, she couldn't tear her gaze from him. What was going on here? She would *not* be attracted to him. What was he playing at teasing her like this? William had been nothing but awful since the day they met. He had a mistress for crying out loud; one, she reminded herself, he refused to get rid of.

But today, this night, right at this moment, as she danced with a man whose flirtatious manner was kind and gentle, her tightly meshed resolve to hate him crumbled a little. Could there be more to the man she had married? His responsibilities were many and great indeed. That, she never doubted. But could he be willing to change for her? Change this toxic marriage between them for the better? It was something she should consider: to meet him half way. Maybe...

But not now, not this night. Tonight was for celebration. For her people to enjoy themselves, free of errands and expectations. Maddie threw herself into the dance. She relaxed and enjoyed the moment and allowed everything and anything that lay between them to slip away—to be a concern for another time. The night was still young and there was more fun to be had.

The laughter at Aimecourt rang out for many hours after.

LATER THAT EVENING—KINGSTON CASTLE

"You say Lady Madeline thinks herself from the future?"

"Yes, m'lady. I heard her with me own ears say just that. Her maid, you know the protective dark one..."

"Yes, I know which one, pray continue," Lady Veronica said, annoyed by the girl's prolonged speech.

"Well, I heard her say to Lady Madeline to keep her mouth closed and not to talk to others about her concern, lest it be misconstrued."

"Did they see you? Did you keep well hidden as I instructed?"

"Of course, m'lady, no one saw me. I used the gate

your mam told you of, just as you instructed. I thinks me could be a spy all the time, if you like."

Lady Veronica walked over to her desk and pulled out a piece of parchment. Her mother would be happy to hear of this, as she herself was. How dare that lowbred whelp demand Lady Veronica stay behind at Kingston Castle while she galloped off with her lover?

Veronica smiled. So, Mistress Rhode thought the people may think the Lady Madeline a witch if they heard Her Ladyship's nonsense uttered aloud. Interesting...

She looked up when she realized the girl still stood before her waiting. "What is it now, Laura?" Her servant shuffled her feet in a nervous manner.

"Payment, m'lady. You promised me if I did ye bidding, I'd be paid."

Lady Veronica took pity on the frightened girl. She had, after all, proved to be a reliable spy on this occasion. She had earned her coin. Picking up a handful, she handed them to the woman.

"Thank you for your assistance, Laura. Do not travel far; I may take you up on your offer."

"Oh thank you, Your Ladyship. Thank you," she repeated as she backed out of the room. The girl's eyes glittered with excitement at having so much coin in her hand.

Lady Veronica picked up her quill and proceeded to write to her mother. Perhaps it was time the lands at Kingston were threatened by the mysterious Scots everyone was afraid of. Perhaps it was time indeed. She laughed.

CHAPTER 7

Two days after the festival, Maddie set out to look for her ring in earnest. Why she had put it off for so long, she did not know. They had been back at Aimecourt for two weeks, more than enough time to search.

However, despite her good intentions; something had always sprung up; a problem with the evening meal, a sudden birth of a baby within the village or a sick serf who needed tending. And it seemed the Lady Madeline was the one expected to help, even though most of the time she had no idea what to do. Her steward hounded her every footstep regarding the household accounts, which was something at least she could make sense of.

It all took significant time, time she did not have if she wanted to find a way to return home. The days seemed to pass her by with considerable speed, ended every night with her under the same coarse blankets, staring out glass-less windows, in a time not her own. Three months had almost passed since her journey into the nether regions of history. It was time she put other matters aside and found the blasted piece of jewellery that transported her here in the first place.

The air was chill, to say the least, as she stood atop one of the four towers of the keep in the early morning mist. Her inside shoes, slippers made of colored goatskin, were layered with snow and ice. She looked between the merlons cut into the stone, and surveyed her vast expanses of land. A fact still hard to comprehend. All this wealth belonged to one family. A family that had denied even the basic rights to its workers. The Lady Madeline of old deserved to be horsewhipped over the living conditions of these people.

Some of her serfs were ill, riddled with lice and dying of what she knew of as dysentery. Regardless of her steward's condemning frown when she mentioned the fact, the working conditions of her people had to change. Not only were they required to work well past sunset, but also their basic dwellings, made from strips of woven wood covered with a mixture of dung, straw and clay, were in dreadful condition. She gave orders for repairs to be undertaken immediately with directions to her carpenters to attend to any matters they deemed necessary.

This Christmas, all the village children were to be fitted with new shoes too. A smile quirked her lips as she thought of the gift she would bestow. Shoes were a well sought after commodity for the poor. Her people, Maddie hoped, would be grateful, and see the gesture as a way of apology for the family's wrongdoing in the past.

She breathed in the clean chilled air and gestured for her maid to come stand beside her.

"Mistress Rhode, what is the clearing I can see over there?" Maddie asked, pointing. "It doesn't look natural. Was there some sort of building there once?"

Her maid nodded, pulling her cloak over her head as she stepped up into the breeze that blew over the stone.

"Aye, m'lady. That's the site of the original village of Aime-court. It hasn't always been within the walls of the castle."

Maddie frowned. "Why was it moved?"

Her maid let out a resigned sigh and looked back over the lands beyond. "Fifteen years ago, m'lady, your father and the then Baron Kingston were at war. I believe it was over land and boundary disputes, but I cannot be certain. Both barons were cruel. Neither flinched when swords fell on the innocent under the care of each household." Mistress Rhode's eyes clouded with pain. "Was a terrible time, m'lady, one I never wish to experience again."

"So they fought over land and then decided to betroth their children to each other. That doesn't make any sense. Why would they do such a thing if they hated each other?" Maddie watched as her maid found her slippered feet fascinating all of a sudden and she wondered what she wasn't being told of the story.

"The king put a stop to the war. He would not condone any further bloodshed between two Norman families. If his Highness lost the feudal services of these two great families, it could have put his own safety in jeopardy, should he need their help. It could not continue any longer."

"So the king arrived and stopped the war, by whatever means. Then, in a deranged attempt to keep his barons from further fighting, he thought to betroth the children to one another?" Maddie said with sarcasm. "Was he mad?" Her maid's eyes widened as she stole a look over her shoulder.

"M'lady Madeline, remember who and where you are. The king's decree is not something any would oppose. Do not jest so aloud. The king threatened war upon Kingston and Aimecourt should the marriage not take place. Your father, a confidant of the king, would never go against his wishes. However, the late Baron of Kingston was furious and held a deep grudge against your father until his death."

"Do you think this is why William dislikes me so?" A peculiar amused look passed over her maid's face. Maddie thought back over her question and frowned, having not thought it funny.

"His Lordship grew up full of hate and loathing of the Baron of Aimecourt and any beneath his rule and care," Mistress Rhode answered, her voice weary.

"Perhaps it would be easier between us should I give Lord William the land they wanted all those years ago. You said yourself you believed it to be over boundaries," Maddie said, watching her maid closely and not missing her servant's pale countenance.

"Many years have passed, child. Leave it be. I'm sure in time His Lordship and yourself will get along well enough."

Maddie caught the guilty line of her maid's face but let it go. What was she hiding? And she was not the only one hiding something. But what? Did William know? Of course he would. With a father who never kept silent over his dislike of the Baron of Aimecourt, how could he not? Maddie wiped away a snowflake as it landed on her cheek, and stepped toward a door leading into the castle.

"Shall we return? It's getting cold."

"Yes, m'lady, let's."

LATER THAT DAY MADDIE STOOD LOOKING DOWN A SNOW-covered road. One they were soon to travel. Somewhere over those hills, between Aimecourt and the church, lay her ring. Surely it did. It had to, for it certainly wasn't anywhere within the castle. Between Mistress Rhode and herself, they had rummaged through every square inch of the place. Including the carriage in which she had landed those many weeks ago. She pulled her cloak closer as a chill ran down her spine.

"Lady Madeline, the carriage is ready. If you will, we should make haste before it grows too late and we're unable to continue our search."

Maddie turned away and walked toward her maid. "Was anyone able to locate and inform Lord William of our plans?"

"Nay, m'lady, but I have notified your steward and asked him to pass on the message as soon as His Lordship returns."

"Thank you." Maddie hastened down the stairs. She hadn't seen William since the night of the winter solstice. She knew he had ridden out yesterday with thirty armed men, but as yet, had not returned. All Sir Alex had said, when she enquired as to the purpose of their journey, was it was nothing of concern. Maddie tried not to worry, knowing William was a seasoned warrior and could take care of himself.

However, these times were far from safe. War, death, and famine were a part of everyday life. Even if the journey were only between family estates, the miles left any open to assault. There was no doubt William could be obnoxious and domineering, but lately he had shown another side of himself. One she could grow to like very much, given enough time and if she was fool enough to do so. No matter what was between them, she wished no harm to befall him.

It took one hour to reach the spot where Mistress Rhode believed Maddie had fallen onto the floor after hitting the rut in the road. Stepping from the carriage, they searched for the missing jewellery. Sir Alex and their coachman even braved the winter chill to look for her missing ring, before the snow became too heavy. They walked, searched the road longer than advisable in such conditions, but without luck. It seemed pointless to have even tried, like searching for a needle in a haystack.

Maddie stood next to the carriage and turned as the sound of approaching horses thundered in the distance. She looked to Sir Alex, whose attention was fixed on a group of men cantering up the road. A prick of alarm shot through her when he tensed and became alert. He came to stand before her, silent and watchful. Maddie stood on her toes and tried to see over his broad shoulders. Hoped against hope she would live to see another day, even if in 1102. She sighed in relief, as none other than her husband, led the party that bore down on them.

Maddie smiled and stepped around Sir Alex, then stopped. The riders who accompanied her husband, were male—all but one. She should have known William's inability to live without his whore wouldn't last. Maddie had an overwhelming urge to smack the condescending smirk off Lady Veronica's face. She swallowed, hating the absurd crush upon her chest. It wasn't like she didn't know of his mistress. He'd never taken the care to hide that from her. So why did the sight of them together make her want to vomit.

At least it explained where he had been these last two days. She pushed away her stupid feminine hurts and let anger coil in her gut. William dismounted and strode toward her, his face a mask of cool indifference. Maddie lifted her chin and watched him, his large woollen cloak making his broad shoulders seem even larger. He grasped her arm and she wrenched free, the thought of him touching her made her skin crawl.

William glared at Sir Alex. "What's the meaning behind you having Lady Madeline out in this weather?"

"It was my choice, my lord. I lost something on the day of our wedding, and I was trying to find it," Maddie said.

After a few tense-filled moments, William glanced at her. "What is it you've lost, Madeline?" he asked.

"It doesn't matter. It's not here." She walked over to the carriage and opened the door, only to have it slammed again by her husband.

"Madeline, you are angry with me." His gaze searched her face. "Why?"

Maddie looked out toward the open fields and forest that lay beyond the road. What was this emotion she was feeling? Some form of annoyance, or the worse and more telling emotion of jealousy. She shook her head. No. She wouldn't be jealous of Lady Veronica. Not ever.

"In the future, please advise me when you sojourn off into the sunset with your mistress. Unless, of course, you do this so I look incompetent to my people. I don't like to ask after my husband only to be informed he has left."

His deep, rumbling chuckle was the opposite response to what she expected. Her stomach flipped as he ran a finger down her cheek and then tweaked her chin.

"My humble apologies, my lady," William said, bowing. "But the matter was urgent and needed my immediate attention."

Or Lady Veronica needed urgent attending.

"Lady Veronica has come to stay, Madeline. There have been reports of the king's enemies roaming these parts, murder and mayhem their only goal. We are Norman, all our homes and lives are at risk. I could not leave her at Kingston castle unprotected." William folded his arms over his chest and Maddie noted he wore chain-mail. Her mouth dried seeing him dressed as a soldier for the first time. If anything, his armour made him even hotter. Not that he'd ever hear those words from her.

"There have been no such reports received at Aimecourt, my lord. I think you must think me a simpleton who is unable to glean your true purpose."

"I do not do this to hurt you, Madeline."

"Whatever," she said as she turned and stepped into her carriage. She could understand him needing to keep his people safe, but surely the Lady Veronica could have been taken anywhere other than her home. Perhaps back to her own family in London, from where she apparently hailed. Or to her brother's, Lord Ribald of Castle Dee.

Her stomach rolled with nausea. She didn't want that conniving, nasty woman to live within her walls. Whenever she saw her, she always had an overwhelming urge to scratch the woman's eyes out. Veronica was obviously happy to be back within arm's reach of William, knew that her presence within Aimecourt would make Maddie look the fool to her people.

"There is nothing left to say between us." The coach lurched as her maid settled into the seat across from her. "Please step away, so I may proceed home," she said, as she looked back to her husband who stood silent beside the door. She leant over and slammed the door shut and tried to ignore the simmering fury that blazed from his eyes.

Why should he be angry? It was she who had the right to be furious. How dare he bring Lady Veronica into her home, especially when she had said no to such a situation? They may have been on their way to being friends, but that was well and truly over now. Perhaps in time their friendship could have progressed into something deeper. Who knew? But not now, not after his actions this day. She would not allow him to sway her with his fake words and easy charm. He'd be lucky if she showed civility toward him again. Be damned if she would welcome that whore into her home with open arms. Damned indeed.

THE GREAT HALL BUSTLED WITH KNIGHTS, LADIES AND servants as the evening meal began. Freshly laid rushes that smelt of herbs and spices crackled beneath Maddie's slippered feet. The peat fire lent a muddy smell to the room. Oddly, it reminded her of home, the atmosphere welcoming. Turning toward the dais, she stopped as she took in the seating arrangements.

Maddie pulled forth all the authority a lady of the manor would have, determined to sit at her allotted station. She straightened her back and walked toward William and Lady Veronica who seemed deep in conversation. An overwhelming urge to throw Veronica to the floor assailed her and Maddie took a calming breath. She would not make a scene, nor let Lady Veronica get the better of her. The room quieted as others watched, noted her presence. She hated William at that moment. How could he allow such a slight against his wife? A wife he knew damn well hated his mistress.

Maddie came to stand beside her seat. Lady Veronica continued to converse with William making it plainly obvious she was being ignored. Heat coursed up her neck. Not one to fight, Maddie would have preferred to slink away and disappear, let them have each other and be done with it. However, this was her home; this was the Lady Madeline's home, not theirs. Maddie owned this grand estate and she would sit on the chair allotted to her by right of birth. Even if she was acting as a stand-in mistress at present.

She looked over the tables and caught the inquisitive,

worried glances of her servants. About to physically remove Veronica herself, she heard her husband hiss at Her Ladyship, which ensured Veronica's departure. Maddie met the whore's laughing gaze as she stepped away, her own eyes hard. It took all her will not to trip her as she walked past. Really, that woman was going to go down, and hopefully by her hand.

Maddie sat, ignored her husband's welcome and gestured to the servants to proceed serving the main meal.

"Madeline, you must understand it was imperative for me to bring Lady Veronica here. I received word from my steward that a Scottish war party was roaming the area. 'Twould have been wrong of me to allow Lady Veronica to stay within a keep still under construction and not as well fortified as Aimecourt."

Maddie refused to be turned by the common sense her husband spoke. She regarded him over the rim of her cup as she took a sip of wine.

"You forget I do not care what happens to Lady Veronica, my lord. She is nothing to me and never will be. Never have I known a more callous, spiteful, and devious woman. I will not make her welcome here or treat her kindly; she has never shown me such a courtesy. And as soon as the trouble abates, I want her gone and you with her. I have written to the king requesting the termination of our marriage. I hope in time we may both be able to move on in our lives to futures we both want and desire." Maddie held her husband's furious gaze and refused to cower.

"Maybe," she continued, "you could make an honest woman of her." If that was even possible. Maddie scooped some chicken broth up with the ladle provided. An ache settled in her chest at the thought of William and Lady Veronica married.

Maddie could feel William's anger as he stared at her.

Well, he should not think her all puff and no wind. She *did* have the nerve. And to prove her point, she had followed through on her threat—she'd sent the messenger off this morning with her letter to King Henry. She would not repent. No longer would she be stepped on.

"I thought..." he paused. "'Twas my understanding that we were gaining a friendship, one I had hoped may become more in time. Perhaps prosper into a marriage of the truest sense," he said.

Maddie turned away from him, not wanting him to see her own conflicted thoughts and feelings on the subject. She frowned as confusion swamped her. For whatever reason, she was stuck in this time, and to survive one had to make the best of the circumstances in which one found oneself. But what was the point of William and herself? They never seemed to get along. Every opportunity he had, he ran back to his mistress. He'd slept with the woman on their wedding day, for God's sake. It didn't matter what the reason; it didn't change the fact it had happened. No matter what he said or felt toward her now, he had an obligation to Lady Veronica, one he needed to recognize and honour. Lady Veronica's venom toward her was solely because she saw her as competition. And perhaps if Maddie placed herself within Lady Veronica's shoes, she would do the same.

No, on second thought, she couldn't agree wholly with that. Had a man up and married someone else, while dating her, she would have hightailed as far away as possible from the situation. Nevertheless, perhaps she should stop being so callous and nasty to Veronica. It wasn't as if any of this was Her Ladyship's fault. And it wasn't in her nature to be catty, scratching and hissing at everyone every minute of every day. She took a sip of her wine and slumped back in her chair.

"You and your kin will always be welcome in time of need within Aimecourt, Lord William, including Lady Veronica. Who in time no doubt will become your wife. The king may have forced us into this marriage, but it would seem we have the power to end it. Do not live your life doing what everyone else thinks is right for you. We are not matched well, and that's the end of it. Our parents and the king were wrong. It is neither of our faults. I'm only sorry you have wasted these weeks when your life could have been spent more pleasantly elsewhere." Maddie tried to keep the spite out of her voice, but it was not easy. The thought of William back in Veronica's bed maddened her. And it shouldn't. She should be happy he stayed away from her, stopped looking at her as if contemplating something that made her insides quiver.

"I'm married to you. I made a vow to you, Madeline. I do not back away from my obligations, whatever they are. What is blessed by God cannot be undone."

"Well, I'm sorry for you, then, because I refuse to be married to a man who sees me as an obligation. We both deserve more," Maddie stated, lowering her voice as others about the hall looked their way.

"It is too late, Madeline. What is done cannot be undone. No letter to our sovereign will change that." William paused when she stood. "Madeline, 'twould be unwise for you to leave this table, if that is your plan. You will finish this discussion, and you will finish it...now!"

Maddie held his maddened stare as she stepped away from her chair. She pushed down the lump which formed in her throat as she strode from the great hall. How could she start a relationship with William? The year 1102 wasn't her time. And this wasn't her life to live. Perhaps she was stuck married to William, but that didn't mean she would allow it to become marriage in truth. It may not be what she wanted to do in her heart, but it was for the best, Lord William was not for her—ever. She stumbled to the stairs as her vision blurred under the multitude of tears.

"M'lady, what is wrong?"

Maddie allowed her maid to usher her upstairs. "Nothing. Mistress Rhode, that the twenty-first century couldn't fix," Maddie said, with a self-deprecating smile.

"Come, m'lady I will put you to bed and make a tisane."

"No," Maddie said, a little too quickly, a shudder of revulsion running though her at the memory of the last tisane. "I just need some sleep. Do not trouble yourself."

Her maid studied her face at her chamber door then conceded. "Perhaps I could sit with you for a time," Mistress Rhode ventured.

Maddie sat on a stool before the hearth. "I'll be fine, really," she answered brightening her features to place more believability behind her words. "I'll see you in the morning."

Her maid protested but eventually departed. Maddie looked back to the fire. The heat of the flames soon dried the tears, but couldn't warm her heart. Her decision was for the best. And perhaps if she kept repeating such words, eventually she would believe them as well.

WILLIAM SWORE AS HE WATCHED MADELINE WALK FROM the hall. What was the woman thinking? He glanced at the empty seat beside him and rubbed his jaw. Such a troublesome wench, to have written the king. But then, he wasn't overly concerned that she had. The king would not want such a powerful Norman family alliance to come apart. Kingston's and Aimecourt's joined forces, were too powerful an ally to lose. The king may sympathize with Madeline over her situation, but he would not allow an annulment of the marriage to take place. At least, that was what William was counting on.

"Lady trouble, m'lord?"

William laughed then groaned at Sir Alex beside him. "Maddening wench. She is too proud, like her father, to see reason."

Sir Alex nodded and sipped his mead. "May I ask what her ladyship has troubled you over?"

"She wrote the king requesting an annulment."

Sir Alex spat his mead out all over the dais. William looked on with disinterest, his thoughts mimicking that of his knight's reaction.

"Nay, she did not."

"Aye, she did. She believes the union can be tossed aside as if it never was. She does not seek my bed," William said, gazing down at his wine.

Sir Alex chortled. "Do ye wish to seek hers?"

"Be lying if I said no. But I've hardly been fair nor treated Madeline kindly since our marriage. 'Twould serve as my own fault should she turn from me and seek another," William said, his eyes alighting on Lady Veronica who sat at the trestle tables before the dias.

"The king will toss such a request to the dung heap, m'lord. 'Tis as certain as the sun rising on the morn." Sir Alex nodded toward William's mistress. "What of Lady Veronica?"

William shrugged. "'Twould seem the association must end. Lady Veronica knew our tryst would be just that, a tryst. I have let it carry on much too long. I will speak to her and inform her of my decision."

Sir Alex poured more wine. "I have known ye, m'lord, for a long time. And never in all that time have ye succumbed to a woman's demand." William gave him a baleful look. "But to win the love of the Lady Madeline will be a difficult task," Sir Alex continued, a smile quirking his lips. "She is strong willed, aye, but she is also kind and passionate about her people. I wish you luck, m'lord; I believe you will need it."

William nodded, his knight's words true and fair. An accursed fool was what he was. To win the love and trust of a woman, predisposed from birth to hate you, did not bode well for him. But he would succeed and win her.

William watched Sir Alex make his way through the great hall and out of the keep. He looked down at his meal and pushed it away, no longer hungry for food or company. Both their strongholds needed an heir. And Madeline, his wife, was required to fulfil her duties and give him one. And soon.

᠁

LADY VERONICA SMILED TO HERSELF, AS SHE IGNORED THE pitiful men who surrounded her. All were trying to win her affections with grand tales of war or female conquests notched upon their belts. They were fun enough to play with, she supposed, always delightful to bed when Lord William was absent, which seemed often these days. She smiled at the young archer who sat beside her. He reminded her of a pathetic dog with doe eyes, panting to do her bidding.

However, he *was* delicious to look at. His arms bulged with rippling muscle. His face, although youthful, showed promise of a future knight, one who would be devilishly handsome. An all-too familiar heat spread between her legs as he took in her gaze, their communication silent, a promise of what was to come...later.

She ran her hand up his inner thigh, reached his drawers, and fondled what was concealed within. He stiffened in her palm. Biting her lip, she fought the desire to straddle him and take him here and now. An archer was just what she needed; one to teach her how to perfect her aim, which always seemed to be a little off during her own practices. She giggled as his hand started to journey under her dress, sending delicious shivers across her skin.

It had been so easy to falsify the letter to Lord William about the outlaw party who roamed the area. She inwardly laughed at her own guile. What a shame it was that the pretty Lady Madeline was going to come to harm by that terrifying company of men. And of course if that did not work, she only had to tell Lord William of the conversation her maid had overheard between his wife and Mistress Rhode not long after their marriage. The conversation reeked of witchcraft, and no lord of the realm wanted to be associated with such slander.

Either way, she would be rid of the Lady Madeline. Justice and death was much more satisfying when achieved by one's own hand. William could no longer be trusted to think logically when it came to his wife. To think he would trial her in the manor court was laughable, the fool. Standing, she beckoned with a silent look for her night's entertainment to follow, which of course he did, in all haste...

CHAPTER 8

M addie sat in the solar, enjoying what little sunlight came through the narrow windows and conceded defeat. The ring was not here. Wasn't anywhere, in fact. She suppressed a scream of frustration. Did it mean she was stuck here in 1102 forever? Was she going to grow old and die in medieval England? A shudder ran down her spine at the revolting thought.

Her attention wandered from her stitching, laying untouched in her lap, to the woman who sat across from her. Lady Veronica, exquisite and conceited as ever, plied her needle with ease. Although, perhaps not at ease herself, if her constant fidgeting was anything to go by. And any wonder, considering the size of the dark blue love-mark that sat above her left breast. The finest piece of lace was no match for the blotch on her skin.

Maddie stabbed the needle through her embroidery. Hated the thought of Veronica and William together. Hated herself more for hating it. She must have been deluded when she'd started to like him before he brought his mistress here. She did not want to feel anything for William, a man who did not care for her or her opinion.

Maddie shook her head. She was not jealous, perhaps only envious that William had someone he loved in this harsh time and she had no one. And never would if she remained stuck in 1102. Maddie looked down at her pitiful stitching, and cringed. It would seem she had no talent whatsoever for the finer arts women employed in this time, the art of being a wife included in her estimation.

"How do you like married life, Lady Madeline? From conversations with William, I understand you care naught for the notion," Veronica said, with a smug smile.

Maddie pushed away the hurt that rose in her chest. It should not surprise her that William would discuss their marriage with his mistress. It was no secret William did not care for her. Why would he see the need to keep their conversations private? He was in love with another, had he not almost told her that himself? It should not shock her to hear such words spoken aloud. However, hearing it from this woman's lips, somehow made it seem all the more awful.

"It is all very well, I suppose," Maddie said striving to keep her voice even and calm. "When one is unable to pick one's own husband, we must, each of us, make the best of situations not always to our taste." Maddie bit back a scathing remark as Veronica laughed. She clenched her jaw as the sound grated against her nerves.

"Yes, poor William, having to proceed with a union he fought so hard to avoid."

Maddie took a calming breath. Was the woman's tongue always forked? Did Veronica speak to her in such a way from sheer hate, or was it unconscious? Somehow, Maddie thought, it was probably both.

"Lord William is a strong man. I'm sure he will survive

the union," Maddie replied in a bored tone. She held her embroidery to the light and made a point of inspecting her work, anything to hide her emotions from this woman.

"Oh? Pray, did you not message the king to annul the marriage, Lady Madeline? I was sure that was what William had said." Veronica tapped her chin, her face one of mock puzzlement. "But perhaps not. We were occupied at the time, with a more pleasurable discourse." Veronica smiled and tilted her head in query. "Why did you do such a thing? The king cannot help you, Lady Madeline. No one can."

Maddie's stomach tightened as she struggled to contain her anger. Never in her life had she wanted to slap another person. But this woman... Maddie took a calming breath, breathed in the muddy scent of burning peat in the fire, and decided to take the higher road. With calm indifference, she met Lady Veronica's piercing stare.

"I don't believe my marriage is any of your concern, Lady Veronica. I do not delve into your private life within my home, for I do not care to know who you bed and what you are doing. It would only be polite if you should avail me the same courtesy." Maddie smiled. "Perhaps next time," she continued, "when you are in such circumstances with my husband, you would remind him to keep me out of his bedroom talk."

Maddie ignored Lady Veronica's laugh. She would not let this witch of a woman see how much her words hurt. Maddie turned back to her embroidery, intently focused on the rose she stitched. How dare William have the audacity to discuss their married life with this woman. Well, she inwardly fumed, he wouldn't do that for much longer. The man was an untrustworthy cad! Thank God she had not fallen for his charm and false words.

"Who I bed?" Veronica asked, one eyebrow raised. "Are you implying I sleep with many instead of one?"

Maddie shrugged. "I do not lie, Lady Veronica. What I say is the truth. Moreover, I believe you forget whose home this is. This is my estate, and not one thing that goes on here escapes my notice or the notice of my servants."

"Well, how diverting that I think as ill of you as you do me," Veronica said matter-of-factly. "It seems your own behaviours are not above reproach."

Maddie put down her embroidery. "What does that mean?"

Lady Veronica sneered. "There is talk, of you and Sir Alex and the close friendship that has sparked between you. He is your constant escort. Forever your champion. The man's praise of you is high and never ending to any who wish to hear it. I do believe you have your own motives for wishing your marriage to be annulled, other than what you claimed to William in any case."

Maddie could not leave the accusation undefended. "Sir Alex is my friend, Lady Veronica, and nothing more. Lord William himself placed me under the protection of his most trusted knight not long after I arrived at Kingston castle. There has been no impropriety on either side. He is to marry a woman who lives south of London within the year. I do not care to hear my name lowered to your level. If I hear any whispers that you have been spreading lies I will throw you from my keep and shut the drawbridge behind you myself. Am I clear?" Maddie said, her voice hard.

"William would never allow you to do such a thing. You bluff," Veronica said, her voice only holding the slightest ounce of doubt. "To think all of this is yours," she said, waving her hand to encompass the room and all beyond, "the daughter of a baron and," she frowned. "Who was your mother?"

Maddie clamped her mouth shut having no idea of her parent's history in this time. But from the vindictive line of Veronica's mouth, Maddie knew it wasn't great.

"Ah, now I remember," Veronica said. "A legitimized bastard by the king's second cousin. Why, I'm surprised you are even allowed the title of lady, Madeline."

Maddie stood. "Watch your mouth, Veronica. You dare to speak of my family in such a way again, and you will be kicked from these walls and by my foot. If anyone has lowered themselves by their actions, it is you, by becoming my husband's doxy." She gestured at Veronica. "You claim to be a lady of class and yet you sleep with a married man. You fool yourself if you believe you are not sullied. You're so dirty, had you fallen over in a puddle of mud, Lady Veronica, I would not have seen you."

The slap echoed loud in the small room. Maddie stumbled before she righted herself. She stood there, her hand against her face, silent and in shock. Her cheek ached and her eyes stung with unshed tears. Something trickled down her face and Maddie knew she was bleeding.

"You will never do that again, Lady Veronica. I warn you now, lay another finger upon me and you will rue the day. I promise you." Maddie walked to the door before the argument went any further.

"I consider myself duly warned," Lady Veronica said smiling.

Maddie glared as best she could with an already swollen eye. "I would heed the warning, if you knew what was good for you."

Lady Veronica's chuckle followed her from the room.

Maddie frowned and wondered, not for the first time, if Lady Veronica's mind was unhinged. What had just happened was no laughing matter. Something was definitely unbalanced with the woman.

Unbalanced and dangerous.

❧

VERONICA LAUGHED AS WILLIAM'S WIFE WALKED FROM THE room. She sat down and picked up her embroidery, her composure serene and relaxed. I will do more than touch you next time, Lady Madeline. This day you have proven to have backbone, but it will not be enough to save you, not with what I have planned. Veronica smiled as she watched the flames within the hearth, a turmoil of ideas flicking in her mind.

"Foolish girl to have threatened me," she uttered. "That, Lady Madeline, you should not have done...ever."

❧

IT DID NOT MATTER HOW MANY COLD COMPRESSES Mistress Rhode administered against her face, nothing, could stop the swelling and instant bruising which marked her skin.

"Do not worry, Mistress Rhode. The swelling will go down in a day or two," Maddie said, a half smile quirking her lips.

"Aye, m'lady you are correct. But 'tis distressing for a well-bred lady to act out in such a way. You should demand Lord William send her to London, or to her brother's home. Lady Veronica deserves punishment," her maid replied, her brow furrowed.

Maddie nodded and walked over to her bed and slumped down on the woollen blankets and animal skin bedding. "She probably thinks she has one over me now because I didn't hit her back."

"I will not deny to being a little confused with your wording, m'lady, but I believe I understand what you imply. 'Tis my opinion that Lady Veronica will now leave, she is not bold enough to stand before your husband and admit to striking you. Lord William will not stand for such insolence. Not even from his mistress."

Maddie removed the damp cloth from her face, the smell of lemons wafting from the linen. "Do you think William will go against my wishes if I tell her to leave?"

Her maid ruffled through the wooden chest, searching for gowns. "'Tis my hope Lord William will stand united with you." Mistress Rhode looked over her shoulder and smiled. "Now come, put down the cloth, we must dress you for supper, m'lady."

Maddie sighed then rose. "What herb did you use in this water? It's got quite a sharp scent."

"Vervain, m'lady. 'Tis used for wounds."

She was not looking forward to the evening meal at all. To have to go down to the Great Hall looking like a woman who had participated in a street brawl was shameful. And what would the castle priest say when he saw her face?

"Lady Madeline, I do not know what you should wear. Your green gown will only accentuate the bruising. Perhaps blue? Purple is most assuredly excluded."

Maddie giggled at her maid's strained expression. "Blue will be fine, Mistress Rhode. It does not matter what I wear. I cannot hide my face in any case."

Mistress Rhode mumbled something under her breath that Maddie did not catch. She stood and allowed the gown to be placed over her head and taking a steadying breath, she walked from the room.

The hall was a buzz of noise. Laughter, the clinking of goblets met her ears as she descended the last steps. Smells of roasting meat made her stomach grumble in hunger as she made her way to the dais. She kept her eyes focused on her seat, ignored the murmurs and gasps of shock, which followed her every footstep. Heat stole up her neck and she pushed away her embarrassment and strove for composure. She could only thank God William had not yet arrived for the evening meal. Seated on her right, with any luck, he would not notice her reddened cheek and swollen eye at all.

However, with such a marred face, it was only a matter of time before he did. She wondered what he would say and do when he found out what his mistress had done. Would he defend his lover? Or would he defend his wife? Maddie looked down the dais and caught Lady Veronica laughing and conversing without a care in the world. Perhaps Veronica's ease this night was an indication William already knew, and had made his choice.

The Great Hall quieted. Maddie looked up and watched William, accompanied by Sir Alex walk into the room, his stride purposeful and sure. She listened to the deep baritone of his voice as he acknowledged his men. Her body tensed and her breathing hitched at William's nearness. Maddie took a large sip of wine to calm her nerves. She needed to get a grip. He probably wouldn't even care his mistress had hit her. Certainly wouldn't stand beside her when she asked for his agreement in sending Veronica away.

Tonight, William wore finery that would befit a king. His long, muscled legs accentuated his height. His broad shoulders masked by the green tunic made him look stronger and deadlier than ever. He almost seemed too powerful, an untouchable man. William reached the dais and her heart accelerated at such masculinity. She swallowed the rising irritation that her body would deceive her in such a way.

Maddie nodded for the priest to start the supper prayer. The priest commenced and she kept her attention fixed on the old minister not wanting William to see her bruised face.

"Good evening, Lady Madeline."

Maddie turned her head the slightest degree and smiled. "Good evening, my lord."

"Are you speaking to me this eve, my lady?" William asked, summoning a footman for wine.

The servant stood before the dais and stared at her, his hands fumbling with William's goblet. Maddie sent the lad a scathing look. "Of course, my lord, what is it you wish to talk about?" Maddie turned her attention back to her meal, took a bite of pork, and flinched as the action of her jaw hurt the muscles in her face. Was the bruise worsening as she sat there? The thumping in her skull had certainly intensified. She swallowed and touched the bruised skin with her fingers to try to determine for herself how bad her eye was.

William cleared his throat. "I looked over the stores of wheat and grain today. I believe with this year's crop, Aimecourt will be well stocked for the winter. It seems between you and your steward, the people under your care are well looked after."

Maddie smiled at the small compliment while a seed of embarrassment lodged in her mind. She had no idea how much wheat, grain or food they held in storage at Aimecourt. In fact, Maddie didn't even know where such supplies were kept. "That is a relief, my lord," she replied.

William sighed and leaned forward in his chair, his

gazed fixed on the revellers eating in the great hall before them. "Madeline, look at me."

The request said in a soothing tone, had no such effect. Maddie shut her eyes and wondered how to explain to William she'd argued with Lady Veronica like a jealous child.

William clasped her jaw and turned her face to look at the wound more closely. Her chin tingled and heat pooled in her stomach by his touch. Maddie pulled her chin from his fingers and sat back. "It's nothing really."

"Who did this?" William asked his voice so cold it sent goose bumps across her skin.

Maddie let out a deep breath. "Lady Veronica and I had a disagreement." Maddie looked away from his gaze, not liking the deadly gleam that she saw there.

"Lady Veronica did this to you, ma chère?"

"Yes, my lord."

William flashed a look at Lady Veronica. Maddie looked between her husband and his mistress, unable to decipher their silent communication.

"Lady Veronica and yourself have quarrelled." William rubbed a hand across his jaw.

Maddie sipped her wine. Quarrelled was a nice way to phrase it she supposed. She looked up and noted for the first time the quietness of the hall. Placing her mug on the table, she faced him. William's jaw worked and his eyes blazed with an emotion she could not place as he stared at her injury. Was he angry with her or Veronica?

"My face is only a little swollen, my lord, it will heal in a day or two." Maddie paused and took a fortifying breath. "There is one request I would make. I want Lady Veronica to leave. It is time she returned to her family and started a life of her own instead of living in ours."

WILLIAM TRIED TO CALM THE RAGE THAT COURSED through him over the state of his wife's face. How dare Veronica lay a hand on Madeline? To mark her like some lowly serf. He unclenched his fist from around his goblet of wine.

"I want to know what happened, Madeline." He adjusted his tone when her eyes widened in fear.

"We argued, my lord. We both said things that hurt the other. It will not happen again."

"Did you hit her?" William regretted the question as soon as he'd asked it. The accusation in her eyes was like a punch to his gut.

"No, I did not. But if she does it again, she'll feel my foot in her backside as she flies out the gate, instead of my hand against her face."

William stifled a laugh. "So I gather you are still enemies."

"Of course we're enemies," Madeline replied a disgusted look on her face.

Wanting to touch her, he ran a finger down her cheek. She flushed and his mind turned to what she'd look like flushed and hot in his bed. His body reacted as it always did around her and he drank in every delightful feature that made up his wife before turning back to his meal.

"It was a jest, my lady. I will have words with Lady Veronica. It will not happen again." His skin heated as her hand clasped his arm.

"I don't want you to have words with her. I want her gone, my lord."

He remembered to breathe as her touch made him burn. "'Tis impossible, Madeline. Lady Veronica is a relative of mine. I will not send her away when Scots are threatening the surrounding lands."

His wife slumped back in her chair, disappointment etched on her lovely features. "So, you'll let her stay here after what she did to me?"

"'Tis not a battle over life and death, ma chère. I will speak to Lady Veronica and she will not touch you again." Madeline's disappointment sliced at him like a sword in battle. William leaned over and kissed the cut on her cheek. She stilled and their eyes locked. Never had he bestowed such a sympathetic gesture to anyone least of all a wife he cared naught for.

But...did he? Did he care naught for her? Or had he started to feel a connection to this woman beside him? He wasn't in love with Madeline. So, what was this new emotion that clutched at his chest and pumped his blood to pounding? Made him ache with need.

The kiss brought him in close proximity to her skin; jasmine wafted to his senses and he forgot where they were. He skimmed the sensitive coil of flesh on her ear with his lips and his body roared to have her, to show her the pleasures a man and woman could have.

"Ma chère, I..."

MADDIE STIFFENED AND PULLED AWAY FROM WILLIAM. A sensual shiver raked her body by his endearment that sounded awfully heartfelt. Forgetting her ire over his refusal to send Lady Veronica away, Maddie said the first thing that popped into her head.

"I thought I might take some riding lessons." She looked up at him and hoped he couldn't hear the unease in her voice. "Would you teach me?" Maddie dipped a piece of bread into her soup and tried to calm her beating heart. If he dared touch her again with those soft lips, she may not have enough wits to change the course of the conversation. She took a sip of mead and still her stomach wouldn't settle. Just his presence made her nervous.

"You already ride, Lady Madeline. In fact, from what I've been told, you're a very good rider. I wouldn't have thought my tuition was required."

Maddie blanched, having completely forgotten William would think that. Damn it!

"Oh...well, maybe we could just ride out one day, you know, together." What was she doing, trying to break her neck as well as her face? She couldn't ride if her life depended on it. She would be lucky to stay on the horse at a walking pace, nevertheless a speed he would assume she could handle.

Maddie held his gaze as William studied her. The puzzled frown of a moment ago now replaced with an all-together different assessment. She peeked down at her gown to ensure all was proper, before she looked back at him. His eyes burned with a heat that smouldered in their depths. William grinned and her heart turned over in her chest from the roguish smirk. Why did she not like this man again? At this point in time, it was very hard to remember such facts.

"'Twould be a pleasure. Shall we say after breaking our fasts, come morn?"

Maddie nodded. Despite her impulsive request that would put her at risk, she now oddly looked forward to a ride with him, away from the castle and its many eyes. Even if it was on horseback.

"Sounds good, my lord," she answered, and chuckled when his own laugh sounded at her odd reply.

The remainder of the dinner progressed pleasantly.

Her husband was attentive and full of banter. Had she not known him, she would have thought he was trying to court her in some way. She sporadically peeked at him. He really was very good-looking, hard and yet yielding when he wanted to be. She had certainly never met anyone like him before. William somehow made all the modern men seem weak of character and body. And this man beside her had a body she found herself gazing at, almost slobbering over quite often.

Six foot four of muscle and brawn; a man who trained daily for battles. Not with guns or bombs, but with swords and axes. Well, he was hard to resist. She watched his lower arm flex as he ate his meal. She licked her lips knowing both arms were capable of wielding a sword with deadly precision.

Heat pooled in her belly when she remembered his sweat-soaked body during one of his training missions with Sir Alex. His body marked with scars of battles past. The sweat had run down his chiselled back, the muscles taut from the ebb and flow of their practice. Her skin heated as the vision flashed before her. Then the way he had treated her at dinner tonight, made her yearn for a man she had no right to want. The thought of that body atop hers, within her, sent her blood to pounding.

Maddie should face facts. She wanted him, no longer wanted to share him with any others. Never did, if she were honest. Somewhere in her female soul, it cried ownership of such a medieval warlord. She was married to him, after all.

And even though all the days and nights which passed in this time were new to her, something about Lord William was awfully familiar. When he turned on the charm like tonight, it was very hard to stay angry with him, to hate him no matter what. Even with his mistress, who continued to live under the same roof.

But could Maddie have him? Win him only to leave? Was she willing to risk her heart, at least for a time, and share it with this man? She already knew without looking at him, the answer to that question.

She looked down to the vexing woman who stood between them. A woman who flirted with an archer from William's army, the lady's hand well occupied under the table. It was not hard to guess what Veronica was doing to the man, considering his flushed visage.

Maddie shook her head in wonder. Did William know his mistress shared her favours with all and sundry? She was not fool enough to think everything that came out of that woman's mouth was truth...

Lady Veronica raised her mug in toast over her newest conquest to her. Maddie stole a look at William, deep in conversation with his steward, and knew he was oblivious to Veronica's conduct.

No. The Lady Veronica de Walter was not a woman to be trusted.

Not ever.

CHAPTER 9

This was not a good idea. Maddie gawked up at the horse. It seemed twice her height and ten times her body weight. It snorted and stomped its mammoth feet— no doubt to declare its dislike for the person who stood before it. She pulled back her hand as the monster tried to bite, wondered what it would do when she sat in its saddle. That was, if she even made it that far. It took all her courage not to run away screaming.

Even to her untrained eye, she could tell the horse was a thoroughbred, its bloodlines as strong as any aristocratic family in this time. The beautiful dark brown coat shone in the morning light. Brushed and well fed, the animal was probably looked after better than some of her people. Still, the beast had the audacity to snicker his dissatisfaction. She made eye contact with the horse as she prepared to step toward it. It stared at her, dared her to come closer. Maddie changed her mind and remained still. She had no death wish and what had she been thinking? Horses were just not her thing. Period.

The stable master stepped forward and held the reins.

With no alternative, Maddie clasped the saddle as William prepared to give her a leg up. She smiled her thanks, and placed her foot in to his linked hands. The horse side-stepped out of her reach and left her hopping on one foot. A shiver stole through her as one of William's arms clasped her waist in support. Her eyes met his for a moment before she stepped away and prepared to mount again. She pushed away the desire that rose within her at William's touch. She needed to concentrate. Keep her mind focused on the animal before her. She needed no distractions today.

"Are you ready, Lady Madeline?"

She nodded while her mind screamed "No!" She silently thanked Mistress Rhode who had the common sense to fit her with hose this morning, now hidden under the woollen gown. It was only a matter of time before she landed on her behind. The extra padding would come in handy.

"When I lift you, throw your leg over the pommel then put your feet in the stirrups. Eurus is a good steed and James has the reins. Naught will happen to you, my lady. Lord's honour," William said, a hand over his heart.

This was unsafe. Maddie clasped the saddle with hands that shook, managed to turn and sit in the soft leather seat without tumbling over the other side. The horse stomped and snorted under her and she stilled, sure, the horse would bolt.

"William, I don't know if I can do this."

"Aye. You can, my lady. 'Tis a while since you rode, that is all. We will keep the pace slow if you like. I chose Eurus this morn because he is your usual mount. I can summon another if you prefer," William said, his features perplexed.

Maddie swallowed the lump of fear now lodged firmly in her throat. A fear the horse instinctively recognized. The

TAMARA GILL

Lady Madeline of old may have been a great rider, but Maddie was not. What was she going to do? Why didn't she keep her big mouth shut? She cursed her stupidity under her breath.

"No, Eurus is fine, my lord. But I would prefer to take it slowly. You are right, it has been some weeks since I rode." Years, if he wanted the truth. He placed her foot into the stirrup. The touch, in no way sensual, brought forth a longing in her she should not feel. She watched entranced as he walked toward his own mount, his stride purposeful. William mounted his own horse with ease and Maddie noted the muscles in his legs flexed as he settled the animal beneath him in total submission.

She remembered to breathe and looked away, knew if he caught her eye at that moment, all her desires would be bared before him. Gosh, her infatuation was bad. Maddie looked down at the stableman and asked him to release the reins. She lifted herself in the saddle and adjusted her seat then clicked her tongue and jerked her body forward to encourage the horse to move on. It did not. Instead, she found herself going around in circles.

"Sit down in the saddle, and tighten your reins a little," William said, his voice amused. Maddie looked up and caught the roguish grin on his lips and it settled her nerves a little. He wouldn't let anything happen to her.

Maddie did as he suggested and tried to relax. Eventually her horse settled beneath her and relented to its rider. In the distance, she heard the slow rumble of the drawbridge being lowered. The stableman walked her mount over to Lord William and handed him the lead rope. Maddie could only imagine what they were thinking. For a woman who was supposed to know horseflesh and how to control such animals it was humiliating to be seen led out

138

like a child. She blushed and shrank into her saddle a little further.

"Are you ready, ma chère?" William asked.

"Yes," Maddie nodded. "Let's go."

He walked, thank God, out to the road that led to Kingston castle, before he veered them away to walk parallel to the sea. The waves ebbed and flowed against the beach and an outcrop of black rocks could be seen further along the shore, the only marring of a stretch of beautiful golden sand.

They sat in silence, both enjoying the freshened sea air and beautiful views. Maddie soon forgot her fear as she looked about. From this vantage, she could see the steep jagged crags that circled the castle. Her home looked dominating and grand, not in the least penetrable.

"This view is magnificent, William." Maddie looked at him, and her breath hitched in her lungs. His smile lit up an already handsome visage and a longing to see him so and often assailed her. Their gazes locked and for a time Maddie couldn't look away. God almighty, could a man be any more delicious?

WILLIAM SMILED LIKING THE SOUND OF HIS NAME SPOKEN from Madeline's delectable, red lips; lips that he longed to touch again, to taste as he had all those weeks ago.

'Twas strange she did not know how to ride. Earlier this morn he had sought out the stable master to ask about her seat. The man confirmed Lady Madeline had as good a seat as any on a horse. Yet, to him she looked like a woman petrified of not only horses, but of heights.

"All this land before you, as far as your eyes can see,

belongs to Aimecourt, Madeline. But of course, you know this already."

He watched as her eyes looked with renewed fervour. Surely, she would know what she owned. Something about her fascination made him wonder if that was in fact the case.

"It's wonderful, isn't it?" she said. Her small backside bobbed up and down in the saddle in her haste to view everything.

William looked away from the delectable sight and gestured for them to continue. He veered their mounts down to the shore, headed for the water to submerge the horses' legs in salt water. The coast stretched for miles, arcing toward the craggy headland. The dense forest, running adjacent to the shore, he would take her to another day. William looked over at Madeline; her hair billowed about her shoulders and accentuated her fair complexion and something in his gut tightened.

"My Lady Madeline looks lost in thought," William said.

"Do I?" Her carefree, warm laugh sent blood pounding to his groin. "I didn't know the Solway coast was so beautiful," Madeline said, her tone wistful.

William pulled up his mount. "That, my lady, is impossible. You have resided here your whole life. And what is this name you call the coast? Solway? I have never heard of this name before."

William frowned as all colour in Madeline's cheeks dissolved. She worked her bottom lip and looked out over the ocean. William thought over his words and could not understand her unease by them.

"Madeline?" he prompted.

"I'm sorry to confuse you, my lord. Solway is a name I made up years ago for the coastline. And I suppose until today I hadn't really stopped and looked at it." She shrugged. "To admire its beauty."

Something inside William's chest thumped hard. He rubbed the chainmail that sat over his heart and smiled. "I believe one should always stop and take a second look. First appearances can often be misleading, my lady."

The silence stretched as the horses made their way along the edge of the surf. A tension, not at all ominous, filled the air between them.

"Lady Madeline, would you allow me to speak freely? I have been meaning to talk with you for some time, but..."

"Of course, if you wish it," she said.

William shifted in his saddle. "I wanted you to know that I have ended my association with Lady Veronica. After what happened between you and further consideration, 'tis only right she leave our home. I have sent word to her family in the hopes they will assist her with her travels. She should depart Aimecourt within a month or so."

He watched the surprise blossom on her face. He supposed his words would come as a shock. Had he not told her only hours ago such a thing was out of the question?

"I hope, my lord, that you do not come to regret your decision. You know I petitioned the king for support to annul our marriage. Perhaps in time, you'll be free to marry whomever you please."

William clenched his jaw at her refusal to admit to what was between them. This tension that went beyond sexual need. He liked her. Had grown to respect her. William would not believe Madeline wanted him to leave. He stared at her profile, her own gaze lost on the waves.

William ran a hand through his hair. "I have forsaken Lady Veronica for our marriage, Lady Madeline. I would have thought words of another kind may have been forthcoming from such a declaration," he stated, annoyed now at her refusal to look at him.

"You never wanted to marry me in the first place, William, why the change of heart?" she asked, her voice blasé.

How could she sound so disinterested? Did she not know how much it irked his pride to concede defeat? Why should he, the Baron of Kingston answer to a woman? He sighed, knew the reason of his capitulation, because he was fond of her, more than he thought ever to be. Also knew force with this woman would never work, nor would a show of temper. Was she not in the least enthused by the idea of a marriage of the truest sense with him?

"I do not want to marry another, Madeline." He reached out and turned her defiant chin. He watched her mouth open, her breath hitch and hold. Knew his stare was penetrating and intense with his desire for her.

"I want you," he said, at last.

MADDIE'S BREATH CAME OUT IN A RUSH. THE HORSE WAS still but the sudden tremble through its withers echoed her own body. She was too close to him. Too, too, close. Her thigh brushed his knee and need bloomed in her stomach as he closed the distance between them and then he kissed her.

Finally...

Fire ignited in her soul. She had wanted this for so long. Had waited for him to see the light and pick her over all others. Unable to stop, Maddie kissed him back. Weeks of repressed longing and desire rose within her. A savage sound that resembled a groan escaped William as his mouth claimed hers. His stubble rasped against her skin, marking her, as his lips took hers repeatedly.

She shivered, clasped the hair at his nape and tried to inch closer to him. Her nipples peaked when her breasts pressed against his chest, the movement sending delicious shivers to her core. Her body started to fracture into a million pleasure pieces as his tongue swept into her mouth. All coherent thought fled. She whimpered when he pulled away. Couldn't tear her attention from his mouth as he spoke.

"Will you be my wife, Madeline, in mind and body?"

William's tone, low and rough, was everything one would think a lust-filled medieval lord's would be and she shivered. Could she give this man before her a shot at being a husband in the truest sense? Should she? That would be a better question to ask. If her assumptions were correct and she returned home one day, would the Madeline of old remember everything that has transpired in her time here? Or would the lady have no memory of these many months and what had passed. She hoped somewhere deep inside the memories would hold, be kept safe. Because she did not want to leave William with a woman who neither loved nor liked him, that would not be fair.

Then again, twenty-first century Maddie would never know. She would be back, safe in her own time oblivious to what transpired after she left. And that, she realized with sickening dread, would be worse than death. For she would be forever wondering what happened.

Was she about to start something that was in no way fair to this man? His past or present course did not signify in the matter. The truth of her situation should stop such nonsense, such desires and wants. She could never do it to him.

She pulled a stray piece of hair away from her face.

Thought back over the many disagreements and knew with certainty that if this man declared he wanted her and no other, he meant it. She watched him, quiet and unsure as he waited for her reply.

Maddie closed her eyes and begged God for forgiveness over her choice.

"I will try, William. But I would prefer to know something first."

"Aye, anything, my lady," William said, his expression searching.

"I would like to know when you stopped sleeping with Lady Veronica."

Her body braced for his reply as he started at her question. Perhaps she should have asked that before her agreement. Please don't say last night, or worse, today. He caught her gaze and held it and it never wavered.

"Not since the day I took liberties with you at Kingston."

Maddie frowned. But that would mean weeks, months even. Her body did a silent little jig. So, the Lady Veronica was a proven liar. Did it also mean her husband was a little besotted with her? "And the serving woman the night you saw me in the bath?"

"Ahh, so you did see me that night," he sighed, the sound one of remorse and regret. "I never slept with the wench, Madeline. I'll admit that I tried. But 'twould seem I did not have the stomach to follow through." He laughed. "Let me declare with all honesty, there was another I wanted in my bed, and it was not her."

Like a schoolgirl on the eve of her first kiss, she grinned knowing William was deadly serious. Maddie swallowed, her throat parched as his gaze heated. "Well then, my lord, I suggest we start as friends and go from there. Does that meet with your approval?"

"Naught would I agree to more, ma chère. Over the past months, you have shown yourself to be a woman of loyalty and kindness. A woman I had not thought existed." William picked up her hand and kissed it. "I would like to get to know you, Lady Madeline, if you would allow."

Maddie's heart stumbled. He was in earnest. He was a man of pride and principles, if she excluded his past faults. And she would love to get to know him. Find out all there was to know about the Baron of Kingston, their homes, people and land.

She cleared her throat of the lump lodged there. "I'd like that, too," she said, as a drop of rain splashed against her cheek.

"'Twould be best to return, the weather looks to change," William said, looking to the west.

Maddie looked up at the sky and noticed the ominous clouds blowing toward them. "Yes, we'd better."

"Would you care to trot? I will not allow you to fall," William said.

Maddie calculated how far they had to travel home, then looked back to the storm billowing behind them. "I'm not sure," she replied as she patted her horse's neck. Felt the whip of its tail slice across her leg for her effort. She pursed her lips and weighed up her options. She could either walk all the way back to the castle, arrive drenched, or she could throw caution to the wind and give it a go. Trust in her husband's words that he would look after her.

"Why not?" she asked, shrugging. "Lead on, my lord."

William leant across and kissed her. Her hand stole to his cheek before he pulled away. The swirling pool of heat in his eyes, masked an inferno her body recognized well.

"It seems my lady wife is brave."

Maddie shivered when he spoke, his breath, fragrant of

mint, caressing her cheek. The compliment warmed her against the imminent storm and its cold wind.

As they cleared the beach, Maddie urged her horse into a trot, happy with her small progress. William kept close by her side, had to grab her only once when she lurched too far one way, and nearly toppled off.

Out of the corner of her eye, Maddie caught the flash of grey in the woods. She squinted as she tried to make out what exactly she thought she saw. Whatever it was, it did not seem to be there now. Perhaps the wind played tricks, or an animal ran for cover. The weather turned for the worst and branches and leaves blew up and whipped at their faces. Maddie turned as she caught the movement once more, this time followed by a whizzing sound. She stilled before some inbuilt sense of foreboding made her lunge forward on her horse.

She gasped as an arrow came directly toward her. The next few seconds played like a movie in slow motion. The arrow thumped into her arm, popped out the other side like some special effect gone wrong. She looked down at it, not comprehending what she saw. What she didn't want to see.

A metallic taste settled in her mouth as she heard William curse from afar. She was going to faint. As her breath hitched, she realized she was still on her horse. She clasped her arm. Someone had just fired an arrow at her, and it was now stuck there.

Oh God, that meant they would have to pull it out. Maddie swallowed. That one thought was enough to make her decline into darkness. A welcome darkness where there was no pain, no anything. She didn't acknowledge the ground as it came up to greet her.

WILLIAM FROZE BEFORE FEAR FOR MADELINE TOOK OVER his uncomprehending mind. He jumped from his horse and swore as he ran to her. She lay partially under her mount's hooves. The horse stood above her in a protective gesture, as if it could save her from further assailants. He gently pushed Eurus away. He did not move her, for fear of injury. He checked her neck. Thanked God it was not broken. She breathed calmly and regularly. A good sign. As for her arm, this was a different matter. He frowned as blood oozed from the wound, the arrowhead clear through both her flesh and woollen gown. He only hoped that when they removed it, it would not bleed excessively. He had lost many a good man to innocent looking wounds.

He scraped her hair from her face, sighed in relief as she murmured his name. Her face, bleached of colour, took his attention back to her wound. He tore his shirt and made a tourniquet around her arm. It would do for now.

"Madeline, can you hear me?"

She did not answer. He had to get her home, keep her safe, warm and out of the gusting wind. Her dress and cloak were no protection against such a storm. He could only pray she did not succumb to fever, as such wounds had a tendency to turn septic. He swallowed the bile that rose in his gullet. He would not think such things. He would not lose her.

William scooped her up and ignored his inner warning that whoever had shot at her may still be around. He looked toward the trees and could see no one. It was not a comfort. He could only hope, since they had hit their prey, they would have crawled back to the hovel they called home. One he would find soon enough.

He mounted his horse and settled her as best he could. Madeline whimpered in unconscious pain and anger tore through him like a sword. How dared someone hurt her?

Try to kill his wife. He turned his horse toward Aimecourt and kicked his mount hard into a full gallop.

His horse, as if sensing its master's distress, needed no urging, knew what it must do. As the gatehouse came into view, William yelled for the sentries to open the drawbridge. His horse never lost stride as he galloped within the outer bailey walls. Sir Alex ran down from the battlements and met him at the doors of the keep.

"She's been shot," William said, as he watched his knight pale when he looked at the wound.

"Pass her to me, my lord," Sir Alex said, his arms outstretched.

William settled her into Sir Alex's embrace while he dismounted. Serfs and servants stopped to stare. Women with concerned faces, the men's set in hard lines of revenge. William understood their emotions and welcomed their support. Whoever had done this to her, his wife, their mistress, would pay.

He walked up to Sir Alex and gently took Madeline back in his arms, just as Mistress Rhode burst through the keep's main doors.

"This way, m'lord," Mistress Rhode yelled. She barked orders for clean linens and hot water to be brought to the Lady Madeline's chamber as they passed the great hall. Staff scurried to do her bidding. Knew by the worried expression, which covered all their visages, that Lady Madeline was in trouble.

William followed her up the stairs, waited as Mistress Rhode pulled the sheets down on his wife's bed. Dread pooled in his soul. He shuddered over the thought of what they were about to do to her. Unconscious she may be, but the pain they would soon inflict could possibly pull her out of that comfort. He settled her as best he could.

William stepped back as water and bandages soon

arrived. All set out close to the bed, close to the ghastly wound that sat open and mangled and could kill her. Mistress Rhode, who seemed very apt in such situations, requested one of the maids to fetch her medicine basket.

"M'lord, come." Mistress Rhode gestured him forward. "I need you to cut away her clothes, while I prepare to remove the arrow.

William cut away her mantle, pulled it out from beneath her. The dress, made of fabric the same colour as the ocean, was soon ruined by his ministrations. As he prepared to cut in and around the arrow, he sent his men out. He did not want anyone but himself to see her stripped of decency.

His conscience pricked as he gazed down at the small, limp form in the bed, a bed too large for one person. How could he have made her sleep here alone these past months? A good woman, who deserved better than his treatment of her. William could only hope he had the opportunity to tell her so and to right his wrongs.

He promised himself that should she survive, he would never treat her in such a way again. He picked up her hand, so cold and pale, and frowned. There was no doubt he had feelings for this woman. His wife and supposed enemy; an enemy no longer.

When had he recognized the emotion that had settled in his chest, for what it was? It was more than esteem, like or admiration, although he held all of those things for her. Comprehension dawned like the rising sun of the east. It warmed his soul and heated his blood. Even if he could not form the words at this time, he would someday.

The thought that he may lose her today, this very night, made him rage against the world. She had not deserved such a callous attack. A woman unarmed, out riding with her husband. He would kill the villain who dared try to take her away from him. That he could promise.

He looked at Sir Alex, the only knight left in the room and walked over to him. "Take thirty men. Search the woods two miles east of here. Where the track leads to the shore; it happened there. Someone aimed at her from the forest. She must have caught a movement before the arrow struck, because she turned." He rubbed his jaw and swallowed. "It was the only thing that saved her. It would have been a clean shot to the heart otherwise," William stated with a shudder.

"Lord William, if you please, we need to remove the arrow," Mistress Rhode said from the bed.

He frowned. He didn't want to hurt Madeline. At least with it lodged in her arm, she lived. What if they pulled it out and she bled to death?

"Yes, m'lord," Sir Alex, replied.

William nodded in acknowledgement as his knight clasped his shoulder in support, his eyes steadfast on his wife.

"If you find whoever did this, kill them—slowly." William's voice brooked no argument.

"I understand," Sir Alex answered.

William watched as Sir Alex strode from the room, yelling orders as he went. He looked back to Madeline and noted the dark circles beneath her eyes. They were losing her. He swallowed and prayed she lived. He came and sat beside her on the bed. What they were about to do had brought tears to the eyes of the strongest men. He watched as she fought for consciousness each time her maid pressed or touched her mangled flesh. He prayed to God not to let her wake before they pulled the arrow from her arm.

He wished he could swap places with her. He would do anything for her at this moment should it lessen her pain.

He strove for calm, needed to keep his head clear, uncomplicated by the feelings he had for his wife.

"Hold her firmly, my lord."

He nodded. Leant over Madeline and secured the one shoulder he could, his other hand hard against her hip. He watched as Mistress Rhode cut the arrowhead away. It enabled them to pull it back out the way it came. He stole a look at Madeline and stilled at her beauty. His hand stole to her cheek where he touched the softest skin he'd ever known.

Mistress Rhode touched his shoulder. "Ready, my lord?"

"Ready," he replied, his attention steady on Madeline.

Mistress Rhode clasped beneath the wound and pulled at the arrow. Madeline jerked under him, and a scream that chilled his blood rent the air.

Madeline pushed at them. "Stop. Please stop! It hurts," she said, sobbing.

"Shhh, ma chère. 'Twill be quick. I promise." William stroked her hair and held her gaze until the fear and panic disappeared from her eyes. "We need to get the arrow out. Now."

Madeline nodded, her lower lip trembling, no doubt in fear. "Okay." She paused and took a calming breath. "Do it. But do it now, before I change my mind."

Mistress Rhode placed a piece of circular wood between Madeline's teeth. "Bite down on this m'lady. 'Twill help with the pain."

William frowned and held her still. Madeline's eyes closed as the arrow pulled free. Only the slightest whimper signified the pain she experienced. His respect for her increased tenfold. A strong woman. The woman for him. He, on the other hand, made the mistake of looking at the wound. He paled.

Mistress Rhode kept calm as she placed another tourniquet around Madeline's arm. Madeline, he saw, winced as the bandage tightened. A maid held the dressing tight, while Mistress Rhode poured water over the entrance and exit wounds. His fists clenched as tears streaked down his wife's cheeks. To clean a wound of such magnitude would be unbearably painful. He leaned forward as she went limp.

"She is well, m'lord. She has slipped into unconsciousness once more, that is all. It is the least of our concerns," Mistress Rhode said

He swallowed; sweat beaded his skin.

"If she bleeds when the tourniquet comes off, there will be nothing I can do, m'lord. We can only pray the vein that has been punctured will clot." She frowned as she packed clean swabs of cloth against Madeline's wounds.

"We need to leave the wound open to heal. If the bleeding does not stop..." A moment passed. "We may have to cauterize the wound. I'm sorry, m'lord."

"How long before we know?" he rasped, his throat tight, his mind a whirl of anxiety. They would find a way in which to save her. He would not lose her now.

"I cannot allow her arm to be much longer without blood." Mistress Rhode paused and inspected Madeline's lower arm and hand. "Too soon, I'm afraid."

CHAPTER 10

The excruciating pain tore through her. Maddie wouldn't have thought a piece of wood could cause so much agony. She winced somewhere between consciousness and sleep as her arm was shifted and prodded. She wanted to shout to whomever it was to leave her alone. Perhaps if she were lucky, it would come out like a splinter. Fester within a day or so and pop out. But right now, all she wanted was that blissful darkness to swallow her again.

Maddie had always fainted easily as a child and as the arrow staked her arm, that same sensation of falling through a void had enveloped her. From that point on, she moved in and out of consciousness, remembering only segments of time.

She remembered William, his grasp on her, hard and secure. The distant sound of horse's hooves, which pounded against the ground. The wind cold on her face, the unbearable ache as her arm jostled through the ride. He'd spoken to her, a plea almost, against her ear, the words a blur, erased by the pain. However, whatever the words he spoke, they comforted her. His tone conveyed more than words ever could.

They were above her now, not only William but also Mistress Rhode. She wanted to smile to reassure them. Their words were harried, fast, scared; they frightened her. They were arguing. Why wouldn't they go away and leave her alone?

A hand, warm and strong, clasped her arm. The other pushed down on her hip. She couldn't move. She opened her eyes, fought the sleep that wanted to take her. Panic assailed her. They were going to pull it out. Oh, God no, please, no. Not without morphine, or whatever medieval drug they had to kick her back into oblivion. Her eyes met William's, they somehow calmed her soul. She could do this. She could.

Okay, maybe not. She stilled, clamped her jaw about a piece of wood as the arrow pulled free. She wanted to scream but her voice didn't cooperate. At that moment, Maddie hated them both equally, with their barbaric doctoring.

Idiotic, bastard, medieval torturers.

Another sharp stab of pain assailed her arm. Fingers prodded then clamped with excruciating pressure. It hurt like hell. Never had she suffered such agony in her life. Another arrow wound would have hurt less.

She passed out.

Minutes or perhaps hours later, Maddie heard them, faint at first, then louder as her senses started to work. How long had she been here? She tried to open her eyes, feeling weak as a newborn babe. She no longer hurt. She was just sleepy. Really sleepy. They said something; words lodged in her brain. Bleeding too much. Death. William, who sounded...unhinged.

She fought the blackness that wanted to take her and opened her eyes. She looked up at him. Panic marked his face. A faint smile lifted her lips as his eyes beckoned her to stay with him. They were warm and inviting, pulled at her. Begged her to give their marriage a chance. Even with herself in this precarious position, her female self crowed over the win. The medieval lord was hers.

She shut her eyes, but stayed awake to listen to them. Liked the sound of their voices, liked them again, now that there was no pain. They were arguing. She frowned; why did they have to touch her arm again? No, she wanted to scream, leave it alone. Her fingertips prickled as the blood flowed back into the digits. Yet something was wrong.

The bed was wet.

She was bleeding.

Bleeding to death.

Her eyes flew open and her gaze landed on William who sat next to her. His brow furrowed, his hand stroked her hair from her face. She didn't want to die. She was young, had her whole life before her. She couldn't let a piece of wood take her out. How embarrassing would that be on a headstone? Killed by stick.

"William, cauterize it," she hazily murmured. It was that or them watch her die. She refused to die in 1102. Not only because of her age, but technically, she hadn't even been born yet, for God's sake. How can you die before that took place? She heard Mistress Rhode gasp in horror. She winced as the tourniquet tightened once more.

"Are you sure, Madeline? 'Twill be extremely painful," William said, his hand stroking her cheek.

She opened her eyes and peered at him. He placed a damp cool cloth upon her brow. Worry and anguish written upon his features, he looked older than his years. A half smile lifted her lips. She didn't need anyone to tell her that, she knew damn well how much it was going to hurt. However, dying was not an option, so they better jab her with that hot poker and be quick about it.

"I know, just get it over with," Maddie stated, nerves knotting in her belly.

"But, m'lord," Mistress Rhode said. "She's a woman. I cannot let you do such a thing to a lady."

"Would you rather she dies?" William asked, his voice hard.

Maddie heard his reply and relaxed, knew he would do as she asked. "Let him, Mistress Rhode. I'll survive. I promise," Maddie said as she braced herself for the burn.

She watched the fire poker came out of the roaring blaze. The tool, wiped with a cloth with no disinfectant used. She inwardly balked, her insides awash with panic over her choice. Had she just asked to be stuck with a dirty hot tool in medieval England? As Mistress Rhode poured a mixture of herbs over the wound, reality hit.

She had.

Oh God, she had.

William held her down, his clasp tight, almost painful.

"I'm scared," Maddie said, biting down on her bottom lip.

"Shush, ma chère. 'Twill be over soon," William said, his eyes haunted.

She caught her maid's silent apology just before the hot metal instrument stabbed fast and long within the wound.

Maddie screamed. What she wouldn't give to be home, under anaesthesia and oblivious right at this moment. Her body fought for release, futile under her husband's tight hold. Blackness assailed her once again.

There was a God after all.

MADDIE LICKED HER LIPS, CRACKED AND AS DRY AS HER mouth. It was so hot in here. Why was it so hot? She kicked at the blankets and sighed in relief as the chilled winter air met her skin. Her maid walked about the room. Her stride no longer panicked but calm and assured. She was out of danger. She had succumbed to a fever; no wonder with the dirty poker Mistress Rhode had used. But she was better now. Maddie stretched out, luxuriated in the soft wools beneath her. Only the slightest twinge of pain tweaked in her arm. This was much more preferable to how she was days ago, when she had wanted to shrivel up and die.

"You're awake, my child."

Maddie smiled. "Yes. Thank you, Mistress Rhode, for all your help."

"You are welcome, m'lady." Mistress Rhode stoked the fire with peat. "Your people believe m'lady's recovery is due to a blessing from God."

Maddie lifted her hand to her hair and felt the matted mess. "No blessing from God, just luck," Maddie said. A lot of luck. Such a fever should have killed her. Perhaps when she'd jumped into the life of Lady Madeline some of her twenty-first century inoculations had come with her. Maddie wiggled up higher on her pillows. "Could I have a bath, do you think?" she asked, wondering if the sweat she could smell was her own.

"Aye, m'lady. I will have one brought up anon,"

Mistress Rhode said, pulling out a clean chemise and bustling out of the room.

Maddie sighed and laid back, her attention fixed on the hearth. The fire, well alight, threw ample heat into the chamber. Her solitude was short lived before her chamber door opened once more.

"Would you care for anything else, m'lady?"

Maddie rubbed the wound on her arm. An annoying itch upon her skin. A good sign and one she would tolerate with gratitude. "No, thank you, Mistress Rhode," she said. "What time is it?"

"The evening meal is about to be served, m'lady."

"I'll be fine here by myself. Go and enjoy your meal, you deserve a night off after all you've done," Maddie said in a sincere tone.

"Nay, m'lady. I will stay and watch over you," her maid replied, shock layered in her weathered face.

Maddie wanted to be alone with her thoughts. She flicked her hand at her maid's protest. "Go. I command it," Maddie said with a smile.

Two knights entered with a wooden bath, followed with pails of steaming water. Maddie assured Mistress Rhode she was well enough to bath herself and was soon left to her own devices. The water felt heavenly against sweat-ravaged and bloodied skin. Maddie looked down at the wound, still red and nasty looking. She cleaned away the blood her maid had missed and tried to clean around the wound without making it bleed. Blissfully clean, Maddie lay back in the tub and closed her eyes. Her mind wandering back to the day of the attack, and what little she could remember.

Figments of that day ran through her mind like a movie. The flash of movement in the woods. William and herself trotting toward home. The attacker must have been on a horse as well. And a very good shot. Perhaps there were Scotsmen roaming the area, bent on revenge for lands stolen years ago. Or perhaps someone closer to home had tried to kill her. And failed.

Maddie shivered in the lukewarm water and stood to get out. Would the assailant try again? And if so, how? People killed one another in medieval England all the time. Was she doomed to join their ranks?

She slumped down on a stool by the fire, her muscles weary after such an effort. She sat there, staring at the rough-hewn mat underfoot before the memory of Lady Veronica conversing with an archer at supper entered her mind. Anger as hot as the poker that jabbed into her wound assailed her. Had Lady Veronica stooped so low? And if so, why would she risk the wrath of William and the king by doing such a thing to a noble lady? Men were wonderful, but they weren't worth killing people over.

Well, not in Maddie's mind at least.

THREE DAYS LATER, MADDIE STOOD OUT OF SIGHT ON THE minstrel stage above the Great Hall. Her little fingernail was growing shorter with every moment that passed. What was Veronica up to? She could see her seated below, the man she flirted with, in awe and practically salivating. The knight in question was none other than Mistress Rhode's younger brother. A man whose mother knew how to use herbs. A man brought up in and around healing remedies and poisons. A shiver stole down Maddie's spine. Was Lady Veronica planning to attack her through the food she ate? Tainting it with foxglove or cowbane?

Her heart sped up as William strode into the hall. Snow sat upon his green mantle as he handed it to a waiting servant before he proceeded to the dais. He paused at Lady Veronica's side. Spoke to the pair before he escorted his ex-mistress to her seat, not far from his own. Maddie pushed away the stab of jealousy that knifed through her seeing them together. She supposed he couldn't ignore the woman due to her status. However, that small fact did not make it any easier to watch.

Doubt crept up her spine like a spider. Had she misread his concern for her when she lay injured? He seemed at the time truly upset at the prospect he could lose her. Was it her imagination or had she hallucinated his troubled countenance?

Perhaps she had. Because William had been noticeably absent since the night he brought her home injured. It was as if he no longer cared how she got on. Unsure as to why he would not check on her, Maddie had plucked up the courage to ask Mistress Rhode of his whereabouts. Only to receive a look of pity followed by a tone meant to soothe, that she had not seen His Lordship at all and could not say.

Perhaps it was best Maddie had not told William of her feelings toward him. How hers had changed after his declaration on the beach. She may have stated that friendship was all she wished, but it was far from the truth. She wanted more. She looked down at the dais, and the many meat dishes now steaming before the diners. Unsure if William's affection was still on offer.

Maddie steeled her back to find out. She looked down and checked her gown. Tonight she wore a supertunic over a kirtle. The cloth embroidered with gold thread, hung halfway down her gown. The dress, with its long sleeves, hid the bandaging on her arm well and accentuated her figure. She felt attractive and alive, and it was time to see just what her husband's thoughts were when it came to their relationship.

Maddie walked into the hall, and whispers sounded loud in the quiet. She ignored Lady Veronica and her tittering. Instead, she smiled and returned her peoples well wishes. William's gaze was on her as Sir Alex stopped and kissed her hand. The knight welcomed her back and proclaimed how happy he was that she was once more among them. In no rush to sit at the dais, Maddie spent some time with the first knight and others who joined them. She thanked Sir Alex when he offered to escort her to her seat. Maddie did not miss the line of tension that pulsed between her and William when she laid her hand on the knight's arm. William stood; dismissing Sir Alex with a glance then helped her to sit.

"Thank you, my lord," Maddie said, as she settled before the populace.

"You are very welcome, my lady."

Heat stole up her cheeks at his words. 'My Lady' had sounded more like a declaration than a name. She beckoned her meal and wine from a servant, and then rallied herself to find out where she stood.

❦

WILLIAM DID NOT MISS MADELINE'S REACTION TO HIM AS she became aware of his fixed attention. He drank her in, like a man starved of water in a desert. A delicious blush sat upon her cheeks, her eyes shining with merriment. She looked well, happy, and whole. He sent a silent prayer up to God for such a blessing.

With a desire he could no longer hide, he picked up her hand. It was soft and delicate within his. He rubbed his thumb across her flesh, and did not miss the slight tremble of her fingers. She was nervous. He bit back the fiendish smirk and kissed the inside of her wrist.

He breathed in her luscious scent of jasmine. Madeline was a flower in bloom and his to pick. Heat coursed down to his groin.

"You bathed," he said, then watched as her blush deepened.

"I did, my lord." A frown puckered her smooth brow. "How did you know?"

"You smell of summertime and...I heard you," William said sipping his wine, his gaze slipping down to the ample flesh bared by her gown.

Madeline threw him a searching look. "You were in your room?"

In his room and pacing like a caged animal with the knowledge his wife was but a wall away. Soaking in warm water, naked. A part of his anatomy tightened painfully at the thought. He knew too well how comely Madeline was when bare of clothes.

"Aye." William cleared his throat and then changed the subject to a less arousing issue. "I had your steward ensure all your needs were met throughout your healing. 'Twas what I thought was best."

"Really? Your absence made me believe you did not care at all," Madeline replied, her tone conveying how much she believed in her words.

William kept a hold of her hand and flattened her palm against his thigh. "'Twas never my intention for you to think so, ma chère. I kept guard most nights and thought of you often. I did not wish to hinder your maid's care."

Madeline's hand tightened on his leg. "Really?" She smiled, her eyes bright. "I had thought you had changed your mind."

"Plague take it, woman, 'tis impossible for me to do so. I stand by my declaration at the beach. You know what I desire," William said, lowering his tone when others looked their way.

Madeline's sigh of relief was audible. "I'm glad, my lord," she said.

Food forgotten, William watched her, did not want to take his eyes from the beautiful vision she made. Impossible to imagine anyone else in her position, married to him. His very own Lady. She consumed him, possessed his mind and heated his blood. He wanted her. Wanted to love her and make her cry out in pleasure. He watched as she picked at her food. Perhaps her appetite veered to a different hunger also.

"You are very comely tonight, ma chère."

"You are welcome to look, William," she replied, her voice cool and steady.

William frowned. Did her heart not pump as unevenly as his own did? "My thanks, my lady. I believe I shall." A ruckus at the trestle tables showed knights partaking in a game of chess. William took a sip of wine and watched her over the rim of the goblet.

"'Tis a welcome sight having you back among your people, ma chère." William leant toward her, his lips but a breath away from her cheek. "I have missed you."

William kissed the soft flesh beneath her ear. Breathed in her perfume, knew to his soul that he would never wish for another. She leaned into the embrace. Her hand stole higher upon his leg. William swallowed when his hose stretched to breaking point. His heart thundered in his ears.

"A little higher, ma chère and 'twould be a surprise if you ended this night a maiden still," he whispered and kissed her neck and helped her hand stroke a little higher.

Madeline laughed the sound resonating with need. She crossed her legs under the table and shifted in her chair.

"Perhaps I should be more obvious, my lord," she said, her eyebrow quirked. "Maybe," she whispered in his ear. 'I should undo your hose before everyone. Do you think you would get the message then?"

His burning desire made it hard to breathe. William looked away to the trestle tables before them, and then placed her hand back in her lap and stood.

"What are you doing?" Maddie asked, frowning.

"'Twould seem our meal is done. Would you not agree, Lady Madeline?" William said, looking down at her.

Madeline rose, her cheeks flaming red. No one who sat within the hall could miss his intentions.

"I would agree, my lord," she answered.

William clasped his wife's hand and pulled her from the hall. His body throbbed with need. Her words echoed in his ear with every step he took. Never had he thought to hear such words from her and his heart had leapt in his chest. He strode up the stairs, eager to be alone with her. He reminded himself that his wife was a virgin, a maiden, untouched...at present.

The spiral staircase continued endlessly. He slowed as they reached their floor. Neither spoke as he pulled her into his room, the first along the corridor.

He slammed the door, and pushed her up against the wood. Madeline's eyes flashed in excitement as he pinned her against the door. Hands on either side of her face, he leaned down and brushed his lips against hers, marvelling at his patience. The kiss, soft at first, hardly a caress at all, turned decadent in an instant when her tongue beckoned his.

William's hands shook as he reached for her fastenings, his fingers fumbling with the delicate lacings at her side. He met her gaze and swore as one cursed cord knotted and held. Madeline's nimble fingers undid his belt. His chest rose and fell with every laboured breath. God's teeth, he groaned when her hand slipped inside his hose. He could wait no longer. She gasped when he produced a knife and cut the fastenings that kept him at bay.

William threw off her dress and chemise then stilled as his eyes took in her lithe form, and curves. Her breasts were high and full, her nipples hard as pebbles. He leaned down and grazed the firm flesh with his tongue. Her moan of delight flowed to his appendage and made him throb. He kneaded her ample breasts and revelled in the bite of pain as she dug her fingers into his skull. He wanted her. Wanted to mark her as his in any way he could. Yet, he held back the roar in his head to do so and continued to tease. He liked giving her pleasure, a pleasure only he would ever bestow.

One hand moved down and grazed her slender hip before clasping her delectable bottom. A shiver stole over her as he brought his hand back around to lie against her stomach. He could smell her need and hear her unvoiced pleas for him to touch her. William met her gaze as his fingers slid between her wet folds. Her breath hitched and his cock ached from the tight passage he felt there.

"'Tis pleasing, my lady?" His voice was hard, rough.

"Yes." Madeline sighed. "You know it is," she said, trembling in his arms.

Maddie had never been so excited in her life. She lifted her leg against William's hip and allowed his fingers to continue their endless, delicious torture. Her hands plied his hair, pulled him close as his mouth sent bolts of lightning to her core. She wanted to scream for him to take her, to stop teasing and put her out of this exquisite anguish.

"William, please," she said, almost sobbing.

His hands came away from her heated core leaving her bereft and unfulfilled. Maddie whimpered in annoyance before he clasped her bottom and lifted her up. The rough wood door behind and the hard masculine flesh before excited her, made her need almost a tangible thing. Her legs encircled his hips and held firm. William's dark gaze captured hers, before she leaned forward and kissed him. His response had a savage edge to it, but also caution.

"Hurry. Don't make me beg."

"Wanton wench," he said, and groaned when she rubbed herself against him seeking release. "I will not, ma chère."

Maddie almost sobbed in anticipation as he rubbed her swollen, needy flesh with his own engorged penis. She moaned and bit her lip in anticipation. Captured his gaze and held it while he slowly slid inside her. His eyes burned with passion and something else she could not name. Maddie smiled and kissed his lips. Let her own love and respect shine from her eyes.

She frowned as unexpected pain assailed her.

"William, stop. It hurts," she said on a gasp.

"Hush, ma chère. 'Twill only hurt for a moment. You are a maid, but not for long."

"But," she stilled, then realized why such a thing was happening. It was not her body. Not really, this body belonged to Lady Madeline of the twelfth century. And of course she was still a virgin. Maddie braced for the stinging burn as William sheathed himself fully. She tried to relax. Tried to remind herself it would stop hurting soon. But he was so large. Not a size any virgin wished to tackle the first time.

"Madeline," William whispered, his voice strained.

His tone pulled her back from the edge of panic.

Maddie opened her eyes and calmed her breathing. William flexed the tiniest bit and the fullness she had longed for moments before took hold. His action was slow. In and out. An endless tattoo that made her mad with desire. She no longer hurt, but craved. Craved his darker wilder self. Wanted him to claim her, hard and fast and for as long as possible.

"William. Please."

Up against the door, he thrust relentlessly into her wet heat. His calloused hands grasped the flesh on her upper legs, the pinch of his hold only adding to her enjoyment.

"I want to please you, Madeline." William kissed her chin, her neck, her upper breasts. Anywhere his mouth could reach.

Maddie's nails bit into his back. "You are." She rested her head against the door and moaned. What was he doing to her? "Please don't stop."

His husky chuckle sounded against her ear. "'Tis not my plan to."

His tongue licked the sweat from her skin and she shivered. Pinned to the door and under his ministrations was consuming and Maddie felt herself coming apart in his arms.

William swore and in two strides, they were on the bed. He kneeled over her and rocked into her heat. Her back arched and she moaned. The raw lust she read on his visage and the utter determination to please left her floundering in ecstasy.

Maddie felt her release upon her. She shifted her legs higher on his hips and the deep penetration pushed her to breaking point. Her hands splayed against the bedding and she clutched at the woollen blankets for purpose. Her body fractured, convulsed around him and came apart. On and on the pleasure points in her body fired and she gasped his name as the orgasm took her.

William's release followed hers and his ragged breath against her ear was like a sensual caress. Maddie wrapped her arms about his back and held him still, not ready to let him go yet.

"You are mine now, wife," William said, kissing her mouth.

Maddie smiled and ran a finger down his stubbled jaw. "That I most assuredly am, my lord," she said. No truer words ever spoken.

❧

HOURS LATER, MADDIE WOKE UP ENTANGLED IN A MIX OF arms and legs. Her limbs were weak, relaxed, and her body very much satisfied. She smirked and bit her lip remembering their heated first time together. She sighed, having never felt such release and pleasure with a man before. It would seem the Baron of Kingston was not only a good kisser, but also a magnificent lover.

The thought of doing it again blazed in her mind and she squirmed. She looked up from the crook of his arm and gazed at him asleep. Even in slumber, he looked dangerous and devilishly handsome. Her pulse leapt as she leant in and kissed his nipple, then ran her tongue around the small-pebbled flesh. He moaned but did not wake.

Determined on her course, Maddie sat up and straddled his waist. His penis, half erect, lay across his leg. She stroked his well-endowed manhood, watched it rise to meet her before she moved over to take him again.

"'Twould seem I married a shameless woman," William said, running a finger down her breast. "What will I do with you, ma chère?"

He sat up and took her lips, in a demanding, hot kiss. Maddie never had a chance to reply as the embrace left her breathless with renewed need. She kissed him back without abandonment, allowed her body to spiral over once more into blissful oblivion.

Only with him. William.

She was lost...

CHAPTER 11

William raised his sword and parried a blow from Sir Alex. The contact reverberated down his arm. He stumbled before he gained his feet. The demonstration to his younger squires in training was supposed to be educational. All he had done since the bout began was demonstrate how to get yourself killed when your mind wandered. And his wandered constantly.

To Madeline...

Her name spun a web of erotic images within his mind. That organ was not the only part of him affected by thoughts of her. A half smile lifted his lips as the image of how he had left her this morn entered his conscious. Sound asleep and in a pool of scattered blankets. A rosy flush upon her cheeks, her body marked by his love. She fired his blood like no other. One look from her and all the demands of a mighty baron flew out of his mind. He had claimed her in truth. He could not leave his bride unsatisfied, and he certainly had not.

"'Tis a strange lord who smiles while preparing for war

with his knights," Sir Alex said, a teasing note to his voice. The young squires smirked from the sideline.

William swore as his sparring partner's blade contacted with his shoulder. He stepped back and shook off the blow, thankful to be using blunt swords. William pushed Madeline and her exquisite long legs out of his head and concentrated on the bout at hand. He would not be made fool in front of his very own men, especially because of a female.

He evaded the next blow before he aimed a hit of his own. The full body strike was so forceful, Sir Alex lost his balance and stumbled. William made use of his dilemma and swiped at his opponent's feet. The ruse worked and his knight stumbled to his knees. William's eyes narrowed at his knight's knowing smirk. He pushed the sword against Sir Alex's throat.

"Good hit, m'lord. Perhaps next time you will nay end up bruised yourself, if your mind's kept upon the task."

William stepped back and allowed Sir Alex to stand. He ignored his knight's insightful laugh when he stood. William sheathed his sword. "Or perhaps my knight should remember who won the bout this day." William smiled and turned to his squires. All eager eyes faced his way. "Perhaps my first knight should learn how to use his puny sword before we spar again." William laughed along with Sir Alex.

Tom, an eager boy from Norfolk stepped forward. "Can we have a go now, m'lord?" William ruffled the small lad's hair and nodded. "Aye. Partner up and start."

William watched for a time. He showed the boys how best to defend a forward strike from the sword before luncheon was upon them.

William wiped the sweat off his face with his tunic, then put it on. The warmth of the castle hit him as he proceeded indoors. He allowed his eyes to adjust to the light before looking about for Madeline. He watched her speak to a serving wench, her face animated, and something within his chest began to ache.

Her emerald gown and red surcoat with gold stitching around the seams suited her. Her hair, strands as soft as silk flowed down her back, only a few locks pulled away from her face. She was beauty personified. And she was his.

William had not believed hair could be so erotic. Last eve, when she had kissed his chest, his stomach, his... The strands that had flowed upon his skin left a burn in their wake. She left him in a constant burn. Tonight they would be together again; only a few short hours to go before he could retire. The minutes ticked by, each one an eternity in time. Perhaps it was too long after all.

MADELINE FELT WILLIAM'S GAZE AS SOON AS HE ENTERED the hall. Like an imaginary line that ran between them, heat moved over her body when she caught his appreciative gaze. There was naked admiration in his expression.

Her body flushed, as if she'd done a stint at the gym. Maddie dragged her attention back to the girl speaking to her, before images of William sparring outside in the bailey entered her mind.

The gallery upstairs was quite a fortunate find, and one she would endeavour to use more often. Especially if it meant she could ogle her husband to her heart's content. That is, however, if she would ever be content when it came to him.

She listened to the kitchen girl and her troubles with the head cook. She tried to keep her mind focused on the girl's problems, but it was really quite difficult when William watched her. Wanted her.

His body today was magnificent. The sweat had run down his back, even in the chill of winter. The muscles flexed, strained under the bout between allies. He seemed preoccupied during the battle. Was it because he thought of her? Did she occupy his mind as much as he did hers?

Maddie informed the serving girl to seek her in the solar tomorrow, as her problems were many. The girl, satisfied, ran along to do her chores. Maddie looked back to where William leaned against a wall, his casual stance no way masking his eagerness for her and she smiled.

He'd pushed back his hair, his body still in the afterglow of swordplay. It reminded her of how she had seen him last in his room. A shiver stole over her skin as she came to stand before him. The smell of masculinity wafted from him and she inwardly sighed at his rough beauty. He stood motionless, his eyes burned as they looked at her.

"Hello, my lord," Maddie said, and melded against his body. She sighed in delight as his hands came around her back and held her tight.

"Good day, ma chère. You look, should I say it, comely."

She laughed and ran her hands up his damp tunic. "Do I? I thought I was shameless, not comely." She grinned at his chuckle. Leant toward him and kissed the tip of his stubbled chin then his lips. For a moment, Maddie forgot where they stood as William's desire for her ignited her own. His tongue swooped into her eager mouth and she moaned feeling his erection hard against her stomach.

Maddie wrapped her arms about his neck and held him close. How she had missed him. More than she liked to admit. Realized she was only half-complete whenever he was absent. She belonged in 1102 and to this particular man. A man she was determined would admit his deeper feelings toward her. And soon.

His hands dug hard in to her hips as he pulled her close. Not a breath of air separated them and her body ached for release. She broke the kiss just as his fingers moved southward toward her bottom.

"What are you doing after luncheon, my lord?" Maddie whispered against his ear, nibbling his lobe. William's understanding laugh rumbled against her chest.

"I will be training the squires, my lady," he replied.

Maddie stilled her ministrations and pulled back. She frowned at his grin. "Well then, that put me in my place," she said and pulled out of his embrace, squeaked when he wrenched her back within his arms.

"And where do you think you're going?" he asked.

"Nowhere, would it seem."

William smiled at her and kissed her lips quickly. "Perhaps I should change before continuing on with the training. It is chilly outside, and my clothing is already damp."

She nodded. "Sounds like a good idea to me."

Maddie peeked over her shoulder at the quiet hall and heat stole up her neck. She looked back at William and grinned.

"I do believe we are being watched," she said.

William surveyed the room. "'Twould seem you are correct in your estimation."

She allowed him to pull her toward the dais, welcomed the heat from the fire behind them as they sat. Maddie caught the eye of Lady Veronica as she settled herself. She tried to look through the woman and not worry that the food she was about to eat may be tainted. It was hard not to wonder what the woman's inner thoughts were. Her eyes, so devoid of warmth and life, were disturbing. There was no doubt in Maddie's mind she had an enemy.

"Are you well, Madeline?"

Surprised by the question, Maddie looked up at William. It took her a moment before she understood his issue. How sweet, he was worried for her womanly bits after his pleasurable exertions. Unconsciously she moved upon her seat. She would admit to being a little sore. However, that would pass within a day or so. And she certainly wouldn't allow it to hinder their love making. Especially as she had a whole afternoon planned around such activity. The squires could wait a day.

"I'm absolutely fine," she said, as she placed her hand upon his leg, her fingers teasingly close to his member. She smiled when he had to clear his throat before he spoke.

"I'm glad for it. I was worried that I may have hurt you with my haste to..."

"Bed me," she finished for him. "No, you didn't, William. Do not concern yourself over such matters."

His body stilled as her hand moved up his leg. Sure no one would see, she inched a little higher and grasped him within her hand. She only just held back a moan as he leaned behind her and nibbled her neck. He purred naughty words only she could hear.

"What are you doing to me, ma chère?"

Loving you. Teasing you. Trying to show you how much I want you every moment of every day. Most of all she wanted to tell him she loved him. Instead, she chose a different answer.

"I don't know. But whatever it is, you're not the only one affected." It was as honest as she could be at this time. Perhaps if he confessed his love it would give her courage to do the same. But at the moment, so soon in their new bonds of trust, perhaps it was better to keep such things to herself.

She clasped his jaw as he went to kiss her cheek and

pulled him into a proper embrace. Her hand wound around his nape and held him there. She didn't care what anyone thought of the Lord and his wife's new found relations. She sighed in reluctance when he pulled away.

"We had better behave, my lady. Are we not supposed to be members of the nobility? Decorum and rule-abiding drilled into our very core."

Maddie shrugged, in no mood for etiquette. "And were we not going to take it slow and try being friends first? We've broken every other rule, why not this one," she said, motioning for the food to be brought out.

At Williams raised brow, Maddie sat back and behaved herself. "Perhaps you are right. But doesn't that also give us the ability to forgo such woeful ideals when it suits us? Like now, for instance." Understanding lit his eyes as he picked up her hand and placed a reverent kiss upon her inner wrist.

"'Twould seem you are right, but we should nonetheless allow our fellow table-men to eat. We seem to be the day's attraction, which is not enabling the populace to sup."

"If you insist, my lord."

"Meet me in the solar after the meal," William said, stabbing into some sort of pie Maddie could not name.

"Of course," she replied, wondering why he wished her in the solar and not their chamber. Inwardly shrugging, Maddie looked down at the slice of pie she, too, had been served, the spicy smell alone enough to extinguish her hunger. Putting down her knife, she picked up a roll.

AFTER A DISCREET TIME HAD PASSED, MADDIE MADE HER way to the solar. She walked into the room and closed the door. Leaning against the wood, she silently watched William.

Her breath hitched in her throat as an invisible energy hummed between them. It took all her restraint not to lick her lips as if to savour his delicious taste in the air. A feminine need to bring this man to his knees assailed her. He was so sure of himself, sitting on his writing table, one leg at ease.

Maddie walked over to the fire, kept clear of the table and gasped in pleasure as he came up behind her. His tall, strong body was hard against her back. His excitement wedged firmly between her buttocks. His hands stroked down her arms, his fingers grazing the sides of her breasts. Maddie leaned her head on his shoulder, her breathing uneven.

She shivered as his lips skimmed her neck. The gentle caress was at odds with his body's tension. She purred as a hand moved across her stomach, paused before travelling lower. Maddie shut her eyes and revelled in the desire—unlike any she had known—that coursed through her veins.

Never had she wanted a man as much as she did this man right at this moment. He fondled her through the gown, rubbed and teased her most sensitive nub. The flames in the hearth were as cold as ice compared to her conflagration.

Maddie clasped his nape and held him close while she enjoyed his ministrations. She rubbed against his own excitement and smiled as his growl of enjoyment huffed against her neck.

"I want you, ma chère."

She undulated in need, desperate for him too. "Yes."

She wavered as all contact stopped, before he picked her up and carried her toward the table. Anticipation swam in her veins at the heated feral look in his eye. She bit her lip and wondered what he planned.

"You look eager, lass," he said, kissing her.

"I am," Maddie said, and blushed. Why, she had no idea, after all they had done together.

He laughed, the sound predatory. She gasped as he turned her and laid her against the rough wood table. He lifted her skirts, uttered a curse, before cool air met the backs of her thighs. The woollen gown pooled about her waist.

Maddie could feel the dampness between her thighs. She shut her eyes, savoured the feel of his hands upon her skin, and only just held back a moan as two digits parted her folds and loved her. She grasped the table for support while he teased, fondled and pressed her ever closer to release. Then, finally, he gave her what she wanted.

He entered her in one swift stroke. Fulfilment and pleasure overwhelmed her and she moaned. His arms came around her in an immovable grip. His chest rasped against her back and left her feeling cherished and wholly loved. His murmurs of delight tickled her ear and sent her insides to quake.

"William," she gasped, unable to form any further words as endless jolts of pleasure spiked throughout her body. He continued to love her, allowed her to enjoy every moment of her orgasm. Maddie squirmed as his hands tightened. His thrusts became less guarded, barbaric. He stiffened before his own release shot deep within her womb. He moaned, a deep satisfied rumble against her back.

"Madeline..."

Tears pricked her eyes as he whispered her name against her back in reverential tone. She fell irrevocably in love with her knight in shining armour, on the spot and without doubt.

❧

MADDIE SAT UP IN BED WITH A START AND WIPED THE SLEEP from her eyes. She looked over to the other side of the bed and noticed William's imprint on the pillow, but the man himself absent.

Mistress Rhode bustled about and opened the tapestries. The morning air—less chilled now spring was on the way flowed into the room. Maddie breathed deep the smell of earth and sea then jumped from the covers.

"M'lady, 'tis a beautiful day. Just the weather for the moot," Mistress Rhode said, pulling out an ornate golden embroidered gown Maddie hadn't seen before.

Maddie looked from the gown back to her maid. "What moot? What are you talking about?"

Her maid stripped her of her chemise and passed her a damp cloth. Maddie walked over to the basin and washed as best she could, missing her shower dreadfully in the twenty-first century.

"The hall moot, m'lady. With your illness, Lord William sat in your stead at the last one. Today, you will once more take your father's chair and rule over your people."

Nerves fluttered in her stomach. Maddie clutched the cloth in her hands and stared at the grey stone wall. "You mean, I have sit before these people, who will come to me with their problems and I will have to make a decision of what's right and wrong," Maddie asked, her fear of public speaking closing her throat.

"Aye, m'lady. The dais is set up already in the bailey. After your morning mass, the moot will begin."

179

Maddie turned to her maid. "I can't. I can't do it," she said, her words muffled as her maid placed a clean chemise over her head.

"'Tis easy, m'lady. As long as you are fair, your people will be pleased."

At her maid's calming tone, Maddie pushed away her fear. Mistress Rhode was right. She had to do this, and would do it well. Hopefully.

The golden gown sat heavy, its intricate stitching adding to the importance of this day. "Do you know what they'll ask me?" Maddie asked, allowing Mistress Rhode to place a silk veil over her hair, a fillet of gold holding it in its place.

"Nay, m'lady. But 'twould seem we will soon find out." Her maid smiled and stepped back. "Now, where did I put those cursed shoes?"

Maddie smiled and waited for Mistress Rhode to find her footwear. She walked over to the narrow window and looked out over the ocean. The calming waters in no way calmed the fear of knowing she would have to sound noble and intelligent to pull off the next few hours without her people thinking she'd gone completely nuts.

MADDIE STEPPED UP ON THE WOODEN DAIS AND LOOKED about at the gathered throng of serfs and vassals. William helped her to her chair and she smiled at him in thanks. Adjusting her seat, she noted Lady Veronica and Sir Alex as part of the crowd.

At a table to her left, the parish clerk sat parchment and quill in hand. Maddie rubbed her forehead, having no idea how to act as judge and jury.

She took a calming breath as the first villager stepped before her.

"Mr. Robert Boyle has been caught baking in a personal oven instead of using the castle oven, m'lady," her steward said, then stepped back. Maddie looked down at the man, his clothes far from clean, his frame ill and sickly looking.

"Why did you do this, Mr Boyle?" she asked, inwardly fuming at such a pathetic offense.

"M'lady, I was ill. I could not make the distance to me front door, nevertheless the castle. 'Tis my only excuse."

Maddie nodded, the sincerity of his voice paying truth to his words. She looked down at the man's pants and noticed the small boy whimpering into his leg. "You could not help your circumstance; therefore I will let you off with a warning, Mr. Boyle. The next time you are ill, send your child to me and I will ensure you are kept fed by my oven."

The man clasped his hat against his chest and bowed. "Oh, thank you, m'lady. You are most kind."

Maddie smiled and nodded to her steward for the next complaint or query.

Overall, the day went well. She gave her blessing to two marriages between her people. Settled a dispute with a farmer who lived outside the castle walls and warned a young woman not to gossip. It was only when a local freeman brought forward one of the village children and stated he had caught the young boy stealing the barony's game did Maddie pause with thought.

She summoned the boy forward and noted his mother stood behind. Again, these people were poor and underfed and Maddie felt an overwhelming desire to take them in and give them everything she owned. "You stole some game from my woods. Is that right, young man?" Maddie asked gently.

"Aye, m'lady. But as I already told him," the boy said, pointing to the local freeman. "I scared a fox off that was killing the rabbit. It would have died anyways and, well, I just helped it. I thought because the rabbit had been in partly eaten, it wasn't fit for ye table, m'lady."

The freeman protested and Maddie ordered him to be quiet. She knew her people expected her to deal a harsh treatment out to the boy due to the fact she hadn't fined or punished anyone this day. She could not. If her people were hungry, it was her fault. She could not bring down the force of the law on an innocent child whose story did sound plausible. And the lad was right, she wouldn't want to eat anything partly eaten by a fox. She sat back.

"Due to the fact the fox had already munched on the rabbit, I will let you off with a warning. But the next time such a situation occurs, I want you to bring it to me so I can gift you the rabbit," Maddie said, winking.

She gasped as the boy ran up on the dais and hugged her. Tears prickled her eyes as his mumbles of how he thought she would kill him, met her ears. Had that been the punishment for such a felony? Maddie rubbed his back then set him away and looked at him.

"You're a child, I would never do that," she said.

The boy nodded but bit his lip. "Ye did last year, m'lady. My friend George——," his voice trailed off when William stepped forward.

Maddie's mouth gaped as she watched the young lad run to his mother. The bile rose in her throat and she sought confirmation with Mistress Rhode that such a thing was true. Her maid's solemn expression was all the answer she needed.

"Come, Madeline. The moot is over. 'Twill be time for supper soon," William said, pulling her from her chair.

Maddie's vision of William blurred in a pool of tears. "Did I really kill a child, William?"

He frowned and nodded. "Aye. The lad had been poaching on both our lands, but was caught on yours. 'Twould be a year ago now you held a trial and found him guilty. He was executed immediately by one of your knights." William paused, his eyes searching. "Why do you cry?"

"Lady Madeline killed a child because he was hungry. That is such a barbaric thing to do." Maddie's voice trembled as the tears streamed down her cheeks. "She should have helped him, not killed him. Given him employ somewhere in the village to keep him out of trouble. Not kill him as if he was nothing."

William pulled her into his arms. "Nay, Madeline. 'Twas no hope for the boy, he was set in his ways. Do not punish yourself. 'Twas what I would have done."

Maddie wrenched out of his arms and walked into the keep then headed for her chamber. She determined to be present at every future moot, and steadfast that all would be dealt fairly with the law. And ensure that no one faced the sword under any circumstance. Ever again.

CHAPTER 12

As the first weeks of spring arrived, Maddie set out to weed the kitchen garden. She stood and breathed in the smell of herbs and spices that slowly rose into the air. After a hard winter, the plants seemed eager to bud and bask in the mild sunlight. A smile played on her lips as she realized she was happy. That she had come to think this wondrous journey back in time a blessing, especially now, as a woman in love.

Finished with the bed before her she sat on the wooden seat, made not a week past, by her husband's decree. The sun was warm on her face, not a breath of wind marred the day. She raised her face toward the heat and thought of William, a man who made every day as warm and bright as that star in the sky.

As the sound of brisk footsteps sounded behind her, Maddie turned to look over her shoulder and smiled as Sir Alex came toward her. She had not seen him for many weeks, the knight having travelled to London for a time.

"Hello, Sir Alex, long time no see."

Sir Alex laughed and sat beside her. "How are you, Lady Madeline? I hope all is well?"

She raised her brows and smiled. "All is very well, Sir Alex. I understand you've been away."

"Yes, to London. In fact, I will be away again shortly. The king has given me permission to marry, so within a few months I shall commence the care of my own holdings in Kent."

Maddie lost some of the joy in seeing her friend again. He would be so far away; she may never see him again. "I cannot say I will be happy to see you go, Sir Alex. Although, of course, I understand you must live your own life and start a family. Congratulations on your future marriage. Please do not forget us up here, and visit whenever you can."

He nodded in assent. "Of course, m'lady. Although, because of the great distance I am not sure 'twill be as often as I'd like." He looked down at her in all seriousness. Maddie shifted on the seat as a fear curled within her belly.

"I do have a missive for you and Lord William from the king, m'lady."

She slumped back and cursed her stupidity at writing the missive. Serve her right if the king did allow the annulment and she lost William through her own foolishness.

"Well, I dare say I will read it tonight. Are you joining us for supper, Sir Alex?"

"Of course," he said, a thoughtful frown upon his brow. He paused. "If there is anything you ever need, you only have to write or send for me. I will keep you safe, m'lady."

Maddie clasped his arm in thanks. Sir Alex was such a nice man and a good friend. She would miss him dearly. However, he deserved a life and happiness like her. It would be selfish to keep him here just for her comfort.

Maddie leant over and kissed his cheek. "Thank you, Sir Alex. I am happy to know I have a friend should the need arise."

Something in his gaze made her pause. For the first time within Sir Alex's company Maddie wasn't sure of his intent. She froze as his hand pulled a stray leaf from her hair. She sat back with a laugh, hoped he had not noticed her unease. His eyes and what she'd seen in them made her uncomfortable.

"Thank you, Sir Alex."

He nodded and continued to stare. She watched a myriad of emotions flow from him before common sense seemed to reign supreme in his mind and he stood and strode away. Maddie frowned after him, worried she had inadvertently hurt her friend somehow. She hoped not, but to her, that was all he was, a friend. She looked back at her garden and mused she should probably get back to it.

⚜

WILLIAM STOOD ACROSS THE BAILEY AND WATCHED Madeline and Sir Alex with a simmering temper. His wife had a genuine attachment to his first knight. He knew it was wholly innocent on her side. However, of the other party involved, he was not so sure. His jaw clenched; foolish bastard to have insinuated the friendship in the first place. All in the hopes Sir Alex would keep his wife away while he bedded his whore.

It would be wrong to blame either of them for the closeness he had allowed to form. From her crestfallen expression, it seemed Sir Alex had informed his wife of his imminent departure. He fought the urge to go to her, give her comfort. Whether wholly for her ease or his own he wasn't sure. Either way, he did not like her distress and it would not hurt to inform his knight whose wife she was.

A red haze settled over his vision as Madeline kissed the man before her. His hand clenched his sword while his mind fought to comprehend what she had done. Was Madeline in love with Sir Alex? A rage welled within him. Had she played him a fool all these weeks? She had certainly never declared her love for him. He turned away, yelled to his page to fetch his horse. Either that or kill them both.

If Madeline thought such goings on would be allowed within their marriage she was very much mistaken. Her excuses this day would want to hold true. Or she would feel the full force of his temper...tonight.

THAT NIGHT AT DINNER, MADDIE SAT AS USUAL NEXT TO William and tried to hide her confusion over her husband's manner. She absently kept up conversation with Sir Bryan, who sat upon her left and wondered what the hell was wrong with William?

She stole a glance at him—his face hard and unread-able—gave no sign as to his thoughts or problem. It had hurt more than she cared to know when he'd greeted her this eve with barely a nod. As for talking to her, which was normally constant, he'd barely made a sound. She frowned, wondered if it was the king's letter that had caused such a turn of countenance, or was it something she had done. What though, she had no idea. As far as she understood, they were getting along marvellously.

"Is something the matter, my lord?"

Maddie kept her eye on William as she waited for his reply. A flush bloomed on her cheeks by his refusal to answer. The only sign he had even heard her was the ticking muscle in his jaw as he continued to stare down at his knights. Out of curiosity, she followed his glare and noted it lodged firmly on Sir Alex. Sir Alex, it seemed, was not the only one to notice William's curiosity.

Maddie's temper snapped. "Don't you dare sit there, William, and ignore me. If you have a problem, bloody well spit it out so I can have the pleasure of putting you back in your place," she said, annoyed.

That question at least warranted her a look. Her husband's cold glare froze her blood as he took a sip of mead. What had she done to have so much hate aimed at her?

"I saw you today, Lady Madeline, embracing another man." He glowered. "Does that answer your question?"

She quirked an eyebrow and glared, her mouth set in a hard line. Was he daft? Obviously. Because if he thought after what they had been doing together over these last week's she would look elsewhere, he was batty in the head.

"Yes, I did. I won't deny it. I found out this morning that Sir Alex is leaving and I was saying goodbye." She put down her knife lest she poke him with it for being an idiot. "Now if you had seen me with my tongue down his throat you should be worried. I like Sir Alex...as a friend, and I was being nice. There was nothing more to it than that. Please don't be angry and become all lordly and painful."

His gaze bored into her. She held her breath, as the seconds that seemed like minutes ticked by. She relaxed when the tension in him slowly drained away. She bit back the urge to tease him on his jealously. Her heart tweaked in her chest as she watched him run a hand across his jaw, a sigh of regret expelled.

He caught her eye, his brow furrowed. "I don't want to lose you, ma chère."

Maddie leant across and kissed him. Basked in the heat his lips always fired in her blood. It melted her heart to know a man of such stature could be insecure when it came to a woman. And not just any woman...but her.

"You're not going to lose me, William. Not to Sir Alex, or anyone. Please trust me as I trust you. Can you do that for me?"

He nodded as something flicked in his eyes that Maddie took as understanding. It may have taken a while, but she now trusted him above all else. And she was probably the one person who should be most wary of the man. Especially since all past action between them had been anything but smooth.

"I apologize, my lady."

She smiled across at him, happy all was well between them once again.

"I need to let you know, Lady Madeline, that I will be away for some weeks to London. I meant to discuss this with you after the meal but since we're both here, it may as well be now. You may be aware I received a missive from the king via Sir Alex's hand today."

Maddie blanched. Had their monarch done as she asked? She didn't want an annulment now. She loved William, wanted to stay with him. Even odder was her desire to stay in 1102, if that was what would keep her within her husband's arms for all time.

"What did the letter say? Sir Alex said it came addressed to us both. Is it bad news?" Maddie asked, fear curdling her supper.

"'Twas bad news, for you at least. I'm sorry to inform you, my dear, but your request for an annulment has been denied. In fact, you are now requested to beget an heir within a year." William chuckled. "Which I might add, a few weeks ago would have been a problem, but not so much these days."

Maddie laughed at his wink.

"Very true, my lord, but why is it you need to travel to London?" She didn't want him to go. The thought of weeks away from him troubled her.

He sighed. "Tedious court business pertaining to Kingston land, nothing you need worry about," he added as he noted her concern. He cleared his throat. "I will also be escorting Lady Veronica back to London, to ensure her safety. Her family have been notified and are expecting her return."

Maddie continued to look at him. She wanted to gauge his reaction to Lady Veronica's forthcoming departure. She inwardly sighed in relief when she noted no remorse or regret etched on his features. But that wasn't where her worries ended. Her stomach clenched in dread. She didn't like the idea of William's ex-lover in such close quarters with him and for weeks on end. The Lady Veronica was sly. There was no doubt about that. Maddie wouldn't trust her as far as she could kick the woman.

No matter William's actions or declarations to her, he still had a history with this lady. And from what she'd beheld in the castle hallway that very first night in 1102, it had once been a passionate one. Unease crept across her skin. Maddie cleared her throat and remembered to hold onto her trust.

"I suppose I will have to bid you farewell," she said. "And hope for the best," she added under her breath.

※

WILLIAM FROWNED AT MADELINE, HAVING NOT QUITE caught her last words. Although he had a good idea what they were. She was uncomfortable with him travelling with Lady Veronica. He threw his knife down and ran a hand through his hair. He wanted to comfort her, reassure her. The last thought on his mind was undertaking an illicit affair with his ex-mistress.

To be frank, they were hardly friends before he took her to his bed. He knew his words to Madeline upon her arrival into his life were cruel and hurtful. He shuddered as he remembered the lies he blurted, denigration that shamed him to his core.

It was no secret Lady Veronica had aimed for their relationship to proceed to marriage. Even now, she blamed Madeline for her loss. However, if anyone was to blame for Lady Veronica's loss of dreams, it was him. Having come to know Madeline as he now did, no other could ever fill her place.

He hated to leave her even for a night, nevertheless weeks at a time. It made it doubly hard knowing she would worry about his faithfulness. He picked up her hand, kissed her delicate fingers, and captured her gaze. Let all the love he held for the marvellous woman shine from his eyes.

"Do not worry, ma chère. You are the only woman I want. There will be no other. As soon as my business is completed, naught will keep me away." He should tell her he loved her. All but worshiped where she stepped. But he could not. He had other ideas as to when he would mention such sentiments. And London featured heavily in that grand scheme.

A half smile lifted her lips. "How will I get on without you around, my lord? I do believe I'll be quite lonely. Certainly afternoons will be filled in an entirely different manner."

"'Twould have to be," William growled, making his

wife laugh. She sighed, her breath warm against his neck when he pulled her into his chest and held her.

"I will miss you, ma chère," he said, looking down.

She ran a finger upon his cheek and touched his lips. "I'll miss you too." She paused. "It's going to be so boring here without you. I'll have nothing to do other than household chores. And I don't really even have them, as the servants carry out most tasks." William smiled at her mulish tone.

"Running a castle is no minor chore, Madeline. You should know that better than most."

"When do you leave?" she asked.

"Next week. A carriage as we speak is on its way up from London to carry Lady Veronica home. We'll leave in a day or two after its arrival."

"Her family's carriage?" Maddie frowned.

"Aye, I believe so."

Maddie looked along the dais to the woman who sat not far away, a smirk of triumph on Lady Veronica's face. Maddie gritted her teeth. She didn't like the sound of that at all.

Two days later, Maddie sat playing a game of checkers with Mistress Rhode and enjoyed a companionable cup of mead while they competed. The afternoon was cool, and spring showers were often. The air smelled fresh and clean, cleaner than she could ever remember. It was a scent only a storm could bestow and reminded her oddly of her childhood.

A ruckus in the courtyard caught their attention.

Simultaneously they rose and made their way to the small window that overlooked the bailey. A carriage arrived, and a second one soon after, piled high with luggage.

Maddie frowned and looked to Mistress Rhode, who appeared as puzzled as herself to whom it could be. Of course, there were to be carriages arriving from London. But they were not due until next week. As far as she was aware, no one else was due to arrive. So who was it?

A woman in a dark blue cloak stepped out of the carriage, holding her back as if in pain. Maddie started as the woman screeched orders to her staff about the unpacking of her luggage, the sound a high pierced squeal. She winced at the voice and a worry started to work up her spine. There was something awfully familiar about the woman, but what, Maddie couldn't place.

Couldn't place that was, until Lady Veronica herself raced down the stairs yelling Mama like a child of five.

"Bloody hell," Maddie muttered, and shrugged as Mistress Rhode chastised her language with a silent look.

"We have guests, m'lady."

Maddie looked back to the sickening sight of Lady Veronica and her mother, no doubt who would be another thorn in her side.

"So it would seem."

CHAPTER 13

Maddie sat and stared at flames that burned as hot as her temper. Lady Ribald not only had no manners, but was also as conniving and vicious as her daughter. The blood flowed thick and similar in that family.

Her Ladyship's room was hastily prepared, but very comfortable for a woman of her stature. The room had a view, which overlooked the sea, a tranquil space with furniture well made from a dark wood. No sooner had the woman walked into the chamber had her nose lifted, a dismissive sniff sounded that proclaimed her distaste. She had then marched back out and declared the room, "unacceptable," and demanded a chamber elsewhere within the keep.

Maddie allowed Her Ladyship to move into her late mother's chamber. Adjacent to her own, the room was used sparingly when the castle housed guests. Situated as close as it was to William and her chamber, many thought it not a proper place to sleep visitors. And Maddie agreed.

If only her troubles with the woman had ended with the one complaint.

But no. Lady Ribald had then waltzed within the solar, her tongue covered with barbs of disgust and contempt for the new Lady of Kingston. As the first words that dripped scorn flowed from the woman's mouth, Maddie's hackles rose.

Being discussed as if invisible was profoundly rude, no matter what century one occupied. Lady Ribald declared to her daughter—who basked in such censure of Maddie —that, "brunettes were the new flavour for Lord William. One of many, and easily discarded when the time came."

Lady Ribald had sat herself down across from Maddie and decreed to her face she had neither looks nor figure to compete with her daughter. That, and quote, "She was utterly baffled by Lord William's change of heart," end quote.

Surprisingly to Maddie, she now couldn't wait for William to depart, just to be free of the woman. She wondered what the time was, the hours seemed the longest she could ever remember. The days stretched endlessly ahead with such visitors.

"I hope your journey, Lady Ribald, was agreeable and without trouble?" Maddie asked, the taste of being polite bitter in her mouth.

Lady Ribald looked back at her, her features mocking. "Do not bother to be polite to me, Lady Madeline. Neither of us should endeavour to be friends. I'm here to collect my daughter, take her away from this evil place and have her marry a respectable gentleman. Something Northern England has lack of."

"Oh, I'm sure you're mistaken, Your Ladyship," Maddie replied, placing her cup of mead on a side table. "For I believe there are plenty of gentlemen." Her eyes took in Lady Veronica, her gaze a study of the woman before her. "As for ladies in these parts, now, I do believe they are scarce on the ground." Silence ensued, but sadly, Maddie reflected, not long enough.

"I will not pretend to misunderstand your meaning. You will not again insinuate another such accusation against my daughter," Lady Ribald replied, her attention flicking about the room.

Maddie looked over to Lady Veronica, who had an air of mock innocence. "I do believe, Lady Ribald, we should not talk of barbs." Maddie held Veronica's eyes as she uttered the last and was pleased to see the woman's face drain of colour. Steeling herself, Maddie turned back to the unwelcome guest and refused to say anymore, lest the conversation turn nastier than it already was.

The ensuing silence was deafening.

"Pray, where is Lord William?" Lady Ribald queried. "'Tis most decidedly rude for him to be absent when guests arrive."

Maddie clamped down the urge to tell Lady Ribald she could go to Hades for all she cared of her opinion. Instead, Maddie said, "Had he known of any, I'm sure he would have been here, Your Ladyship. As it happens, he will be back by nightfall. They are out hunting game today. I'm sure you would look forward to a hearty meal after such wearisome travels."

"In that, you are correct, Lady Madeline."

Maddie sighed and looked over to Mistress Rhode for help. Surely she could escape this lion's den. She realized with a sinking heart she would get no help from that quarter, as her maid shook her head in denial. Lady Ribald flicked an invisible piece of lint from her gown, her face a mask of distaste. Maddie wondered what next to expect from the woman.

Something about Lady Ribald made her skin crawl. What, Maddie couldn't put her finger on. And quite frankly, at this point in time, she didn't want to.

As she lay under the many blankets alone that night, her mind turned to William. She missed him tonight. It worried her that he had not returned home after his day of hunting. She also reflected that since she had been unable to hold her temper in check, all of Aimecourt now knew of the animosity that flowed between herself and Veronica's family.

Maddie rolled over and touched the place where William's head should be. She pulled the feathered pillow toward her and inhaled his scent and an ache settled in her chest. She hoped he was okay and didn't leave her alone in this medieval world. It was many hours later that sleep finally claimed her.

ॐ

SOMETIME AFTER DAWN, MADDIE WOKE UP WITH A GASP OF shock as a man as cold as the arctic ice caps, cuddled her under the blankets. She relaxed as the familiar sound of his voice soothed the worry that she was about to be raped by an iceberg.

"Mmmm, you're warm," William mumbled against her neck, making her shiver from the chill of his lips.

Maddie puffed out a gulp of air when his frozen feet wound around her own. "And you're freezing! Did you only now get home? What happened to keep you away?" she asked.

"Hunting too far a field and knowing we wouldn't make it back before nightfall. We decided to set up camp." His arms pulled her into his side. It seemed he had missed her as much as she did him. A sigh of contentment brushed her neck and his body slowly warmed against hers.

"When the sky started to light, I proceeded home. My men will arrive later this morn with our varied and good hunting."

Maddie rolled over and kissed his chest, revelled in his now familiar scent. "I'm glad you're home. Although, after I tell you something, I'm not sure you will be."

William made an unintelligible sound but didn't answer. Maddie stole a look up at him and noticed his almost comatose state. His eyes closed and shadowed with grey sleepless circles. She sighed and left the news of their guests for later. He deserved some rest. As much as she wanted to confide in him the happenings at home since his leaving, she allowed sleep to take them both. Sleep, much easier now that she lay where she belonged, in the arms of her husband, cold as they were.

Waking some hours later, Maddie was happy to feel arms made of steel still banded around her waist. They were crispy warm under the blankets. The sun had burnt away the cold frosty morn and she could hear the birds twittering outside.

She rolled and faced William, then smiled when she noticed him awake. A shiver of expectation ran through her as his eyes burned with an entirely new heat.

"Good morning, husband."

"It is that, wife," he replied before he rolled her onto her back and pulled up her chemise.

Maddie grinned and allowed him his way. "And what, pray tell, do you think you're doing?" she asked, amused.

He kissed her, his mouth paying homage to her plump bottom lip. "Seducing you."

Maddie ran her hands up his neck and bit her lip as he moved against her, moisture pooling between her legs.

Eager, Maddie wrapped them around his waist. She pushed a lock of hair from his eyes, her heart thumping erratically in her chest. "You've already done that," Maddie said on a gasp when he rubbed against her.

William moaned and thrust, deep and hard into her core. His jaw clenched. "You're everything to me, Madeline," he said holding her gaze.

Maddie pulled him down for a kiss and revelled in the urgency she could feel emanating from him. His lips moved to her chin, her neck, her breasts. The corded muscles along his spine flexed under her palms.

"Madeline..."

Maddie heard his hearts plea in his whisper. His hair fell over his face and shrouded his eyes. But she didn't need to see the windows of his soul to know what she meant to him. In every touch, kiss and look he bestowed, he proclaimed a love that would last for all time.

Not yet ready to end this delightful interlude, Maddie pushed hard against his chest. William's eyes blazed when he guessed her intention. A contented sigh escaped Madeline when he settled beneath her. The tough Baron of Kingston, hers to do with as she pleased; she liked the idea of that.

A moan tore free as she lowered herself upon his swollen phallus. His hands, urgent and rough upon her breasts, sent a wild thrill through her blood. His thumbs grazed the peaked buds, as he thrust into her, filling her. Maddie felt the rough hair on his chest, the muscles on his abdomen hard and chiselled to perfection. It didn't take long for a strong and delicious climax to flow throughout her body. William groaned as she tightened and convulsed about him, his gaze holding her captive.

Satiated and sleepy, William flipped her over to lie on her stomach and anticipation ran throughout every fibre of her being. His manhood slid against her bottom and sparked electric waves to her core. A need to reach that delicious pinnacle again blossomed. William kissed her back, nibbling along her spine until Maddie couldn't stand it any longer.

"William, please," she whispered into the bedding.

He claimed her, showed her how truly medieval and dominant a man could be in this time. It probably should have scared her; instead, Maddie revelled in his desire. Welcomed the frantic pace that left her shattered in pleasure and her husband's seed deep in her womb.

Her lungs fought for breath, matched the breathing of William's sweat-covered body. He shifted and came to lie beside her while Maddie dozed in absolute contentment. William pulled her into his embrace and wrapped her in his arms. The smell of sex and William met her senses. No sweeter perfume she knew or would ever know.

৩৯৫১

"Do not tell me, Veronica, that you have allowed that trollop of Aimecourt to get her claws into Lord William?"

Veronica held her mother's furious stare. That was a temper she was loath to spark. The woman could be cruel and callous at will. Years of court life may have camouflaged her mother's vindictive nature. But only to a point. Any who worked for Her Ladyship or carried the same blood in their veins knew not to overstep the bounds when the woman's displeasure was roused.

Veronica pushed down her nerves and stood silent as her mother tried to leash her anger. She swallowed, tried to remember her own irritation at her parent's lack of help with the matter.

"It would have been fine, had you convinced the king the marriage should not have proceeded in the first place," she whispered heatedly.

"Do not try me any more than you already have, daughter. I'm far past caring." Her mother's gaze darted around the solar. Her fists, clenching and unclenching in her lap, spoke of a woman who tried to hold her temper in check. Veronica took a step back.

"You know what it means to me to see this family crushed. I have not spent the last fifteen years at court raising a daughter of another man, allowed my peers to look at me with disdain and censure for it all to come apart now."

Veronica frowned. Her mother's anger ran deep. And all because of the man who had spurned her all those years ago.

"I understand, mother, and there are still things we can do," she pleaded. "I know my first strike did not succeed as we'd hoped, but I have news. A man who is in service here knows of a woman who may be able to help us." Veronica smirked. "Without his knowing it, of course."

"What have you in mind?"

Veronica walked over and sat beside her mother. She looked around the room and ensured no one lingered to listen to their conversation.

"Lady Madeline's maid is of Welsh blood, and her mother is some sort of healer. Her family travels to these parts yearly and is now, as we speak, on their way here. From what I can gather, they are but a week's travel from our doors." Veronica paused.

"Go on, child, what is your plan?"

"Remember a few months ago, I told you my servant overheard Madeline tell Mistress Rhode she thought herself from the future."

Lady Ribald sat back, startled and looked at Veronica as if her wits were missing. "Yes, I remember. However, the way you worded your missive, I assumed Lady Madeline meant in relation to the future with the Baron of Kingston. Is this not that case? Do you mean to tell me, the woman actually believes herself from the future, literally?" Lady Ribald asked.

"I believe she meant the latter, Mama. Apparently, that night, Lady Madeline and her maid agreed, should they not find a ring Lady Madeline is missing, Mistress Rhode would consult her mother. I do not know of the ring they speak. But I believe they mean to ask the healer if there is indeed some way to send her home, back to this future she speaks of."

"What era does this woman think she is from, pray tell?"

"That, Mama, I could not say. But I believe many, many years into the future." Veronica laughed and her mother cringed. "Do you not see what we could do?" She continued.

Lady Ribald sat back and contemplated the tale. "I believe, my child, that we should accuse the Lady of Kingston of black magic."

"Why black magic, Mama?" Veronica asked, frowning.

Lady Ribald smiled. "Because, my dear, black magic is thought dangerous, the devil's hand. I doubt the Baron of Kingston would welcome a wife labelled such. With any luck, her people will turn against her. Demand the demons spawn burn at the stake. It would ruin Aimecourt and the proud pompous name, once and for all."

Veronica slumped back into her chair and smirked. "And your revenge will be complete."

Lady Ribald glared. "And not before time."

THREE DAYS LATER, MADELINE WATCHED FROM THE kitchen garden as Lord William spoke to Lady Veronica beside the washroom. Oblivious to her scrutiny, she wondered why the two of them would talk in such a secluded location within the bailey. The urge to go to him and demand he explain grew within.

William stood with hands on hips, his voice, when loud enough to hear, was hard and uncompromising. It should have put any on guard; however, Lady Veronica seemed unfazed by his manner and tone. Maddie watched as Veronica's own temper got away from her. Her arms waved about like linen in the wind. Endless words raining down on her William's head, none of them polite.

Maddie glanced around the normally private area of the bailey and noticed the many eyes this argument had pulled forth. Her stomach clenched and nausea lodged in her throat when William pulled Veronica into the wash-room. Maddie put down her wooden hand shovel and stood. Why would he do that? What did he have to say that demanded such privacy? Or was there another nefarious reason behind his logic?

Maddie shook herself from such thoughts. She trusted William, wholly. There was no cause for alarm. He was obviously protecting Lady Veronica from censure.

Maddie walked over to the low wall around the garden and leaned on the cold stone. Her whole body chilled when two giggling washerwomen ran from the shed.

Maddie's mind warred with trust, her love and her ability to think straight, seeing her husband take a woman who once graced his bed into a private dwelling. Should she go and confront them. Did she want to?

But if she did and his innocence prevailed, how could

she ever look at William and declare her trust when it was obvious by her actions that she had none? No, she trusted him. Would trust what she saw in his eyes and his actions toward her. It didn't stop her praying to God to let it be so.

Ten minutes later Maddie still sat against the stone wall and tried to will her damn eyes to stop filling with water. William would not cheat on her. Not after everything they had been through these past months. She punched the ground as another quick glance at the washroom showed the door shut tight with no sign of either party emerging.

She looked down at her dust-covered boots stretched out before her. Pushed the nausea away and wondered what she would do if he were unfaithful. She shook her head; William would not do it to her. Lady Veronica would, given the chance. But not William. Please not, William.

A door slammed and pulled her from her troubled thoughts. She peeked around the stone and watched William stride away. His body taut, his mouth a hard, uncompromising line. A hand ran through his hair before she lost sight of him entering the keep. Was it annoyance or some other emotion that flittered across his features? Maddie turned her attention back to the washroom and watched as Lady Veronica stepped out into the sunlight.

Lady Veronica patted her hair then looked down at her bodice, pulling at it discreetly. Maddie shut her eyes to block out the vision. She swallowed and released the soil held tight in her fist. She wouldn't believe it. Lady Veronica was playing another one of her games. Maddie hoped it wasn't she who'd been played.

She stood and dusted off her gown. Her mind was a chorus of thoughts and accusations. She needed to get away from here. Needed time to think. She headed to the stable.

Maddie charged a serf to saddle Eurus. Her mind taunted her with images of William and Veronica. Had William lied to her? Had their relationship only progressed so his affair with his mistress could continue? Keep the wife happy and satisfied, and continue discreetly with the lover. Had that been William's goal all along? Surely she wouldn't be unlucky enough for it to happen to her again. Once in any lifetime was ample heartache. Was she cursed? Did divinity declare that whenever Maddie fell in love that the fellow who held her heart would then have the right to crush it?

She allowed Eurus to trot from the outer bailey, holding his reins firm so the horse would keep a slow pace. Not again, she could not have been used again. He had better have been faithful, or Kingston would find itself once more at war with Aimecourt. And King Henry could go to the devil himself if he thought to intrude. One could not be married to a dead man.

CHAPTER 14

W illiam stormed into the castle. He took the stairs two at a time, his body shaking. Lady Veronica was beyond help. He had never known a woman to be so vindictive or sly. He wondered what he had ever seen in her all those months they were together. Part of him knew it was a purely physical relationship, no matter what she said to Madeline.

The act she had put on today over their imminent departure was beyond endurance. He had allowed her to stroll with him as a gesture of peace. For all that he had allowed to pass between them, she still deserved respect. And for a time he had thought his actions were welcome. He breathed deep, knew that to be a lie. She had allowed his inconsequential talk as a means to woo him once more. And when that hadn't worked, acted like the blasted banshee she'd become renowned as.

He walked into his room and strode to Madeline's door. Aggravation flowed through his veins at seeing it empty. Where was she? He needed her. Needed her calm and logical presence of mind to ease his anger. Damn

Veronica. How she still thought to continue an affair was beyond him. He shook his head and walked back to his chamber.

He had more than amply filled his obligation to the woman. He had told her honestly of his wish to be with Madeline. Furthermore, he had bequeathed funds upon Veronica. What more did she want?

He sat before the hearth and kicked off his boots in irritation. He sighed and leaned his head back against the chair, his thoughts on the troubled conversation with Veronica. Plague take her, the weeks ahead for him loomed like the white Cliffs of Dover. The trip south would be an endless strain with a woman he was sure revelled in unrest.

Veronica's words sounded loud in his mind.

"William, why do you no longer come to my bed? You must know how much I miss you, my darling," She had purred, throwing her arms about his neck.

William shrugged free and stepped back. "'Twould be because I am married, Lady Veronica. And that I find my wife most suitable to my needs and taste. I require no other."

Lady Veronica flinched at his words, before she masked her hurt behind a cool visage. Ignored his slight and stepped closer, ran her hand up the back of his thigh before it stopped on his buttock. Revulsion seared his blood at her sigh of delight.

"I miss our bed sport, my lord." She leant up and kissed his jaw, ran her tongue along his stubbled growth. "Maybe one last time? Before I'm gone forever. What say you?" she whispered a breath from his mouth.

William lifted his head from the repulsive act and stopped her ministrations. He cursed his weak body for hardening at such a flagrant invitation by a woman he no longer viewed as attractive. Madeline had changed him.

Made him the man he ought to have been, from the day he became a baron. No longer was he the lord who took his delight in all and sundry. He was married. Married to a woman he loved. He needed no other. His body may react as a man's would to such flagrant invites, but he would never again act on such inducements. He had promised fidelity to Madeline and he would stand by that promise. He wanted nothing other than to make Madeline happy. It was no chore to give up the pleasures of the flesh with unnamed and quickly forgotten women.

"I think not, Lady Veronica," he said.

Veronica's pout reminded him of an insolent child. "Come, my lord, no one knows we are here. Your body remembers. Why else would it be straining under your tunic? " He clamped his jaw as her hand wrapped around him. "You're hard, William. Let me make you harder."

He lifted her fully away from him, her touch, although brazen, made his insides crawl. "I said no, Lady Veronica. 'Twould be wise for you to listen." He ignored her gasp of shock as he strode to the door. He paused and turned, met her eyes before he spoke his next words. "Be ready to depart Aimecourt in two weeks. And do not try to make trouble with Madeline, my lady. 'Twould be unwise for you to try to hurt her in any way. I will not have her hurt by your lies or actions. Do I make myself clear?"

Hours later Maddie returned to the keep. Eurus plodded along and slowly ate up the distance toward home. She looked up at the grey imposing stones of Aimecourt. Many things were clearer in her mind. The fresh spring wind was chill against her flesh, yet in her haste to depart, she had forgotten to take her mantle. She rode over a slight incline, and the gatehouse and drawbridge came into view. Maddie patted Eurus and looked to see Sir Alex, his aggravated pace wearing a track into the gravel. She waved and received a stance of an irate soldier in reply, hands on hips and legs spread. Maddie wondered what was wrong.

Dread coiled in her stomach at the thought that William may have been hurt in some way. She pulled her bored mount before him and looked into the outer bailey. All seemed calm and normal. Serfs went about their chores. The blacksmith pummelled steel. The children ran and played in the safety of the walls. Maddie frowned. "Has something happened, Sir Alex? Is everything okay?"

"All is well...now, Lady Madeline. Although the castle's lord is another matter," he stated, a worried note to his words.

"Over what?" Maddie asked.

"Your outing, m'lady. I do believe your husband would have started to behead his men had you not returned soon. As it is, thirty of Kingston's best knights are out searching for you. What possessed you to venture out without me or some other escort?"

Maddie clamped her mouth shut, not wanting to answer that. Certainly not to Sir Alex, who didn't need to know it was William who had made the ride a necessity in the first place. The hours away had cleared her head. She had yet to find out the happenings inside that washroom today, but otherwise she had calmed down and rationalized what she saw.

"I needed some time alone, Sir Alex. I thought a ride would be just the thing, and thankfully it was," she said.

"Madeline!"

Her head whipped toward the keep as William's irritated yell met her ears. She watched, entranced, as he strode toward her, livid as ever and handsome, too. She made herself keep the horse still, refused her body the instinct to flee. His face sported a red tint she had only pulled forth a few times since her arrival in his life. She sighed and knew she owed her servants an apology for having to put up with the baron's raging anger over these last few hours.

Maddie smiled her sweetest as William drew near. Her ploy to distract him worked. She inwardly smiled as his temper gave way to other emotions he had for her. Worry, love, and relief crossed his features.

William helped her dismount. He pulled her into his arms, and Maddie forgot her annoyance at him and kissed him instead.

WILLIAM WALKED MADELINE INTO HER HORSE'S SIDE AND ravished her sweet mouth, heard whom he assumed to be Sir Alex walk away mumbling something under his breath about the two of them taking it inside. He ignored his knight and continued the delightful welcome his wife had bestowed on him before conscious thought took hold. The little vixen had distracted him on purpose.

He lifted his head and glared down at her. His heart once again settled in his chest, beating at a more reasonable speed. She was safe. She was home, that was all that mattered. Fear had taken hold when informed of her leaving the safety of the fortification. He had sent men out immediately and sent word for the whereabouts of the Lady Veronica. He would not take any chances again when it came to Madeline's life. He wasn't stupid not to know who had aimed to take her life all those weeks ago. He knew with certainty that Veronica had tried and failed.

If the woman had not been who she was, she would already be dead.

"What are you about, going out alone? Especially after what happened the last time you ventured such?" She glared at him, her defiant chin lifting. "'Tis dangerous for you to go out alone. Promise me you will never do so again," he said, giving her shoulders a little shake to carry the truth of his words.

"If you recall, my lord, I happened to be escorted the last time, and that didn't seem to help me. I was still shot," Maddie said, wiggling from his hold. "And anyway, as you can see I ventured home safely, perhaps all my future rides should be unaccompanied."

"Don't be sarcastic, it doesn't suit you." A smirk lifted his lips. He should not be amused by her words. William concentrated on his ire. "Madeline, had you been caught by Scottish men they would have raped you. Killed you. You will not do it again," he said.

"Really," she replied her voice bland and unfazed by his tone.

Madeline handed her horse to a waiting serf and walked toward the bailey. William strode after her, his temper simmering in his blood.

"Is that an order, husband?" Madeline asked.

William winced at the endearment in her question. Knew such accolades usually preceded an argument. "A mere request. One I would like you to adhere to."

Maddie looked at him mockingly. "Sounds like an order to me, no matter how you word it, my lord," she said.

William clamped his jaw shut. To force her now would ensue she repudiate his request. He clasped her hand, placed it on his arm, and inwardly smiled when a sigh of acquiescence met his ears.

"Fine, I won't do it again, if it makes you happy. I only rode out today because I had something on my mind and I needed time to think. Alone," she said, not meeting his eyes.

William frowned. "What is wrong, ma chère?" She pulled her hand from his sleeve and clasped them before her.

"I saw you, earlier today, talking with Lady Veronica. I watched you pull her into the washroom. I also know you were in there for over ten minutes." She halted and turned to face him, her face a mask of displeasure. "What took so long in that washroom, my lord?"

"You do not trust me?" William asked.

Maddie sighed and licked her lips. "I do, William. I want to, but," she shook her head. "Please tell me."

"I explained once more to Lady Veronica, that she and I are finished. I reminded her to prepare for the upcoming journey to London," he said.

Maddie pushed away a strand of stray hair from her eye and watched him. "I will only ask this once, William. And then I promise never to do so again." His jaw clenched. "Is that the truth?"

"Naught happened, Madeline. I swear on my life and my name as a nobleman." William lent down and tipped up her chin then kissed her.

"You are the only one I desire, wife. The only one I want to warm my bed, just as you do my heart."

Maddie smiled and hugged him. He returned the embrace, encircling her with his arms and pulling her close.

"Okay, I believe you. Thank you, William."

"You are very welcome, ma chère, and do not ever ask me again," he said.

She nodded. "I promise."

CHAPTER 15

Maddie looked out over the ocean, her mind a mixture of thoughts, regrets, and yearnings. The day had finally arrived. Tomorrow she would see Mistress Rhodes' mother. This time tomorrow night she could be back in the twenty-first century. A pain settled in her chest at the thought of living nine-hundred years away from William. Torture would be easier to bear.

Whether Maddie liked it or not, William had wiggled under her skin and imbedded himself into her heart. Her life in Greenwich seemed foreign now. Would she be able to merge back into society after all that had happened, all her experiences in medieval England? Could she live without her soul mate?

A resounding no echoed in her mind.

Guilt assailed her. She had friends in the future who were, no doubt, worried about her. Her friend Jackie would be frantic by now. Months gone with no word would be deemed suspicious by the authorities. They would think her dead. Then there was her business. Was her shop okay? Was Maria, her only employee, still opening the store? Or had everything been frozen until she returned or until she was declared dead?

Maddie absently watched the gulls swoop down toward the ocean in search of food. Dusk settled over the land and the first stars twinkled on the horizon. Then again, time travel may not work in any way she thought. Time in the future may have stood still or worse zoomed ahead. If she ever returned home, perhaps her home wasn't even there.

She sighed and turned her mind to less worrisome thoughts, like her bath being filled. She wiped at her eyes, laid her towel upon a stool, and then poured her favourite lavender scent in the water and set to soak her weary body for a time.

Silent tears fell into the water as her thoughts turned over in her mind. She missed her old life. Who would not? A single twenty-first century girl, self-employed and free to do as she pleased, the world was her oyster, hers to discover at will. Men she may have sworn off thanks to her ex's misdemeanours, but otherwise she had been happy. However, it all seemed to fade in glamor as her life here with William came into focus. She loved him, loved everything about the temperamental, affectionate Baron of Kingston.

And if she were honest with herself, she didn't want to go home. No matter how much guilt consumed her over leaving everything and everyone she loved, the thought of leaving William was worse. She couldn't do it. Wouldn't do it. Even if she were to find that blasted ring sometime into the future, she would ensure herself that it made it into the sea away from her. She would not allow it to send her home. She could not live without him. It was as simple as that.

"Madeline?"

Startled, Maddie sat up in the water.

"William, what is it?" she said. His gaze was troubled, a muscle flexing in his jaw.

"Are you pleased, Madeline?" he asked.

Maddie sat back and frowned in puzzlement. "What do you mean? You know I'm happy." To a point, she supposed. William shook his head not believing her words and she fought the urge to squirm. She swallowed.

"'Tis my belief you are not, ma chère." William sat on the bed and placed his arms across his knees. "You are distant. Often lost in thought. 'Twould seem most days I can find you gazing out the windows and oblivious to the castle life that goes on about you." William sighed. "You are troubled and I wish to know why. Right now."

Maddie ran her fingers through the water and wondered if William was open of mind enough to hear her tale. Would he believe her or send her to a convent for women who were unwanted or unhinged? Fear assailed her before she calmed. William would not send her away. It was not in his character to do so.

"Do you doubt me still over Lady Veronica?" he asked, frowning.

Maddie sat up and hugged her knees. "No." She turned and looked at him. "I trust you, William."

"Then what is it?" He stood and paced to the window. "Are you unhappy in the marriage?" Maddie shook her head. "Then what, woman?" William bellowed.

"I want to tell you something. But it is a confusing tale and one I think you may not believe. You may even think me addled in the mind," she said, with a passing smile.

"You have naught to worry about, Madeline. If you are in need of telling me of your worries, I promise to listen to your tale." William walked over to the stool beside her bath and sat. His arm reached into the water and picked up the bar of soap she had dropped.

"Really, you would listen if I told you a story that is so beyond rational thought to be unbelievable?" Maddie asked. William picked up her foot, his rough hands tickling.

"If you wish it, yes," he said.

"Okay, I'll tell you. But please don't say anything until I finish. Promise?"

William nodded. "I promise."

Maddie began her story. She ignored his frowns and starts at her wording and life before this time. She explained everything: finding herself in a carriage on her way to the church, her first meeting with him. How she had thought it odd, a man she had made up in her dream did not like her. She told him of the ring she had found. How she thought it was her way home, told him of the inscription with their names on it. She told him everything right up to this moment in time as she sat within a luke-warm bath telling him of her tale.

Silence ensued at the end of her bizarre story. Her skin pricked in goose bumps, and not because the water had turned tepid. His quietness unnerved her; she could not read his blank features. Would he send her away? Would he burn her at the stake for witchcraft? Maddie worked her bottom lip with her teeth. Perhaps she ought to calm down and wait to hear what he thought before jumping to conclusions.

"Well," she asked at length, "what do you think?"

William stood and strode out the room.

Maddie's heart stopped in her chest. "Where are you going? William?" she called, receiving no answer. Terrible thoughts of him fetching his knights to carry her away froze her blood before his returning footsteps sounded loud on the floor. Maddie clasped the tub, her knuckles white on the rim when he walked into her chamber. "William, what are you doing?"

"Open it," he said, and handed her a pewter box. An awfully familiar pewter box.

"It can't be." Maddie shook her head. Her attention fixed on the dragon etched onto the lid.

"Open it, Madeline. Then tell me what you think of my belated wedding gift."

Maddie opened the box, using a nail to flick the latch. It sprung open. A small ring encircled with diamonds glittered up at her. She picked it up with shaking fingers. Her eyes welled with tears as she read the inscription upon the pewter. *Willelm ○ Madaline*, just as she knew it would be. "I don't know what to say," she said, at length.

"'Twould seem I do, ma chère. When I first met you, I cursed God for placing such a beautiful enemy before me. 'Tis no secret my desire for you made me cruel and unkind when we first married. I beg your forgiveness for this."

"But I could not fathom how the Baron of Aimecourt could sire a woman of such inner strength and goodwill. And now I know he did not. For you are not she. A gift from a time far beyond my reach." William walked to the window, his gaze lost on the ocean. "When we struck our own bargain regarding our marriage, I had my steward find out everything about the Lady Madeline. From all reports, she was a tyrant, a spoiled, hard woman who never gave a quarter. You, Madeline, are nothing of the kind. You are sweet. You treat your serfs as equals. And you are far too lenient during your hall moots."

Maddie laughed and sat back in her bath.

"My mother was a healer," William stated from the window. "She often spoke of things that could not be explained. I used to wonder as a boy if what she said may be possible, but as I grew, so too, did my disbelief of such magic." He laughed, the sound mocking. "Perhaps I should not have."

"You believe me? You won't send me away?"

William walked back over to the bath and frowned. "Why would I wish to send you away? You are not mad." William sat. "No one knew of this ring but me, Madeline. No one. I believe what you say."

Relief poured through Maddie like a balm. Months of worry lifted from her shoulders at his words. "You don't know how happy I am to hear that," she said.

"I could no sooner live without air than live without you." William paused. "I love you."

Maddie bolted upright and water splashed over the sides of the tub. "You love me?"

"'Twould seem that I do, ma chère," he said, as his finger ran across her cheek. His lips skimmed across her collarbone and shivers of expectation ran through her.

"You know I cannot wear the ring, William, don't you," Maddie said and pulled away to look at him.

"Why do you think that?" he asked.

"Because, the last time I placed it on my finger I landed in 1102. What if I put it on and it sends me back to my time, to 2011?"

"You're from the year 2011?" Williams shock was clear on his face. "'Tis impossible," he muttered. He met her eyes and started to laugh.

"Yes, I am. It would seem, Lord William, I have a tendency to like extremely old men."

"You mean because I am over nine-hundred years older than you?" he asked, amusement in his tone.

"Yes," Maddie said.

"Well, I am glad for it. And if you think the ring may take you back, you know I would prefer you not to wear it. I desire above all else for you to stay with me, Madeline. I want to have a life with you. I find myself looking and craving you every minute of every day. And if that ring has the power to take you from me, I will destroy it myself."

She clasped his jaw, tears of joy running down her cheeks. Maddie kissed him. Allowed herself to revel in his love.

"I will wear the ring on a ribbon around my neck. Keep it close to my heart, where you are, my lord."

William pulled her from the water, her wet body drenching his clothes. "Does that mean I occupy some of that organ of yours, my love?"

"You occupy all of it. I love you, William. You know I love you, I will always do so," Maddie said.

William kissed her, his tongue swept into her mouth and claimed her. His hands ran over her body, leaving fire in their wake. The kiss intoxicated Maddie's senses and aroused her instantly.

"I want you. I want to feel your heat around me. Love me, Madeline."

Maddie stepped out of the bath and pushed William toward the bed. With a mischievous smirk, she took her time with the laces of his tunic. Kissed his skin as the material slowly parted. His chest, hard and muscular, rose and fell swiftly under his laboured breath.

She loved his body, took delight in touching the strong, corded muscles. She ran her hand down his stomach and smiled when William growled at her direction. His small-pebbled nipple called for her to lick it. She did, just as her hand came to sit on the front of his hose. Maddie curved her fingers around him and stroked.

"Do you like that, my lord?"

William opened his eyes and swallowed before he spoke.

"Your touch is pleasing," he said.

Maddie pulled the laces free and met William's intense

gaze. Their barely leached need thrummed through every bead of sweat, every twitch of muscle. With one finger, she ran over the swollen head of his member and then slid it down the engorged vein to its base. Her lips, eager for his taste, feathered kisses down his chest, her other hand holding him down.

"Let me pleasure you."

William made a pained noise. "You are—" his voice trailed off when her lips moved toward his navel. Maddie smiled and kissed the bands of muscle that encircled his abdomen. His heart beat fast, a symphony of beats that matched hers.

She bent her knees and looked up one last time at William. The pained expectation written on his face was an image she would never forget. She turned back to his well-endowed appendage and took in his size. He was quite large. She wet her lips then bent forward, licked the head of his penis and tasted the salty residue that sat there. William's hips undulated a fraction and Maddie used the movement to her advantage and took him fully into her mouth.

William's hands clasped her hair. "Madeline," he groaned. "Oh, 'tis heaven on earth."

Maddie put all her love and desire into pleasing him as best she could. His hips rocked and set in a rhythm with her mouth. She took him deep and used her teeth to rasp against his velvety skin.

Determined to give him as much pleasure as he always bestowed on her, Maddie gently massaged his balls. They sat high and hard against his phallus.

His hold on her hair increased. "Oh, Madeline...don't—"

The sweetest nectar on earth shot into her mouth with an explosive cry from William. Maddie didn't stop until

William was spent between her lips. She kissed her way back up his chest, her own shiver of anticipation running through her at William's wild eyes.

She smiled and kissed him...hard.

He picked her up and threw her onto the bed, the soft woollens and furs cushioning her fall.

Maddie lay back and laughed when William divested himself of his hose, still sitting about his ankles. She bit her bottom lip as he crawled onto the bed and over her.

"Think yourself a clever minx, my love," he said, grinning. He bent over her breast, his stubble opposite to the smooth slide of his lips on her skin. He took a nipple into his mouth and flicked his tongue before sitting back and staring down at her.

Maddie lifted her knees and placed her wet, needy sex against William's already hard penis. She undulated against him and sighed, pleasure hot in her veins, when the head of his cock entered her.

"I'm very clever, my lord. Do you not think so?" she asked, trying to take him in further.

William's eyes closed before his intense gaze snapped back to her. "I do. Now 'tis my turn to show you how talented your husband is," he said, placing a kiss on her lips.

"Mmmm," Maddie murmured. "Prove it," she said.

William did. Many times over.

EONS LATER, WILLIAM LAY BESIDE HIS WIFE, HIS HEART A beating drum in his chest, his breathing laboured. Never had he had a woman of noble birth bestow such a loving gift on him, as Madeline had. The memory of her hot mouth determined in its course made his cock twitch.

He looked down at her, nestled in his arm, her cheeks rosy and her eyes smoky with satisfaction. William kissed her hair and breathed in the fragrant scent of berries.

"Do all women of your time, ma chère, engage in such active bed sport?" he asked.

Madeline looked up at him, her arm coming about his waist. "They do, husband. Well, most do," she said.

William chuckled. "'Tis my thinking I'd like this future you speak of, my lady."

Maddie laughed. "Oh, you would, would you?"

"'Twould seem so." He paused. "Does this mean you would favour me with your delicious lips another time?" William ventured.

"Aye husband, I would," Madeline answered. "Wherever and whenever you want. I am your wife; I aim to please my lord."

William laughed and kissed her teasing lips. "Minx," he said, and kissed her again, for good measure.

※

MADDIE SMILED AND NODDED AS SHE WAS INTRODUCED TO Tshilaba, her maid's elderly mother. The cavalcade of Rhodes family carriages that arrived early yesterday morn brought merriment to the people of Aimecourt. Maddie had watched the caravans make camp beyond the castle walls. Their horses were left to roam, the children ran about in the meadows. The Welsh men made good use of their time, already repairing damaged vehicles and buying supplies from Aimecourt's stores.

Nerves rolled about in Maddie's stomach over meeting the wise woman. Tshilaba sat before her, the old woman's eyes otherworldly and sharp. Maddie had the suspicion that the woman was already aware of her secret.

"Would you like any refreshment, Tshilaba?" Maddie asked, smiling.

The old woman's eyes flicked to William, who sat beside Maddie, then settled once more on her. Fear crept across Maddie's skin like a spider.

"No, my child. Not at this time," she answered, her eyes sharp and calculating. "May have your palm, m'lady?" she said.

Maddie looked at William, his face a mask of calm and little suspicious. She steeled her resolve and placed her hand within the old woman's clasp. The lady's hands, cool to the touch, ran over her skin. Her fingers, with protruding knuckles, followed the lines of Maddie's palm, the blue veins in her skin. Her hand tingled under the touch and then heated before it settled back to normal.

"You are a long way from home, my child," Tshilaba stated, her eyes closing.

William leaned forward, a frown upon his brow. Maddie didn't respond. Instead, she sat silently and waited for whatever else the wise woman would say.

The lady hummed, her lips puckered as if ready for a kiss. Maddie looked over at Mistress Rhode, and received a comforting smile. They waited in silence, the only sounds from the castle grounds beyond—a hammer here, a yell there—breaking the quiet in the room.

"A ring. Show it to me."

Maddie started before she pulled out her most treasured and feared gift. She pulled the necklace over her head and laid it in the woman's outstretched hand. The wise woman humphed and then sat back in her chair and closed her eyes.

"Hmmm, this ring holds power. A great power, much stronger than my own. Do not wear it, my child, if that is your question this day. Do so and your soul will cease to exist here," Tshilaba said, looking at the ring in detail.

William clasped Maddie's hand. "What did you see?" he asked.

Tshilaba smiled knowingly. "Many things. A future. Lands and places nothing like we know. I understand your doubt over what you have been told, m'lord. Little as those doubts are. But 'twould be wise for you not to. Lady Madeline speaks the truth. The ring has the power to send her home."

Madeline met the old woman's eyes, her own full of the fears that such a thing could occur.

"It is up to you, my child, what you do with it," Tshilaba said.

Maddie's head spun with the declaration. She could go home and anytime she wished. She reached out and took the ring from Tshilaba. A shiver stole through her as the pewter band settled against her chest. Her hand tightened around William's. She should get rid of it.

The wise woman, her eyes shut, her hands waving blindly before her made a sound of displeasure. "There are people," she said, "who I feel harbour a great threat to you and yours, m'lord."

"What threat?" William asked, the furrows on his brow deep.

Maddie looked at Mistress Rhode then back to Tshilaba. The wise woman's sight was distant, her eyes under her lids darting about as if privy to visions unseen by those around her.

"They are faces, m'lord. Blurry in my mind's sight. I do not know whom it is that harbours to destroy you. But I do know they will try," Tshilaba declared.

Maddie's blood froze in her veins. The wise woman

stilled, her eyes snapping open. Ancient orbs stared at William.

"Tell me, m'lord, would you be prepared to wait for your time with Lady Madeline?"

Maddie swallowed. What did that mean? She looked at William, who sat like set in stone. Maddie shifted in her chair, uncomfortable by the turn of events.

"I'm married to Lady Madeline. There is no need to wait for her," he laughed, the sound strained.

Maddie kept her eyes on the wise woman, who nodded slowly. "Answer the question, m'lord. It is all I need to know," she said, her brows raised.

William cursed and stood. His face marked in strain, he turned and walked to the door. Maddie turned in her chair and met his gaze, his features softening in affection when he looked at her. "I would wait all eternity for her," he said, and left.

Maddie's eyes prickled with tears. She looked back to Tshilaba and tried to smile. Mistress Rhode stood and poured wine for them all.

"I do not mean to frighten you, m'lady. But there are other forces at play here. Your future may not be within your control."

"What do you mean?" Maddie asked. Every word from the woman seemed cryptic. The lady looked at her with sad eyes. An awful premonition that something bad was going to happen settled in Maddie's belly.

"You were born many years into the future. 1102 is not your time, m'lady. Your future here is not for you to decide," Tshilaba said.

More cryptic words. Maddie strove for calm. Did the woman not know? Or did she not want to say?

"I will not leave, Lord William. Nor will I allow anyone to make me go. Some other dimension placed me here, and it can now live with its choice. I will not be sent home to a future now foreign to me," Maddie said.

Tshilaba stole a speaking glance to her daughter. "This was a mistake, m'lady, an error in the makeup of this world." The wise woman paused and took a sip of wine. "The magic that sent you here will correct its fault. 'Tis as certain as the sun warming the soil and bringing forth life."

Maddie placed her wine down with shaking hands. "You are wrong, wise woman," Maddie said, refusing to believe such words. "He's my soul mate, why put me here in the first place to find him to only throw me back when I do?" she asked, her voice trembling.

"I do not know, my child," Tshilaba said, her eyes consoling. "Perhaps I am wrong."

Maddie swallowed the lump in her throat. No, the wise woman wasn't wrong. She shouldn't be here. She had known it from the very first when she landed in the carriage. Their love was doomed. And now they both knew it.

CHAPTER 16

William watched his wife stride from her friend's cottage. A smile tweaked his lips when Beth, a cook in the castle, ran out and passed Madeline her forgotten mantle. He looked up at the sky, the breeze warm on his face; but change was in the air.

Spring was upon them. Pruning and new plantings would take place. William walked along the battlements and stopped to look fondly over Aimecourt. A home he had never thought to call such. Nor love as much as its mistress.

He looked down at the carriages loaded with trunks and supplies for the journey south. And conceded he did not wish to leave. Did not wish to lose one ounce of time he had with Madeline. The wise woman's words chilled his skin on this warm day.

A bellow from the bailey yard pulled William from his thoughts. "Are we sparring, m'lord? Or do you have other...more urgent matters to attend?" Sir Alex said, his laughing voice carrying across the distance.

William climbed down the stone steps and walked

toward his first knight. He rolled his shoulders and unsheathed his sword, prepared his stance.

"'Tis your lucky day, Sir Alex. I have need to bloody someone's lip. Better yours than any others," he said.

Sir Alex laughed then lunged.

Swords clashed and rang throughout the yard. Sir Alex swiped at his chest and William threw himself back, the wind from the steel ruffling his tunic. He parried back, sliced high at his knights attempt to unbalance him, before falling low to fend off another strike.

"'Tis the best you can do, Sir Alex?" he mocked, coming to a stand.

Sir Alex grinned and lunged. His sword swiped to William's side. William counter hit his knight's blade. Their strengths, well matched, held a moment, neither giving in. William won the battle then waited for his knight's next move. They circled each other, both men gauging how best to strike.

Sir Alex stabbed forward. William hit the blade to the side, circled his blade around, and flicked the sword out of Sir Alex's hand. It landed with a thump some distance away from its owner.

William threw his own sword away. His breath burnt fire in his chest. He barrelled into Sir Alex and took him down. Punches rained. His knight landed a solid blow to his nose. William ignored his blood and punched Sir Alex's jaw, the sound of cracking teeth making him smirk.

They gained their feet. William wiped his nose with the back of his hand. Sir Alex working his jaw, ensuring it still functioned properly. They both started as a woman's voice rang out from the crowd that surrounded them.

William shook his head at his wife's boldness. He inwardly sighed and watched her walk toward them. Her flawless skin was marred with a smudge of dirt. William fought the urge to smile.

"What do you think you two are doing?" Madeline said, hands on hips.

William crossed his arms over his chest. "Training," he answered. "'Tis not your concern, my lady."

Maddie's jaw fell open. "I didn't think training for war would warrant fist fighting. Do you intend to get that close to your enemy?" Maddie asked, a sarcastic tone to her words.

William's lips twitched. "Aye, when the need arises," he said.

Maddie's gaze snapped to Sir Alex when he swayed. She gestured toward William's first knight. "How long were you going to continue punching each other to a pulp? I think our villages have seen enough testosterone induced madness for one afternoon."

"For as long as this testosterone you speak of, ma chère, takes to wear off."

Maddie frowned at her slip, William noted. She flushed. "It seems to be a constant in this time. A hormone that doesn't wear off for centuries," she quipped back, smiling.

"Glad to hear it," William said, his eyes locked on hers. Maddie looked around at the knights that stood watching their lord and lady argue. She smiled down at the squires, their bright eyes gazing up at her.

"Well then, don't let me detain you from your training," she said and turned into the crowd.

"Will you tend my wounds later, my lady?" William yelled when she made the keep's door.

Maddie looked back at him and shook her head. "Perhaps," she shrugged and walked inside.

William laughed as his wife retreated into the castle.

৩৯৫

THE NEXT DAY, MADDIE WATCHED FROM THE KEEP AS William made final preparations for his departure to London. Lady Veronica and Lady Ribald had already settled into their carriage.

Maddie pasted on a smile and tried to hide her unease over William accompanying Lady Veronica all those miles. Tried to hold onto instead how he awoke her this morn. The love and passion in his every touch should reassure her mind. And it did, to a point.

William finished speaking to his page, turned, and strode toward her. His chain mail hung over his broad shoulders, his sword swaying with every stride. Her mouth dried and she sighed. William grinned as if knowing his person pleased her, which of course it did. Maddie walked off the steps and straight into his arms and hugged him. Never wanted to let go.

"Please stay safe, William." She felt his kiss at the crown of her head and she held him tighter.

"I will, ma chère."

She fought the tears that threatened. "And hurry back, won't you?" she said, the words almost a plea.

"I will, love. I shall not be gone long. Sir Alex will ensure you're kept safe. The castle itself is impenetrable as long as you stay within its walls."

Maddie looked up at him, his strong, callused hands cupping her chin. He kissed her. A chaste goodbye. Maddie swallowed her tears and willed herself to be strong. Yet, her lip trembled.

"Keep well, wife."

"Of course, husband."

She watched him mount his horse, the action swift. The conveyances pulled away and set off. She kept watch until the drawbridge rose and cut off her view. She looked to Mistress Rhode and shrugged, not sure what to do. She was the lady of a castle. Ruler and responsible for of all the people who lived here. And now, she was on her own.

THREE WEEKS AFTER WILLIAM'S DEPARTURE, SHE HEARD the first word from him. He had arrived in London quicker than he had anticipated, because Lady Veronica and Lady Ribald had decided to stay at their family home in Cheshire with Veronica's brother, Lord Ribald.

It surprised Maddie. She had not known Lady Veronica was close to her brother. Although she was thankful that the woman would no longer be around William. It was silly and immature of her to continue to worry. But old habits died hard. Once burned, twice shy and all that.

She looked out her bedroom window and watched the waves crash against the jagged stone below. What was William doing right now? Did he miss her as much as she did him? London, even in 1102, was a thriving metropolis, full of life. Court balls and dinners were held most nights.

Maddie pushed away her upset. She missed him, would miss him dreadfully until his return. But she was the Lady Madeline, she would hold the fort and keep everyone safe. She had a castle to run and she would not wallow away, helpless and pathetic, scared of the unknown. She would keep herself busy until his return and stop counting the minutes since he had left.

By the time the second month of William's absence had come and gone, Maddie was no longer just sick with worry but volatile. Not one word from him, other than his original missive that notified them of his arrival in London unharmed and that he would be home as soon as may be. What was this business he had? What was he doing that was taking so long?

Maddie snatched up her blunt sword made by the castle's blacksmith and walked out into the bailey. She twisted her wrist and worked the weapon, mentally prepared herself for her coming practice with Sir Alex.

"Ah, so the Lady Madeline has come back for her second bout. I must say it pleases my soul that I can beat such a fearsome warrior such as yourself, m'lady," Sir Alex said, leaning away from the keeps wall.

Maddie laughed and watched him swing his sword. "You will not be laughing my good sir, when I whoop your butt."

Sir Alex shook his head. "Your speech is most strange at times, m'lady. Pray tell, what does 'whoop' mean?" he asked, with a quizzical brow.

"It means, Sir Alex that I'm going to beat you soundly." Maddie shifted her feet for better balance. "Now, if you have finished trying to delay our match, lift up your sword and prove to all who are watching that you are indeed a man."

"I am all man, m'lady. Do not doubt that," he said, one eyebrow raised.

Maddie smiled. "We shall see," she said, and lunged.

Sir Alex fought with her for a time and continually stopped to show her where she had gone wrong. Her arm ached from the strain of holding a sword. Maddie wondered how knights kept up such warfare for days on end.

The metal dragged her arm down, pinched at muscles she hadn't known she owned. With every strike, Sir Alex counteracted and pushed her back. Maddie gasped when the castle's cold stone met her back then frowned when Sir Alex pinned her there with his weapon.

"Do you yield, m'lady?"

"I yield," she said and laughed then stilled at Sir Alex's stricken look.

"What's wrong, Sir Alex?" She followed his stare and noticed the large red welt just below her collarbone. It would be black and blue by morning.

"When did you do that?" she said more to herself than to Sir Alex.

"Lady Madeline, my sincerest apologies. I did not mean you any harm."

Maddie started to giggle. "Good sir, do not worry. I assure you I'm quite fine. It is only a bruise. Did I not ask you to teach me the ways of the sword?"

She stepped away from the wall. "Well, I had better get this looked at." She paused and looked at her friend whose features still showed distress. "It really is quite all right. Do not look so worried, Sir Alex, I will survive," she said, patting his arm.

"It is not your neck on the line, Lady Madeline, when your husband finds out I have hit you. It will be I who bruises then," he stated.

"Lord William is not here, Sir Alex. I'm sure by the time he does arrive home the bruising will be gone," she said, trying not to sound bitter over his absence.

"Lord William will be back, m'lady. How could he not with a wife such as you to return to."

Maddie smiled at the knight's compliment. But it did not change the fact they had said farewell to William nearly three months ago. "Yes, I daresay you are right;

maybe even today we will be graced with his presence."
She walked away; she had no stomach for further reassurance or pitying stares. "I will see you at supper. Thank you again for the sword practice," she said, smiling.

"You are welcome, m'lady."

Maddie walked into the keep and headed for her chamber. Called to a maid to fetch Mistress Rhode to attend her. Each of the stone steps to her floor seemed steeper this day. The all familiar longing settled in her chest. She missed William, longed for him more with every day that passed. She just wanted him home and back with her. Was it too much to ask? Maddie hadn't thought so.

Mistress Rhode diverted her thoughts over the next hour. Her maid's flustered countenance over her wound was enjoyable to watch. That was until her maid started to put leeches over the bruising. Maddie cursed aloud and wondered why she had thought learning to sword fight had been a good idea. It was not.

CASTLE DEE, CHESHIRE

"She is at Aimecourt and alone, you say, Veronica?" Lord Ribald asked, looking down at his seated sister.

"Yes. The Baron of Kingston is away in London. From a letter received last week from a friend, it seems the king has kept him busy at court. He looks to return, but cannot for some weeks yet, by the king's decree."

Lord Ribald contemplated his sister's words, rubbing his hand across his jaw. What should they do? Strike now while she was unprotected by her husband? Or wait for a more opportune moment? Men were prepared now, waiting for his summons. He could be at Aimecourt within a day or two and have the Lady Madeline dispensed without problem.

Yet Aimecourt was still a most trusted ally of the king, more so than any other Norman holding in northern England. It could prove troublesome; if the assassin was traced to his door, he would be killed and his family disgraced. He sat and drummed his fingers on the table. No, they would have to go about this some other way.

"You said in your letters that rumours had started about Lady Madeline. What is the basis behind these tales? Is it known that the woman believes herself from the future, and is possibly a witch? Or do her people believe she is addled in the mind in some way?"

"I believe she still assumes herself from the future. The servants are talking; their unease is starting to show. Talk is rife throughout the castle that the Lady Madeline is not all what she seems. Especially as the woman is a complete opposite from what she once was. I shared my concern with certain members of the household when I could," Veronica smirked. "It is also understood there is a ring, which is attached somehow to her coming back in time. I have not found this piece of jewellery on my searches. Although 'tis thought Lord William bestowed a similar gift to her prior to his departure."

"Do you know which century Lady Madeline believes herself from?" he asked, his mind a whir of thoughts.

"No, I do not, brother. But my maid has informed me there was a meeting between the Lady Madeline and her maid's mother, a wise woman from Wales. From what my source could gather, Madeline believes this woman could help her return home. Apparently the ring can be used as a means for this."

Lord Ribald twisted his goblet in his hands. He nodded and smiled as the path to travel opened out like a well cobbled road in his mind. "'Twould be best, I believe, if we continue our plan to mark her as a witch or sorceress of some kind. People are afraid of other worldly beings, and her villagers no exception, no matter how well she treats them." He took a sip of wine. "She will be killed or sent away. You will marry Lord William and Aimecourt will finally be ours." He raised his cup in toast then took another sip.

"Brother, I do not believe Lord William will have me. Furthermore, I no longer want him," Veronica said. Lord Ribald looked up and focused on her. Had not missed the venom in his sister's tone.

"Why not? What have you done to displease him?"

Veronica swallowed and he noted the sweat beading on her brow. "Nothing that I was not told to do," she said. "I believe he suspects me of the arrow attack on Madeline. He thinks I harbour trouble for her ladyship. I may have been his mistress, but I still have my pride." Veronica paused. "Mother's revenge is not the only reason I want to see her dead. Lord William deserves to be hurt, too."

"Why kill her at all, if we cannot get you back where you were, married to a man and mistress to two of the greatest holdings in England." His fist slammed against the table. He welcomed the fear that entered his sister's eyes.

"Because I want her dead, that is why," Veronica said. "Her death would hurt Lord William very badly. Secondly, I would love nothing better than for Aimecourt to slip under Kingston rule. The high and mighty Vincent name a dream long gone. I believe Mother would be happy with this plan and concur. Both of us would get our revenge this way," she said.

Her brother strode to the window. The last rays of the day's sun were warm on his skin.

"We shall proceed to undermine her in the

surrounding areas of Aimecourt and the castle itself. Bring the claim of witchcraft against her and let her be damned like her father. Either way, we will ensure she does not survive. Mother will agree to this. Rumours are untraceable. And you will get your revenge, little sister."

Veronica smiled and toasted him. "Thank you, brother. That is very kind. I look forward to it with relish."

Lord Ribald huffed and stared out at his land. His thoughts were on the Lady Madeline and the fun that was about to begin.

CHAPTER 17

The horns sounded loud and clear. Maddie started in her chair, her earlier thoughts lost in the flickering flames in the hearth. She looked to Mistress Rhode, who sat bent over her embroidery.

"'Twould be Lord William, m'lady."

Maddie ran to the window and looked out to the hills she could see over the outer castle walls. Noted some dust rising on a distant hill. "Do you think so? I can't make out the party from here," she said.

"It is he, m'lady. The horn sounded the lord's sign," Mistress Rhode said, continuing to sew.

"He has his own tune?"

"Aye," her maid said, laughter in her eyes.

Maddie turned back to the view, her body a chorus of nerves and excitement. Three months, one week, and two days had seemed such a long time. William was home. Finally.

She clasped Mistress Rhodes' hand and pulled her from the room. Almost ran through the Great Hall and out into the bailey. A gruelling half hour later, a cavalcade of horses passed over the drawbridge, a page riding out front, holding the family flag.

Maddie spotted William and her smile felt huge on her face. But she could not stop the absurd gesture if she tried. He was home, and he was safe.

Maddie stood and waited for him to dismount, watched him pass the reins of his horse to a serf who stood in wait. His eyes searched the yard and came to rest on her. Her body quivered in response to his wolfish smile.

She drank up his every feature. His clothes, although fine, were dusty from the many miles of travel, his face weary but happy. His horse moved away at a slow pace, sweat coating its hair beneath the saddle, spittle frothed at its mouth. They had ridden hard, eager for home, it would seem.

William walked toward her, stood looking down at her before he picked her up and kissed her soundly. Maddie's arms twined around his neck, her hands twisting in the lengthened locks at his nape.

"I missed you, William." She hugged him close. "What took you so long?" she mumbled into his shoulder.

William laughed and set her down. "The king. I have missed you too, ma chère."

Maddie drew him down for another kiss. His mouth, warm and eager for more, took control of the embrace. His arms around her waist tightened. Maddie mewled in protest when he pulled away. She stepped back and made a point of taking in his dusty appearance.

"Would you like a bath, my lord?"

"'Twould be welcome indeed," he said, winking.

A member of the troop that had accompanied William came up and bowed. Maddie stood beside him and clasped William's hand, not willing to forgo all contact while he discussed details concerning security.

His business at an end, William turned and ushered her inside. Maddie sent orders for a bath to be prepared immediately for his lordship. Maids scattered to do her bidding. Making their chamber, Maddie paused to open the door and felt William's lips graze the back of her neck. Anticipation shivered through her as his breath caressed her skin. She leaned into the embrace and revelled in his touch.

"'Tis best if we took this inside, ma chère," he whispered against her ear. Maddie chuckled and opened the door and stepped aside to allow him enter. He paused in the center of the room and started to remove his armour. She walked over to him, and bent to undo the buckles on his leg armour. She placed them on the trunk then came to help with his chain mail.

He seemed so much larger after his long absence. The stubble on his jaw was a dark growth, his hair, in need of washing, was longer and unkempt. Maddie took a calming breath and could almost smell the male power that resonated from him.

She went and lay the chainmail down just as the bath and water arrived. William sat down before the hearth and sighed.

Maddie followed the servants to the door and closed it behind them.

"You're tired, William." She came and sat before him and pulled off his boots. "You have dark shadows beneath your eyes."

William leaned forward and kissed her. "I'm tired. But never too tired for you, ma chère."

She threw him a smile then pulled the tunic over his head. "Did you finish your business in London?"

He pulled a folded piece of fabric from a pouch on his belt and handed it to her. Maddie frowned at the dark blue velvet. "What is it?" she asked looking up.

William started to take down her hair. "Open it and find out."

Maddie did as he asked and gasped when a golden bangle sparkled bright in the cloth. Its heavy weight spoke of its expense. Not to mention the various coloured stones set in the band.

"For me," she asked, smiling.

"Nay, 'tis for the farmer's wife," William said, laughing.

Maddie slipped the bracelet around her wrist and gazed down at it lovingly. "It's beautiful, William. Thank you."

"Took many weeks to make. Delayed my return, not to mention the king and the many reports he required of Kingston, Aimecourt and," he paused. "Our marriage," William said, meeting her eye.

"Do I still have to beget you an heir before the year is up?" Maddie asked, twisting the bangle in the firelight, liking the way the stones glittered up at her.

"Aye."

At his single worded response, Maddie looked away from her gift. "What's the matter?"

William stood and stretched, then undressed and stepped into the bath. Maddie walked over to where she kept her soap and walked toward him.

"Do ye still wear the ring?" he asked.

Maddie frowned and pulled it forth from her gown. "I do. William," she said, rubbing the soap through his hair. "I think I should throw it away. It makes me uneasy."

William nodded. "'Twould seem we have the same affliction then. When we return to Kingston we will dispense with it there. It is a family ring. I should keep it at least for our future generations."

Maddie collected a jug and rinsed his hair. "Okay." She

paused. "Did Lady Veronica cause trouble when you left her?"

William looked at her knowingly and smiled. "Nay. Not a cursed word from her."

Maddie laughed and started to lather his dark, sun-bronzed arms. "Did the king mention the letter I sent him?" Maddie shook her head. "I feel like such an idiot for writing him. What he must have thought."

William grinned and flicked her nose with his finger. "Addled wits, I believe his words were." William frowned. "'Twas the main reason for my journey, Madeline. King Henry had received word that you were not of sound mind. I'm afraid our audience with Tshilaba has reached his ears and added wood to the fire."

Maddie dropped the soap then scrounged around in the water for it. "What is his thinking now?" she asked, images of being burnt alive at the stake for witchcraft or Satan worship whizzing through her mind.

William grinned and passed her the soap when her hand grasped another round object. "I explained to his majesty Tshilaba's history with Aimecourt. How her daughter has been your maid since birth. That your change of character is solely due to me and your content-ment at being married to a man of strong character and abilities you cannot deny."

Maddie snorted and scrubbed down his legs, made a point of washing between them most decidedly. "Abilities, my lord? Why," she said, with a mock sigh. "It has been so long, one could almost forget a husbands 'abilities.'"

Maddie gasped as William stood and stepped from the bath, his strong arms picking her up and tossing her over his shoulder like a bag of grain. Maddie shrieked and slapped his naked bottom. William growled, then tossed her on the bed.

"'Twould be an appropriate time for reacquainting ourselves, I believe, my lady," he said, pulling her slippers from her feet.

Maddie bit her lip and allowed William to undress her. "Aye husband. I'm in need of thorough tutoring," she said, laying back and revelling in his homecoming.

William kissed her and proved an excellent teacher.

THE FOLLOWING MORN, MADDIE SAT IN THE GREAT HALL sewing in front of the massive fire and watched the third servant that day to cross their chest in her presence. She looked to Mistress Rhode, busy with her own needle and wondered what was going on.

"Someone just did it again," she said.

"Mistress Rhode looked up and frowned. Maddie did not miss the concern that flickered in her eye. "Ignore it, m'lady. Silly superstitions, that is all."

"Why are they crossing themselves only around me? What does it mean when someone does that?" Maddie asked, looking toward the door as another serf walked past.

Her maid winced. "M'lady, do not fret, all is well."

"Mistress Rhode, you will answer my question, or I'll...I'll make you fix my atrocious needlework."

Her maid laughed. "Well then, pass it over," she gestured.

"Mistress Rhode," Maddie begged. "Please." She needed to know what was happening around here. Everyone seemed to be acting strangely. Even the priest recommended more prayer time. Surely five times a day was ample enough already. Her maid sighed, and sat back in her chair.

"It means, my child that they believe you may bring them bad luck, harm them in some way unless they seek the protection of God."

Maddie felt her jaw drop. A prickle of fear trickled down her spine. "They think me a witch?" she said, at length.

"I do not know, m'lady. The villagers are becoming more and more superstitious and I do not understand where the concern is coming from. I have tried to stem their fears, but nothing I say seems to sway them."

Maddie clasped her rosary. First the king, and now her people were suspicious of her. "What will happen if they continue this way? Will I be forced to prove my innocence?" she asked.

A pained expression crossed her maid's face. Maddie swallowed her rising panic and looked around the hall. Her glare dared the castle staff that went about their chores to cross themselves.

How dare they think such things of her? She wasn't a witch, she was just some poor twenty-first century chit who happened to accidentally land in twelfth century.

"Do not worry, my child. Lord William will see it settled."

"Do you think someone knows about me and what I told you when I first arrived?" she whispered.

"I do not think so, m'lady. I believe someone," she said, her brow puckered, "is determined to ruin you any way they can."

Maddie gaped. "You suspect Lady Veronica, don't you? But how could she? She is settled with her brother, many miles away in Cheshire," Maddie said.

"'Twould be wise, my dear, not to underestimate Lady Veronica and her family. I do believe they are known far and wide as powerful allies of the king, however, not the most savory ones."

Maddie frowned over her maid's words. Was Veronica in some way placing the seed of doubt in her people's minds? But that was impossible, unless someone here was working for her.

She jumped as the great hall door swung open and knights entered seeking their evening meal. Maddie glanced at them as she packed away her sewing. At least none of them followed the latest craze and crossed themselves. She absently smiled at Sir Alex as she made her way upstairs.

Perhaps Mistress Rhode was correct. Perhaps she should stop worrying and allow it to all blow over. Surely it would if she ignored it. She stopped and stared, incredulous, at a laundress passing on the stairs crossing herself. Hurried past Madeline like the devil himself was chasing her brown skirts.

It took all Maddie's will not to dismiss the woman on the spot.

This was absurd and something had to be done about it.

⚜

"Do you think it possible, William?" Maddie asked, looking over the knights breaking their fast in the hall.

"What would she have to gain from it, Madeline? She has no cause to strike against you," he said, chewing a leg of some cooked animal.

Maddie furrowed her brow and wondered what it was the woman wanted to achieve. For William was right. Lady Veronica couldn't gain anything, per se. But she could eliminate her from the face of the earth out of spite and jealousy. A woman scorned and all that. Maddie tapped her finger against the dais, only halting when William placed his hand over hers.

"She wouldn't dare touch you," he declared, his eyes holding a feral edge only his enemies would see.

"William, people are crossing themselves when I walk past. They think I'm a witch or something." She shook her head, baffled. He lifted her hand and kissed her fingers, a consoling smile quirked his lips. It didn't make her feel any better.

"William, stop. I'm scared. What if they decide to burn me at the stake?"

"They would have to get through me first, ma chère. And I can guarantee you that will never happen. We don't burn witches in 1102," he said, grinning.

"William, stop being an arse, it's not funny," she said, staring blandly at him when he choked on his mead. And it wasn't funny. Not only was she out of her time, but she was in one that was hard, guarded, and unforgivable to the strange. She couldn't stop the fear that in some way her people now feared her. She looked away, not really knowing what to do.

"'Twill be alright, ma chère. I have spoken to certain members of the staff to quell such notions in the household. No one knows what happened to you on the day of our wedding, and I intend to keep it that way. You'll see, all this worry will be for naught."

Maddie tried to smile as he chastely kissed her lips. She hoped that was true. However, something inside her was screaming for care. Something was not quite right here at Aimecourt. Someone was out for her blood. She looked around the hall as William continued his banter with his knights and wondered who it was among the servants who would dare slander her name.

Most, she noted, stood to the side, in wait for a summons or task. None looked like troublemakers. Her gaze moved over the few that stood patiently, further to the end of the room. Maddie's inspection stopped on a young woman, perhaps in her early teens. Her eyes gave her away. They flicked about, reminded her of a nosy squirrel on the prowl for a chestnut.

Maddie sat up and looked at her, waited for the girl's gaze to meet her own, silently hoping her actions were not the start of some sort of paranoia.

The young woman's gaze eventually came to settle on the dais. She glanced along the seats. Maddie raised her brows as the girl looked at her and she frowned when the woman physically blanched and scuttled away like vermin.

She was the one.

Maddie sat and looked at the empty doorway the servant had gone through. She had never seen her before, not even when the Lady Veronica had been in residence. William pulled her into the conversation and Maddie attempted to listen. Tomorrow she would find out who the girl was and then have it out with the little traitor. And she would see who ended up on the stake. Well, perhaps she wasn't that blood thirsty. But the woman would think twice before she thought to earn coin by doing bad deeds. She would make sure of it.

THE NEXT MORNING, MADELINE RODE OUT WITH WILLIAM, her unease almost palatable between them.

"I tell you, William, the servant I cannot find is the spy, and I bet my bottom dollar she's travelled back to Lady Veronica after the look I gave her last night."

William settled his mount under him, looked over at his

wife, and fought the urge to chuckle at her language. "Madeline—"

"What? Don't be silly. Stop your worrying. You'll protect me." she said, interrupting him. She pulled Eurus up and glared. "I've heard it all, William, and I'm telling you, Veronica and her family are up to something. I just know it," she declared, her voice fervent.

William frowned, met her gaze when he realized she was angry, and annoyed at him. He supposed it was not fair to dismiss her concerns continually. She could be, after all, correct.

"It's all right for you. You're not the one on their radar," she mumbled, and urged her mount forward.

William ran a hand through his hair and took a fortifying breath. "I have men on the girl's trail, Madeline. If she is in fact headed back to Castle Dee, we will know it soon enough. She'll not get away." He paused at her continued glare. "Lady Veronica and her brother are still in Cheshire. Do not worry, ma chère. I would never let anything happen to you."

Madeline looked away from him, her eyes lost on the land before them. Guilt swamped him when she worked her bottom lip, a habit she had when nervous or upset. "I have told you they cannot harm you. They will never have the opportunity." He paused. "I received word yesterday that Kingston's fortification is near complete. It will make the castle as impenetrable as Aimecourt. You will be safe in both homes, my love. No one will touch a hair on your body. I won't allow it."

His wife continued to look away.

"More and more people are crossing themselves, William. I even caught Beth about to do it the other day and she's my friend. Or was," she mumbled.

William started at Madeline's words. The people held

strong to their beliefs, proved hard to sway at times. But to believe Madeline was cursed or evil in some way was a form of insanity in itself. As for Lady Veronica and her family, he would deal with them. Punish them before the king for their misdeeds.

"I have threatened dismissal and expulsion to any who use the sign. It will pass, Madeline, you will see. You must continue with your normal duties. Eventually, some other problem will catch their attention and they will move on. We know there is no truth to the tale. You must stop your worry, for it will begin to make you sick," he said, frowning at her pallor.

"What if they burn me alive?" She asked him, her eyes overly bright.

"Madeline, look at me."

He clasped her reins and drew her mount in next to his when she chose to ignore his request. He turned her face and lifted her chin. Let her see in his eyes he spoke the truth and would not let her down. He controlled his temper at her people. People she had bestowed nothing but kindness on from the very day she set foot in Aimecourt.

"I would never allow that. Nor would the king," he stated. He kissed her, tried to give reassurance and comfort through his embrace. "You must stop, ma chère. Know that I will protect you always."

Madeline nodded but did not smile. "I feel ill all the time, William. I've been trying to win back my peoples' love, but nothing seems to work. The king is already suspicious of me. What if my villagers' unease reaches his ear and he decides to investigate for himself?"

William shook his head at her concern. "'Twill not happen. The king trusts my word. And you being the daughter of a most trusted and well-liked baron, he will not see harm come to you."

"What if it's not enough? My father has been dead for many years now. Loyalties change."

"King Henry's do not," William said.

They continued their ride east and eventually stumbled upon a clearing in the woods. The air was cooler here under the shadows of the trees, smelling of forest undergrowth, earthy and damp with a tang of sea air. Maddie halted Eurus and climbed down, watched as William did the same. They walked their mounts for a time, both silent in thought.

"I don't want to lose you, William. I don't want to leave my life here," Maddie said, looking up at him.

William let go of his horse and turned to her. "I know, my love. I refuse to lose you either." He pulled her into his arms and rubbed her back in a show of comfort. "This will go away, I promise. Come...sit and tell me of your home, the one before mine."

Maddie smiled, delighted at his interest. "Well, it's very different," she said. "People tend to only ride horses for pleasure, not for a means of travel. We have a vehicle much like a wagon, but it has an engine which powers it instead of the horse."

"An engine?" William queried.

Madeline laughed. "Yes, an engine. It's a...well, I suppose you could say it's like a living thing, but man-made. It's alive in a sense. It runs and pulls the wagon—or car, as we call them—along at high speeds," she said.

"How fast?"

Maddie looked over the glade in thought. "Well, extremely fast. Horses for instance can walk about four miles per hour. A car can travel up to speeds of one hundred miles per hour or more if they're racing them."

William raised his brow. "'Tis my belief you are lying, Lady Madeline."

Madeline chuckled. "I assure you, I'm not. People, women and men, drive these vehicles every day."

"Have you?" he asked.

"Of course. I have a car, poor worn out thing that it is. But yes, I can drive."

"And what did you do before coming to my time? What was your life like, ma chère?"

"Boring," she said, sighing. "Well, that's probably not quite true. I owned a shop. An antique store where I sold treasures of old. I also belonged to a group called the Thames Mudlarks. We have permission to search the Thames banks for ancient artefacts. That was how I came upon your ring." She kissed him quickly. "And I live with my best friend above my shop in Greenwich." She shrugged. "That's about it."

"You live by yourself in this time?" William couldn't hide the astonishment from his tone.

"Yes, it's not uncommon for a woman to live like this. Women have more freedom than they do now. We do not need the sanctity of marriage to have relations with a man nor to have children. We can buy property and live on our own. Vote for different political parties. We have the same right as any man. It's a good life," she stated.

"Women do not need the vows of marriage to be with a man." William stilled at the abhorrent thought. "Were you one of these women?"

Maddie heard the steel that entered his voice. She cast a wary look and wondered if it was safer to lie than to tell the truth. "I trust you, William as I hope you trust me," she said. "I was such a woman. I will not lie to you."

William's jaw clenched as he sat speechless on the leaf

litter beside her. Maddie kept silent and allowed him to calm his temper. "How?" he frowned. "When we had…"

"Sex," Maddie finished for him, clasping his hand.

"Yes, sex. You were still…a maid."

"All I can gather is that when I came back into this time, my soul entered Lady Madeline's of old. And of course Lady Madeline was a maid, but me inside was not. Does that make sense?" she asked.

William frowned, his gaze on the horses that stood under an oak, their heads bent down in rest. "It does." He paused, before adding, "Were you bedding these men, Madeline?"

Maddie swallowed her fear of telling him the truth. "I had, but not many," she added, when his forehead puckered, his face turning to stone. "I was more career-oriented. I wanted to make my business a success, small as it was. It didn't leave a lot of time for men."

"I do not like the idea of you with anyone besides me."

Maddie clasped his cheek and turned him toward her. "All that came before you were nothing, a passing fancy, no more," she said. "I do not believe my fancy for you will pass, my lord. Ever," she whispered against his ear.

"Who was it?"

"What?" Maddie sat back, confused.

"Who was the man who made you enforce this rule of self-hibernation from life?"

She sighed. "An arse who thought he could get away with cheating on me. Of course, I found out. Women always do in the end." She shrugged, surprisingly not fazed by it anymore. "It's history now. I don't care."

"I'm sorry, ma chère."

He sounded so remorseful. Maddie frowned. "It wasn't your fault, why are you apologizing?"

"'Twould seem I did the same."

She sighed and kissed him quickly, wanted to wipe the haunted edge from his eyes. "The circumstances were a little different, William. You were already in a relationship with Lady Veronica. Some people in my society would say I was the scarlet woman who stepped between two lovers." He didn't look convinced.

"'Twas wrong of me. I should never have done it. I'm truly sorry, ma chère."

William stood and stared into the grove beyond, lost in thought. Maddie sat and watched him, her heart filling with love. He was sorry. And she loved him all the more for it.

"You have no need to apologize any longer, William. I trust you with my whole heart."

"Come here," he said.

Maddie's blood quickened at his lowered tone. She stood and was soon clasped tight in his embrace. His lips came down and brushed across hers. She sighed and ran her arms down his back. Delighted in the sensual onslaught his wicked kiss promised. Her knees buckled when he pulled her against his sex.

"William...?"

"A moment longer, ma chère," he replied, kissing her neck, her shoulder, her...

Maddie laughed and allowed him a lot longer.

CHAPTER 18

Over the weeks that followed her talk with William, Maddie made a determined effort to cease the rumours about herself and mend her ways with her people.

Daily, Maddie spoke with the villagers, welcomed their ideas and thoughts on the castle's running's. She threw herself into healing the old and sick. Spent nights tending the infirm and ensuring they were well cared for during their last hours on earth or nursed them back to health.

With summer half gone and autumn looming before them, Maddie checked the stores and was happy to see them full. There had been more than enough seed for the spring planting. The summer so far had been good to the crops, and there would be a plentiful harvest before the first snows fell. She had not seen the young lady whom she thought a spy. Nor had she heard a word of Lady Veronica, which pleased her to no end.

Maddie had obeyed the priest's advice and started to attend mass religiously. No one could think a woman who dallied in witchcraft could be so devout. And they did not.

In time, her people stopped crossing themselves. With every day that passed in this time, Maddie grew accustomed to her role and her new way of life. She loved it here. Would not let anybody stand in her way of living in this life she had come to adore.

William too had stopped looking at her people with death in his eyes. The flicker of steel once more replaced with contentment Maddie felt to the core of her being. Aimecourt was a peaceful place to live. And she intended to keep it that way.

Mistress Rhode, who was asleep in an adjacent chair, started at the sound of her own snoring. "Oh, m'lady, I am most sorry. 'Twould seem I fell asleep."

Maddie laughed and stretched her legs out toward the fire. "Apology accepted. I enjoy your snores," she said.

Mistress Rhode bloomed bright red then stood and placed a log of wood on the fire. She walked to the window and looked out over the bailey. "Autumn is coming on. It would be wise to leave for Kingston soon," her maid said, walking back to her chair.

Maddie looked into the flicking flames and thought about the home that they were soon to reside in. Kingston, a castle she had loathed due to the man that occupied it. It seemed so long ago now, not to mention foreign to think of William with anything other than love.

She smiled thinking of him. Could not wait to see his home with fresh eyes and make a life with him there as well.

"I would think Lord William will travel regularly between the two holdings, m'lady. Will you travel with him, do you believe?" her maid asked, picking up her embroidery.

"I should think so. They are reasonably close," Maddie replied, yawning. She thought of their future and wondered not for the first time if they would have two sons, one to inherit an estate each. She hoped it would be so and that they'd be blessed with children soon.

She could picture her children now, blonde hair and rosy cheeks, handsome like their father and proud. And maybe a little outspokenness bred into them as well, her own gift to them. She looked down at her atrocious needlework and cringed.

"'Tis shocking that you do not know how to sew, m'lady. 'Twill be my life's ambition to teach you, that I promise," Mistress Rhode said, taking her embroidery away from her.

"You may teach my daughters," Maddie said, laughing. "I'm past help, I think."

Mistress Rhode tittered. They both turned as a knock at the door sounded before it opened.

"M'lady, Sir Alex is ready to leave. Do you wish to farewell him?" a serving maid asked, curtsying.

Maddie thanked the girl and stood. She swiftly walked toward the great hall before exiting the doors and entering the bailey beyond. She willed herself not to cry over her friend's departure. She would miss him, but he had his own wife and future to grasp and keep him happy.

Maddie walked out and shaded her eyes from the midmorning sun. William stood beside Sir Alex, their conversation quiet, their expressions serious. Maddie looked around and noted the saddled guards that Sir Alex would take with him. At least she could be secure in his safety. It eased her mind that over the following weeks, Sir Alex would be well looked after.

She walked toward them and smiled when they noticed her approach. She stood before Sir Alex and clasped his hands.

"So, the time has come, Sir Alex, when you finally get

to leave us. I cannot say I am happy, for we shall miss you. But I understand why you must go. Please travel safely and notify us of your arrival at your home in Kent."

"Thank you, m'lady. I shall indeed let you know when we arrive," Sir Alex replied, smiling.

She held his gaze and bit her lip to stop it from quivering. Unable to thank him enough for his kindness when she first arrived, Maddie leant up and hugged him. Hugged her friend whom she trusted like a brother.

She ignored the startled gasps that sounded about her. "Thank you for being my friend, sir," she said, her voice thick with emotion. "It meant a great deal to me, as you know. I hope that one day I may be able to pay you back in some way. Perhaps you and your wife may visit one year," Maddie said, stepping back.

Sir Alex cast a quick glance at William, before he nodded and strode toward his horse. She watched him mount and settle in the saddle. His horse pranced under him, eager to be gone.

"We shall, m'lady. Thank you."

Maddie walked over to William and hugged his waist. She swallowed the lump that formed in her throat. "We wish you well, Sir Alex, on your future nuptials. May your union be blessed with many children and love," she said, meaning every word.

"Thank you, m'lady. It is my wish also." Sir Alex's turned to William. "My Lord William, thank you for your tutelage over the years. You need only write me, and I'll return to offer my assistance and protection should the need arise."

William nodded but did not speak. She waved her friend and his guards off and watched them leave the safety of the castle walls. She wished him well and hoped his wife would make him as content as she was in her marriage.

Williams hand clasped her arm, his grip almost severe. "What are you doing?" she asked, frowning up at him when he tried to pull her toward the keep. Maddie wrenched away and stumbled. "What has gotten into you?" she asked, puzzled.

"Me!" he said, his eyes astonished. "I think, madam, that it is I, who should be asking all the questions. What do you think you're doing, hugging my knight like a forlorn lover?"

Maddie tried to hide the smile that appeared on her lips, but forlorn was really too stupid a word. "Are you angry over the hug, my lord? I didn't mean anything by it, William. I was only saying goodbye," she said, truthfully.

"'Twould be unwise to laugh at me, Madeline. You know you cannot hug my knights. People will think you are fast and loose. That I allow my wife to cuckold me under my own roof."

Maddie lost her good humour by his words. "No, you weren't the one who was cuckolded under their own roof. That would be me, my lord," she said, her words as sharp as a whip. "Moreover, I do not go around hugging your knights. I said goodbye to Sir Alex and hugged him. He was my friend. He did everything to try to buffer your manners toward me when I first arrived. I will not apologize or regret my actions this day. Not for you or anyone living here in this medieval time."

William stilled, his jaw clenching and unclenching. Maddie stormed past him, only to be pulled to a halt up against his chest. "It is not safe, Madeline." He leant close to her ear. "You are no longer in your time, my lady. Actions such as those cannot continue. I only say this to keep you safe."

Maddie stepped back and crossed her arms, her body shaking in anger. She stood looking at him and allowed what he said to penetrate her mind. She met his eyes and noted the sincerity of his plight. She sighed.

"Fine, I will not do it again. But nor will I be spoken to or treated like a wife without sense. You cannot drag me about and chastise me like a child. I'm your wife and deserve to be spoken to with respect. If you have a problem, don't clutch at me and then bombard me with accusations. Just talk to me, I can guarantee you'll receive a better reception." Maddie walked over to the door and paused before she turned back and met his gaze. "I didn't mean anything by it, William. You know that it's you I love. If your anger was partly from the stance of a jealous husband, you were being absurd."

William gave her a long look. He took a deep breath and closed the space between them before he pulled her into his arms.

"Point taken, ma chère." He sighed and pulled her close and Maddie relaxed in his arms. "I'm a jealous cad. Could not stand to see you held by another," he said. "I wanted to kill him."

"And I'm sorry for bringing up your past with Lady Veronica. I won't continue to hold that against you when I'm angry, William. That wasn't fair. But, I won't apologize for saying goodbye to my friend."

William nodded. "Well then, I guess we're even."

Maddie pulled him back to her mouth, murmuring against his lips. "I guess we are. Truce?"

"Truce," he said, before he deepened the kiss.

259

THEY DEPARTED AIMECOURT AT THE END OF THE following month. From the safety of the carriage, Maddie watched William ride most of the way on his steed. The road trip had been fun, just her and her maid. She had taught Mistress Rhode how to play canasta, which now she was thoroughly engrossed. Now, however, Maddie had opted for snap as she tried to lighten the mood. Her maid, it seemed, had a very competitive streak.

"Oh, m'lady, Lord William will be greatly pleased, I think, on how his fortification has progressed."

Maddie looked out the window and gazed at the stone structure that was Kingston Castle. She nodded in total agreement. She looked out the other side of the carriage and saw the rapt attention and pride William had on his visage. She smiled, knew there would not be many who would not be.

"Halt the carriage."

Maddie grabbed the seat as the carriage rocked to a stop. She looked inquiringly to William.

"Madeline, come, join me. I wish you to ride with me," he said, motioning her forward.

She stepped from the carriage and allowed William to help her mount his horse. He pulled her up before him and walked the horse to the castle beyond. "I wish to show Lady Madeline our home and lands. Ride on," he said to his new first knight. "We shall follow shortly. No more than an hour at most."

"M'lord," Sir Torent said, frowning. "'Tis not safe, m'lord. We have not secured the land this side of Kingston."

William waved his knight's apprehension away. "All is well, Sir Torent. I thank you for your concern, but I shall proceed as planned. Continue home, we will meet there shortly."

They proceeded to canter along the forest's perimeter. Maddie relaxed and sat back within William's arms, enjoyed the smell of fresh pine and the horse as it cantered beneath them. She stroked William's hand that held her in place, strong and secure.

"Where are we going?"

"I've never shown you Kingston from this standpoint before, ma chère. I wished for you to see it. Once we are through the trees beyond, we will come out on the western side of the castle. The views are best from there."

She smiled up at him. "I'd love to see it, my lord."

They continued in silence for some minutes before the shadows of the darkened canopy of forest enclosed around them. Maddie's stomach knotted with an unknown fear. The forest seemed to have eyes, watching and tracking their direction. Maddie froze when William stiffened behind her. His clasp on her was painfully tight. Concerned.

"William?"

"Shush, we're not alone. No matter what happens, stay close to me, Madeline, and do as I say."

"Okay," she said, her heart thumping hard in her chest, the hairs at the base of her neck rising.

"Halt and dismount, my lord, or you both die."

Maddie frowned at the unfamiliar voice. Were the rumours of Scots true? Did they stalk the woods around Norman strongholds to kill the people like sport?

No.

Understanding dawned in a blinding light. This was a planned attack. One she should have known was coming. William halted his steed as fifty armed men emerged from the undergrowth, surrounding them and blocking their way. Crossbows were aimed with deadly precision at their person. The horse whinnied and stomped in protest beneath them. Maddie felt like doing the same.

Shit!

"What do you want, Lord Ribald?" William asked, his voice bored.

Maddie's eyes sought the man who emerged from the trees. He was beautiful, like a golden god, but one out to do harm. The menace and madness that sat behind his scowl made him a man no one would trust. Her body coiled in fear when Lady Veronica, too, stepped forward. Maddie clutched at William's hand sick with fear.

"William, perhaps if we tried to make a run for—"

Lord Ribald laughed the sound mocking. "Do not bother, my lady," he said, halting her quiet words. "Nothing can save you now."

Maddie swallowed. What the hell did that mean?

"You'll never get away with this." William's voice was strong, sure, but tension throbbed through his body. Their situation was not good. Even a warrior of William's ability could not fight off a small army of men on his own.

"Oh, I think we will. You see, no one knows we are here. These men have sworn to secrecy on pain of death. They will not cross me. 'Twill be my word, Lord William against your own. And I'm inclined to think the king would believe me in this instance."

William's foot connected with a knight Maddie had not seen move. The man's hands slid from her dress when he fell to the ground unconscious. Maddie gasped and clutched at William's arm as the horse shied from the blow.

"William?" she said, the quiver in her voice clear for all to hear.

"All is well, ma chère. I will not let them harm you."

"Brave words from a man in a situation that makes him

powerless, wouldn't you say?" Lord Ribald said, laughing with his men.

"You will hang if you touch her. King's decree or not, you will die if Lady Madeline is injured in any way," William stated, his voice menacing.

Lord Ribald's face hardened, his eyes glittered with danger. "Get off the horse...now. I will not ask again."

William cursed behind her then helped her to dismount. No sooner had her feet touched the ground a man from the garrison twisted her hands behind her back and pulled her against him. His putrid breath assailed her senses along with his unwashed scent. She gagged as William roared in fury, his steps toward her captor deadly, his sword swinging free.

The prick of a blade, cold and deadly, met the skin on her neck. She stilled and met William's eyes. He halted. His attention focused on the soldier.

They were in trouble. Maddie tried to stop her shaking lest the blade cut her skin. She blinked the tears away and watched William be disarmed, he, too, powerless to defend himself. Maddie fought the urge to panic. To lose control now would help neither of them.

She watched a sword poke at William's back. William glared at the knight but walked to the other side of the clearing. The distance seemed miles away from her.

"I'll allow you to remain unbound, my lord. But move from where your feet now rest and the Lady Madeline dies," Lord Ribald said, smiling, his eyes vacant of warmth.

"Well, well, well. If it isn't the pathetic Lady Madeline, all vulnerable and scared."

Maddie glared at Lady Veronica who stood before her. "I'm not scared of you, Lady Veronica. If you care to free my arms, I'm more than willing to demonstrate how much I dislike you."

Lady Veronica chuckled. "You're such a fool. It is a shame you will die by another's hand this day. I did what I could, myself, but it wasn't enough." Veronica shrugged. "If only my arrow had pierced your heart and not your arm."

Maddie felt the blood drain from her face. "So you admit to striking me with the arrow?" Maddie looked to William and noted his eyes fixed on Lady Veronica. She shivered at the menace she recognized there.

"I did. 'Twas a shame it did not work. I would have loved to bury you in the ground," Lady Veronica said, walking around her.

"You're sick and so is your brother. You will not get away with this," Maddie said, hoping her words were true.

Lord Ribald smiled and walked toward her. His eyes feasted on her body like a starving man would eye a roast turkey dinner. He was pure evil and dangerous. "But we will, my lady," Lord Ribald said, and freed his sword.

"Get away from her." William roared.

Maddie stilled, expected him to impale her with the sharp metal. He did not. Merely held it before her face, twisting the shiny blade before her vision, tormenting her. He ran a finger along the sharpened edge and Maddie cringed when he started to bleed. She refused to succumb to fear, at least outwardly. Lord Ribald licked his cut and smiled.

"Tsk, tsk, tsk, Lord William. I will not kill the woman you love with the sword." Lord Ribald's attempt at a smile ended up resembling a snarl. She gasped as he pulled his weapon away and kissed her. Her knee came up to meet his jewels. Lord Ribald doubled over and clutched at himself in obvious pain. His knights looked at one another, their unease palatable.

Maddie smirked. "Oh, dear," she said. "I do apologize, Lord Ribald. But did you not know it was rude to proposition a woman so, when she was already married?"

He stood and faced her, sweat beading his brow. Maddie had no time to brace herself for the blow. The strike to her face momentarily blocked all consciousness. Nothing but blackness assailed her and her knees buckled.

"I'm going to kill you the first chance I get, Lord Ribald. Let her go. She has nothing to do with your spite. Your argument is with me. Fight me. Or are you too much of a coward to face such a challenge?" William yelled.

Maddie gasped when the knight behind her pulled her back up to stand. His hands around her wrists stung and pinched. She heard Lord Ribald reply, his voice unaffected and bored.

"On the contrary, Lord William. However, I cannot be bothered to clash swords with you. You see, I have already won."

Maddie willed her wits to return. "Why this revenge, Lady Veronica? What did I ever do to you?" Her head pounded and her voice sounded strange. Maddie tried to wipe her bloodied and swollen lip against her shoulder.

"Why should I tell you anything?" Lady Veronica said, walking over to her brother and throwing Maddie a dismissive glance over her shoulder.

Maddie shrugged. "Since I'm to die today anyway, what could it hurt."

"Tell her," a voice said, from the other side of the grove.

Lady Ribald, Veronica's mother emerged from the shadows. Her gown of dark green velvet camouflaged her well in the trees. Her ladyship's face held the same hate and revenge that her children bore. Maddie wondered what was wrong with them all.

"I do not care to, Mother. I'd rather her die not ever knowing," Veronica said, her mouth set in a pout.

Lady Ribald came to stand next to her daughter, her eyes void of emotion. "Then I shall tell her."

Lady Ribald clasped her hands before her and met Maddie's gaze. "The reason we have always hated you, Lady Madeline, is not so much for yourself. Although you were a thorn in my side I could have well lived without. 'Tis not the reason. Why today will be your last is merely because of your parentage," she said.

"Why," Maddie asked, baffled. "Why strike against a child who has nothing to do with what their parents have done."

Lady Ribald laughed. "Your father mistreated me badly many years ago, threw me out in the middle of the night and without a coin to my name." Her voice hardened in hate, her eyes looking past Maddie as if seeing the past. "Even when I begged him to help me, the mother of his child, he refused."

Maddie gasped and looked at Veronica. No, the woman could not be her half-sister. Lady Ribald cackled, understood Maddie's train of thought.

"Yes, Veronica shares your blood. But not for long. With your death, the Aimecourt bloodline will cease to exist. The lands to the once great family bequeathed to the Baron of Kingston. Your family forgotten. I have never forgiven your father. He should not have turned against me. I am not inclined to forgiveness. He should have taken heed."

Maddie looked to William. "Was that why our fathers fought a war all those years ago? The conflict was never over lands, was it? It was over my father having an affair with a woman who was unmarried and of aristocratic blood."

William nodded. "'Tis correct, Madeline." William turned to Lady Ribald and pointed his finger. "You knew the risks when entering a liaison with a married man. You knew Anthony Vincent was a cold, heartless baron. Father was wrong to have listened to you all those years ago. Your foolish error was never worth the war we started. Nor is your revenge on Madeline," he said, his hate for them tangible in the air.

Maddie reeled. She was going to die today and all because of a woman's scorn. She shook her head at the absurdness of it all.

Maddie struggled when the knight pulled her arms higher behind her back. She bit back a scream. "I'm surprised, Lady Ribald, that you would go to all this trouble for revenge. Have you spent years planning this? Pathetic way to live a life. Almost makes me feel sorry for you, my lady. I may die today, but you gave your life away many years ago. Wasted it on revenge and hate, when you could have turned your back on such disappointments and moved on. Like any sane person would," she said, her upper arm muscles burning.

Maddie looked over at William and ignored Lady Ribald and her hastened steps toward her. A cry tore from her lips as Lady Ribald's hand slapped her face. William blurred in her vision.

"So," Lady Ribald said, rubbing her palm. "Shall we move on with this?"

"You will never get away with this," William declared. "Kingston and Aimecourt are favoured by the king. He will hear of this treatment, and you will be lucky if it is only hanging that stretches your ugly necks."

Maddie's attention flicked to Lord Ribald when he

walked toward her. Her skin crawled as his finger traced down her neck and onto her chest before he lifted the necklace and sat it over her gown.

"'Tis the beauty of our plan, Lord William. The king will believe us."

"Why so sure?" William asked, his eyes wholly focused on Lord Ribald's back.

"Because of me."

Maddie gasped as Sir Alex stepped from behind the armed knights circling them. He smiled and looked at her, his features no longer declared friendship. He pushed the hood from his head, condescension twisting his lips into an unattractive sneer. Tears welled in Maddie's eyes. She watched with sickening comprehension Lady Veronica walk toward Sir Alex. Their attraction was clear for all to see. They loved each other? But...how? When?

"I'm going to kill you," William said, quiet savagery to his words. A shiver stole down Maddie's spine at the menace in his tone.

Sir Alex laughed, pulled Veronica against him and looked down at her with warmth. "You could try, Lord William. But why would you kill a favoured knight. One who even now is on his holding in Kent?" He kissed Veronica. "Enjoying some welcomed time with his future wife," he said, his eyes intent.

"You're going to marry...her?" Maddie asked.

Sir Alex laughed. "Don't sound so surprised, Lady Madeline. Do you think you are the only person who should find happiness in life?"

Maddie swallowed. "No. I believe everyone is due such gifts. But I do not believe you will find it with her," she said, nodding her head in Veronica's direction.

"Jealous, my lady," Lord Ribald said, smirking.

Maddie looked at him with disdain. "Hardly. I just

think your future brother-in-law's an idiot." Maddie looked at William and smiled, his answering chuckle warming her chilled blood.

"Edward!" Lady Ribald yelled, looking at her son.

Maddie fought her restraints as a sword-wielding knight came to stand before William. Their eyes met as the blade came to sit before his heart.

"What are you doing," Maddie asked, looking to Lord Ribald.

Lord Ribald sniggered then ripped the necklace from her neck. She gasped as the ribbon bit into her flesh. Maddie kicked toward his shins and missed when he stood back, his focus on the ring in his palm.

"Beautiful. Even more so, since it will send you back to whence you came." Lord Ribald paused. "You see, Lady Madeline, we know your fears and are willing to test your absurd theory. If it works, William will live without the woman he loves for the rest of his life. Not only because you will cease to exist, but because we will kill the Lady Madeline of old who will remain." He ran his finger over her lips, his eyes heating with every word. Maddie looked away from the rotting soul that filled Lord Ribald's eyes. "Perhaps I will kill you with a sword after all." He laughed. "Revenge is sweet, is it not?"

"You will face punishment one day, Lord Ribald. It may not be by my hand, or that of my family. But there is a greater judge who all men must bow to. And when you do, I think you'll find your head will come to sit next to your knees," Maddie said.

"Smart words will not save you now, Lady Madeline."

Maddie fought as he grabbed her hair and twisted it. "Let me go. Don't—"

"Calm yourself, my lady. I will not force the ring on

you. You will do it for us." He shrugged. "For entertainment, you understand," he answered.

"You're a mad, sick, medieval bastard," Maddie yelled into his face. He laughed, then looked at the knight still holding her. "Release her."

Maddie stumbled when the man threw her forward. She righted herself and rubbed her shaking arms, bit the inside of her lip as the blood started to flow back in her veins.

"Put the ring on, Lady Madeline, or watch Lord William die," he paused. "Slowly."

"Kill us both and you would never get away with it. Not even you are brave enough, Lord Ribald," William said, his voice cold. Maddie looked at the ring Lord Ribald held out to her then looked to William. She had not missed the trace of desperation in her husband's tone.

"Would you like to test my resolve, my dear?" he said, his eyes not moving from hers.

William shook his head. "Don't put the ring on, Madeline! Do not listen to a word he says."

Maddie frowned. Should she call Lord Ribald's bluff? Would he kill William and then her? With the unhinged look in his eyes she realized he would do both and enjoy every minute of it. Tears pricked her eyes as her gaze met that of her husband's. She fought the nausea in her stomach and took the ring. She looked down at the pewter band that was uncomfortably hot to hold.

"William?" She looked across at him.

"Madeline, don't. Please..." he begged.

"They're going to kill you. I cannot allow that," she said, hating to see him distraught.

"He will not. He cannot, unless Lord Ribald wants to die himself. The king is privy to our life and what lay between us. My men will tell the king of the servant spy belonging to Lady Veronica and he will see the falsehood behind Lord Ribald's tale. He will remember the animosity between our two families and the reason for it," William said with a pointed look at Lady Ribald. "Our sovereign is no fool," he continued. "Do not doubt my word."

Lord Ribald looked at William in surprise. A blossom of hope rose within Maddie.

"Not as close to the king as you would have us believe, Lord Ribald," William said, his words laced with sarcasm. "Foolish man," he declared.

"The servant you speak of is already dead. My men are loyal, and we have been careful not to be seen in these parts. Lady Madeline's death will not be traced to me. Your threats, my lord, are for naught," Lord Ribald answered.

William met her gaze. The silence between them, a death-blow in itself. Maddie shook her head not wanting this to be her last moment with him.

Hunting horns sounded.

"You are too late, Lord Ribald. My men are upon us."

Lord Ribald looked at her, his lifeless eyes dismissing William's words. "I always follow through on a threat."

Maddie screamed as cold, razor sharp steel sliced through her abdomen. She clasped Lord Ribald's shoulder as he wrenched the blade free from her body. She looked down at the red stain growing large on her dress. She placed her hand there in a feeble attempt to stop the bleeding. She looked up and noted the feral excitement that swirled across his face.

"Madeline. No!" William roared, more men holding him from her.

"'Twould be wise to put the ring on, my lady. Before even your future life is lost to you." Lord Ribald said, sheathing his sword.

Maddie dropped to her knees. The trees whizzed around her. She clasped at the leaf litter beneath her hands and fought to breathe. She looked to where William stood and tried to smile through the pain. "I love you," she whispered.

"Madeline!"

"You are everything to me," she said, unclenching her fist to clasp the ring. "I wish we had more time. I want you to know that Aimecourt and its people are proud to have you as their lord."

"Don't put that ring on, Madeline," William yelled. "Please, I beg you."

Maddie ignored the men who laughed around them. Her mind frantically took in William's every feature, captured his image for the empty years ahead of her. The lump in her throat burned as hot as the ring. She hesitated over her choice to obey Lord Ribald. But she refused to be the cause of William's death. She would rather be alone for the rest of her days than be the cause of his demise. And if she stayed, she was dead anyway. There was no hope.

"I love you, William. I think," she winced, gasped, as pain tore through her. "That I loved you since the day you kissed me in the woodshed."

"Madeline..."

"I will miss you forever."

"I love you, ma chère."

"My patience wanes," Lord Ribald said, his eyes hard but glittering in anticipation.

Maddie took one last look at William as she slipped the ring on her left hand. Nothing happened at first and a rare spark of hope that she was meant to stay blossomed in her mind. Not that such a thing would be good now, as they had ensured her death. No sooner had she had the thought, noises of her previous life assailed her. She heard a car horn, traffic sounds, a TV news program.

Her eyes met William' as the life she loved started to blur. An image of a different kind started to form. She had been here before. It was all so awfully familiar. She tried to scream, hold on to the past that had started to fade. William's eyes, frantic and unsure, held onto her. A gaze that would haunt her forever. The last of the trees melted and spun away and a new picture appeared before her.

Maddie looked up at her work desk, her night light on, her computer with the star simulation screensaver working away. She was home in Greenwich. Her hand strayed to her stomach: no stab wound marred her skin and no pain assailed her body other than the ache in her heart. She looked down at her hand, her eyes unsurprised to see the ring gone also. Her eyes welled with tears. Just as William was, nine-hundred years dead.

CHAPTER 19

W hat had happened? Lady Madeline lay down upon the cool leaf bed of the forest and inhaled the damp air into her lungs. Lungs that burned with every breath she took. What was going on? She clutched at the wound in her stomach and knew the minutes she had left in this world were few. How could travelling to the church to marry the Baron of Kingston have gone so wrong? And why did she not remember how she got here this day? Or where here was. Or why men, many of them, stood around her.

Horns sounded in the distance.

Shouts and commands rang out. Madeline shut her eyes and blocked out the images. She did not want her last thoughts in this world to be gruesome. The way she was dying was horrific enough. She clutched at the leaves underhand as pain sliced through her. She wanted someone to help her. She did not want to die alone. Why had this happened to her? It was not fair.

She looked over to a man whom another held. He fought against his restraints, his eyes furious and cold. She focused on the one she assumed had stabbed her, his face mocking, his blade bloodied. Calmness swamped her as she watched the mighty lord. He looked familiar for some unknown reason, but she could not remember meeting such a man.

Madeline shut her eyes as tiredness filled her veins. She fought the dark, opened them and stared at the canopy of trees above. The green branches swayed in the wind, their creaks sounded soft against the words of men around her. So this was it. This was her end. A tear rolled down her cheek, one she neither had the will to wipe or stem. At least it was a memorable death, she supposed. Even if, perhaps, a little too soon in her short four and twenty years of life. She shut her eyes in wait. It would not be long now...

🐾

WILLIAM WATCHED MADELINE UPON THE GROUND, HER body squirming in pain. He met Lord Ribald's laughing eyes and watched the bastard clean his sword on a nearby branch. Revenge, such as he'd never known, fired his blood. Promised the laughing smirk on Lord Ribald lips, would be cut from his face. In fact, the murderer would be lucky to keep his head atop his shoulders before this night fell.

William's blood pounded in his veins and he would kill them all. He would avenge Madeline. Or he would die in the battle of doing so. His knights, their war cry loud in the forest, rode into the clearing. They made fast work of the Lord Ribald's small war party. William joined the melee and killed the knights who had kept him from Madeline with their own swords. The knight's puzzlement over the unexpected attack from Kingston men was all the time William needed to strike them dead.

His soldiers, better trained and more loyal, did not take long to control the murderers who followed the crazed Lord Ribald of Castle Dee. William tore through men as the wind tore through the trees. Every knight who stepped toward him met his blade, was sliced down, and his eyes never left those of his prey.

William's mind replayed the tormenting scene of Madeline's body lurching back as a blade tore through her flesh. Her face one of shock, pain, then comprehension. Lord Ribald had stabbed her with no remorse or pity and William had lost her. She was gone. Lord Ribald would pay with his life.

His hand flexed on his bloodied sword. His gaze focused on Lord Ribald standing before him. No men from Castle Dee stood, all were cut down, dead or dying. William's knights surrounded the baron.

"'Twould be foolish for you to kill a baron, Lord William," Ribald said, his voice no longer smug. The man's gaze darted about, looking for an escape that was not there.

"Then I am a fool," William stated. The blow was clean. He watched absently as Lord Ribald's head rolled to the ground. The dead baron's body stood upright for a moment before collapsing forward.

He welcomed the death of a man who had taken his wife.

Justice.

William dropped his sword on the ground.

"M'lord," Sir Torent said. "She is here."

William turned and found his first knight holding Madeline's hand, his other upon her stomach holding a bandage against the wound that was already soaked through. William ran to her. He kneeled and grief tore through him twofold. The woman's eyes had dimmed, her lifeblood already a part of the forest floor. It was not his wife, but the woman whom he was supposed to have married those many months ago who lay before him.

His Madeline was gone.

Her chest rose the smallest fraction, her breath shallow. William took in her wound. Beheading was too good a death for the bastard. Lord Ribald's strike had been lethal in its appointment. He looked down and noted that the gash severed upwards within her abdomen. Madeline's death would be painful and at length, no one deserved such an ending. Especially her. An innocent woman who paid for wrong doings of someone else's past. William looked down at the frightened woman, her features uncomprehending and confused. He swallowed the lump in his throat as his wife's eyes met his. Madeline's eyes.

"Pray...I do not understand?"

William wiped the hair from her face, her brow covered in a sheen of sweat. What could he say? There was nothing he could tell this woman in the short time she had left that would make any sense. He shook his head.

"Keep your strength, my lady. Do not talk." His eyes met those of his first knight. She will be gone soon enough, the silent words between them.

"But..." Madeline said, and then proceeded to wheeze as if struggling for breath.

William's eyes narrowed, wished her gone and out of pain. "'Twas not your fault, Lady Madeline. Your travels this day put you between battles not of your making. I'm sorry," he said.

"You know me?" she asked.

William's heart crumbled in his chest. "I know who you are, my lady."

Madeline's eyes closed, her breathing slowed with every second. It was his fault. He should never have started relations with Lady Veronica. He should not have allowed his father's hatred toward the Baron of Aimecourt to cloud his judgement.

"I'm cold."

William pulled Madeline into his arms and held her tight. Tears rolled down his face as his wife breathed her last. He shut his eyes at the pain that consumed him. He had lost them both. He looked over Madeline's shoulder and met those of his enemies who still lived, of Veronica and her mother, and his hatred had no limits.

"Kill them."

"M'lord, is that wise? How will you explain their deaths to the king?" His first knight said with concern.

"I will not. Bury them. Their disappearances are not my concern," William said, his eyes hard, unforgivable.

"William, please. I did not mean—" Veronica pleaded.

"Thank God 'tis not me at the end of the blade that will kill you, Veronica." William looked to his men. "Kill them or face me."

The women's screams rang out and then silenced moments later. Sir Alex and Lord Ribald in wait for them at the gates of hell. William clutched at the limp form in his arms, her body cold and lifeless. He clamped his jaw and stood. Settled her in his arms and started to walk toward Kingston Castle.

Their home...

His men stood aside and watched in silence as he carried Madeline from the grove. His tunic soon dampened from her blood. William tried to remind himself that this woman in his arms was not the woman he loved, but another.

A cold comfort that did not work.

He clutched her desperately against him and held her close to his heart. The wind lifted her hair, wafted a scent of lavender, the hint of jasmine. Memories assailed him. He staggered before he righted his footing.

Madeline...

It broke his control.

He yelled and cursed God for taking her from him. It was too soon. They had not said goodbye. Were never given the chance.

This was wrong.

They were meant to be.

They would be.

Even if it took all eternity.

CHAPTER 20

"Maddie, what are you doing?"

Maddie gasped, her hands clenching on the leather book in her hands. She controlled her breathing and reminded herself she was safe. Back in the twenty-first century where no one wanted to kill her. Only when Jackie repeated the question a second time did she answer.

"I'm looking up my family history. I remember mum saying she kept all the records in a box. But I can't find it anywhere." Maddie stood and dusted off her pants, her teeth working her bottom lip. "What if I've lost them? What if I threw them out by accident after their deaths?"

Jackie came into the attic and started her own search. "Don't worry, we'll find what you're looking for. But I still think you need to let go of this dream you've had."

"It wasn't a dream," Maddie snapped back and instantly contrite when Jackie's eyes widened in shock. "I'm sorry. I didn't mean to snap at you. But it wasn't a dream." Maddie shook her head, not willing to believe that for a moment. Not after all the months she'd spent with William. No, it couldn't possibly have been a dream.

Jackie dragged out a box from under some linen throws and started to look. "Even if you find this family tree book, what good will it do you? Your experience happened nine-hundred years ago. Lord William is long gone. He can't come back." Jackie's face was a look of sorrow and concern. "I worry for you, Maddie, that's all. I've never seen you like this before."

Maddie turned her back so her friend wouldn't see the stream of tears that were ever-present. She didn't need Jackie to be concerned, she was concerned enough herself. Even if she found the book and noted Lady Madeline was a distant relative, what would she get out of it? It may prove in some small way that what had happened did, in fact, occur, but what use of such knowledge. Jackie was right. There was no going back, and no way in which to see William again. Maddie wiped her nose with the back of her hand then turned and sought out another box not previously searched. "I'll be all right," she said to her friend. "I know there's no going back. I just miss him, that's all."

"He sounds wonderful," Jackie said, with a consolatory smile.

Maddie nodded. "He was."

They searched for some time in quiet, both silent with their own thoughts. After an hour or so, Maddie went downstairs and made a coffee for them both.

"Maddie!" Jackie called her voice muffled by the two floors above. "I think I've found it."

Maddie left their coffees on the counter and ran up the stairs. She burst into the attic and walked over to Jackie who sat on an old chest, her face alight and looking at an old tome she held on her lap.

Maddie sat next to her. "Let me see."

The book was thick and its pages discoloured with

time. The once-smooth leather binding was now ripped down the spine, parts of it rotted away entirely. Maddie looked down on the first page and noted the ancient text, some of it in French due to her Norman descent. The first record was in 1018 in a town named Falaise. Maddie shook her head in awe.

"Do you think the book is that old?" Jackie asked, her fingers lightly touching the page.

"I don't believe so," Maddie said. "I doubt paper of the eleventh century would have lasted so long, especially the way mum had it stored." Maddie frowned. "No, I believe the book has been rewritten at some time."

"Is there any mention of Lady Madeline?" Jackie asked.

Maddie turned to another page seeking out the year 1078. Eventually she found a notation. It read: Lady Madeline Vincent, born Aimecourt Castle, Cumberland 1078. Died Kingston Castle, Cumberland 1103. Mêlée, the cause of death.

Jackie frowned and met Maddie's gaze. "I don't understand. How is it that you're related if she died."

Maddie went back a page and looked at her parents' parentage and family. Both had siblings who married and had children. So she did have family that were alive in that time, but who knew where they had been. "It must be through one of these other family lines, I suppose," Maddie said

"But your last name is St. Clair," Jackie said.

Maddie frowned. "I must stem from a female child who married and their name changed."

"Is there any mention of William?"

Maddie bit her lip to mask the pain his name brought forth in her chest. She read all the notes around Lady Madeline's entry. "Look Jackie," Maddie said, pointing to an entry on the page. "It states the Baron of Kingston died some months later. His body never recovered." Maddie met Jackie's eyes. "He died." Her vision blurred.

Jackie placed a comforting arm about her shoulders. "Well, of course he did, Maddie. It was so very long ago. And England wasn't the tamest then. I'm so sorry."

Maddie bit her trembling lip. So was she. She looked back down to the entry. So Lady Madeline and Lord William weren't a figment of her imagination. They had lived and Madeline was a distant relative. "I never knew of these people before, Jackie. I'm telling you the truth. So how could I know of them now?"

Jackie rubbed her arm. "I don't know. Perhaps what you experienced really did happen. Stranger things have been known to occur," she said, smiling. "Maybe you are one of the lucky ones to have been blessed."

Maddie shut the book and clasped it to her chest. "Do you think they still stand?"

"What?" Jackie asked, her brow furrowed.

"Aimecourt and Kingston Castle."

"I don't know. I suppose some form of what was once there maybe still standing." Jackie paused. "What are you thinking of doing?"

"I think I may take a little trip," Maddie replied, standing and walking toward the attic door. "Could you look after my shop while I'm away? I shouldn't be more than a week."

Jackie stood and followed. "Do you think this is wise? It's one thing to believe what you do, but to now go and see an estate that is probably rubble...I don't think it's healthy."

"I'm only going to have a look. I have to say goodbye. I'll be back by the week's end and ready to move on, I promise," Maddie said.

Jackie smiled and hugged her. "Okay, I'll watch the shop. But be careful and come home safely."

Maddie nodded and walked into her room to pack. "I will, I promise."

WILLIAM DOWELL SAT UP IN BED; A COLD SWEAT RAKED HIS body, leaving him confused and uneasy. He clutched his chest, had a moment of panic where he thought he might be having a heart attack. Surely at thirty-two years of age he was a little young for that. He sighed in relief as the pain gradually subsided.

He pulled his legs from under the blankets and sat over the edge of the bed. He swiped a hand through his hair while he tried to think of the reoccurring dream that had been haunting his nights for weeks. Never had he dreamed such reality before. Everything was so vivid and real, he could almost believe he had lived it in the flesh.

"Mmmm, darling, come back to bed."

William looked in thought down at the lithe form next to him, a feminine hand straying from under the quilts to run down his back. Once he would have turned and laid claim in the early morning, but not today. In fact, by day's end, he'd be lucky if his lover ever spoke to him again. He sighed and walked to the window that overlooked his estate, land that had been in the family for generations. He watched the morning sun burn away the frost that covered the ground.

He dressed quickly and quit the room, his steps down the staircase sure and purposeful. There had to be something wrong with him. Perhaps he ought to see a doctor. William paused at the base of the stairs and tried to remember when last he'd seen one.

He walked into the breakfast room and sat down to coffee already steaming at his customary place. He couldn't keep on like this.

"The usual, Mr. Dowell?"

William looked up at his butler and nodded. "Thank you, George." Within moments his breakfast sat before him; the smell of bacon and eggs wafted up, but didn't spark his appetite like it usually did.

"What time would you like the car brought around for your travel into Egremont?"

William swore when he remembered the annual fair held in the closest town to his estate. One of the oldest families in the region, he acted yearly as the benefactor and opener of the daily festivities. William looked at his watch. "Have it out front in a half hour. And could you instruct Paul to come directly home to escort Sue to the airport, she'll be leaving today."

His butler started but bowed. "Yes, sir."

William rubbed a hand over his jaw. What was he doing? Going to push a woman out of his bed and home because of another who haunted his dreams. Obviously, he was mad or very much on the way to being so. Perhaps he ought to make an appointment to see that kind of doctor.

"On behalf of my forefathers and proud citizens of Cumbria, I now proclaim the Egremont Medieval Fair open!"

William smiled and cut the red ribbon before stepping aside and allowing the populace to march through the town square in their costumes and fanfare. He nodded and spoke to the people while images of another time assailed his mind.

Serfs working the fields, their hands work worn and dirty. A great hall with a dais and a blazing fire behind. Rushes underfoot and knights supping at table. A woman more beautiful than he'd ever thought possible sat before them all, her shoulders strong yet delicate. Her laughter as she spoke to the lord beside her carefree and honest. The lord smiled down at the woman, his expression filled with love.

The sound of drums pulled William from his strange thought. He looked out to the townspeople and concentrated on the goings-on around him. He glanced across the sea of heads waving at the parade and spotted his driver waiting by the car.

William frowned and looked down when a slight tug on his jacket caught his attention.

"Are you opening the castle today, Mr. Dowell?"

William bent down to speak to the little girl with golden curls and the bluest eyes he'd ever seen. "I am. Are you going to come and have a look?"

"Me mum is going to take me up." She turned her head as if contemplating something. "Why don't you live there anymore?"

William laughed. "Well, it burnt down in a great fire in 1784 and the family didn't have the funds to rebuild it. So we built a smaller home not far from the site instead."

"And now you let people go through it."

"We do," William answered, smiling.

William looked up as the little girl's parent rushed over and apologized. He waved the woman's concern away and said goodbye. Then turned on his heel and moved toward his car.

"Home, Mr. Dowell?" His driver asked.

"Yes, but go via the castle, Paul. I want to check something."

William twisted the family ring around his little finger on the drive back to the estate. Foreboding sat heavy in his stomach. But why, he couldn't figure. The car made a turn and William looked out the window and glimpsed the castle huddled in the valley beneath. A hazy memory of a wagon and horses coming over the crest swam in his mind. A woman stepping down from the vehicle then lifted up to sit before a man on horseback.

William slumped back in the car seat. Why was he seeing these pictures? Always the same woman and man. But who was the man? His features were hazy and never clear.

The car pulled to a stop. William stepped out and walked toward the gatehouse, unchanged since the day the castle was built. He walked into the outer bailey and toward the ruined keep, its four walls still intact and some higher floors as well, but inaccessible due to the main stairwell having collapsed in the fire.

William stopped as another vision swam in his mind. He turned and walked into a small stone shed beside the gatehouse and noted the woodshed sign on the door. His throat closed over and his mind reeled at a memory.

He had been here before.

With the woman from his dreams and he had kissed her. He touched a hand to his lip and could still feel the sting of that nip. And the memory of Lady Madeline finally became clear.

His wife.

His love.

His life.

William walked back out into the bailey and saw Kingston Castle as it once was. A working medieval village. His home and sanctuary. Pain tore through him at seeing the place of his birth brought low by an accidental fire and passing years. He stumbled and held the woodshed door for support.

People milled about the grounds, some picnicking while others walked the battlements all in awe of this once grand home. And all unaware that William Dowell, once the Baron of Kingston Castle, was among them, torn between two times and with not the faintest idea on what to do next.

৩৶৩

MADDIE'S HAND RAN DOWN THE COLD STONE OF KINGSTON Castle's gatehouse, her mind bedazzled once again by the estate.

She stepped into the shadow of the doors and walked toward the outer bailey. It was all here but different from what she remembered. Where there was once dirt, cobbles now lay. Buildings that once stood tall and proud now lay in ruin. Signage was their only link to what they once were used for.

Maddie walked toward the keep and smiled when she remembered the first time she came here. She looked up to the building and remembered the dread that assailed her. Her fear of not knowing what type of man she had married. How wrong had her fears been. For he had been the best of men. Perhaps a little blind to her charms at first, but she'd soon fixed that little problem.

Maddie pushed the longing for him down in her heart and walked into the castle. She headed along the corridor that led into the great hall. Rushes no longer crunched under foot. A fire did not burn. There was no dais or trestle tables.

She looked about the vacant space. Walked toward the

hearth and bent down to touch the blackened bricks from fires past.

"It's not possible."

Maddie jumped and hit her head on the stone mantle. She turned and searched the room then sighted a figure that stood in a doorway. Her heart thumped hard in her chest. "William?" she said. Her feet, like lead, wouldn't move. "Is that you?"

"Yes." William walked into the light and Maddie felt her mouth drop open. Gone were the hose, tunics and chain mail and in their place stood a suit cut to this modern man's perfect form.

Maddie pinched her arm to check she was not asleep and having this wonderful dream. "How?" she asked.

William slipped a ring off his finger. "This," he said. "I found it some weeks ago. Apparently, it's an old family heirloom. I'm not normally superstitious but since the day I placed it on my finger I've been having dreams." He met her eyes. "About you." He paused and walked closer to her. "I believe the ring has somehow given me access to a past life of mine."

Maddie took a step then stopped. "So, you remember everything about this past life and the life you are living now?"

"I do. Seems the ring has changed the way it works over the past nine-hundred years," William said, smiling at her for the first time.

Maddie walked the rest of the way and stopped before him. She took in his features, not one difference could she notice. Unable to stop herself, she cupped his face and revelled in the warmth beneath her palms. His jaw was so familiar and comforting after weeks of unhappiness. "Are you real, or a figment of imagination?"

William clasped her hands and brought them before

him. "I'm no ghost, Madeline. I was born William Dowell in 1978 but I have the memory of William Dowell, Baron of Kingston as well."

Maddie stepped back. "Do you remember everything about my life with William?" she asked. This was so strange. She almost felt like she was cheating on William just talking to this man before her.

"I do. I remember everything about you and me. Everything," he said, with emphasis. Maddie's stomach flip-flopped at the heat in his gaze.

"You look just like him." Maddie bit her lip trying to stem the tears that threatened. "What happened to you?" she asked, sniffing.

"You died in my arms. Well, the Lady Madeline who was left behind did." William walked over to a glassless window and stood with his back to her. "I was crazed, angry, and desperate for you. I went into a stupor of drink. Travelled to London and stayed there. I could not face life at Kingston or Aimecourt."

Maddie came to stand beside him. "History states you died some three months after my death. How did you die?"

"I don't know." William paused then looked down at her, his eyes haunted with grief and remorse. "I did return home when I remembered how you believed I would be a good lord to our people. I could not fail you again. I had already failed once by letting Lord Ribald take your life."

Maddie clasped his hand and frowned. "You never failed me, William. You brought me back to life," she said, meaning every word.

He grinned. "One night at Kingston I placed the ring on my finger. It had not even entered my conscious that the ring may throw me into your time. But I believe it did. And into a life of a future relation," William said, his fingers massaging the top of her hand. "After that it was like I had two memories but one life. It was very strange and I still don't believe what has happened to me."

Maddie nodded, her mind a whirr of thoughts. "That day in the woods, had I not put that ring on I would have died too, William. Perhaps you may think me a coward for doing it, but I didn't want to die. In some small part of my mind, I held onto the hope that I would see you again. I found you once; surely there was a possibility of finding you again."

"I never thought you a coward, Madeline."

Maddie heard the truth behind his words. She turned his hand and looked down at the ring. She ran a finger over the smooth metal and looked up at him. "I never thought you may enter my time and find me."

William smiled. "I have an ache to hold you. Can I?" he asked.

Maddie went willingly into his arms and welcomed the familiar strength and warmth of his embrace. A healing balm to her heartbroken soul.

"I've missed you, Madeline." His hold increased. "God, you have no idea how much."

Maddie pulled back and looked up at him. Could not thank divinity enough in having William back. "I've missed you too." She leant up and kissed him then pulled him into her arms. Never wanting to let him go again.

"Say something to make this real. Tell me something that only William would know," Maddie asked.

He laughed a sound as familiar as Maddie's own. "Will you come for a walk with me, ma chère? I believe I was to show you my castle's stone enforcements."

Tears welled in her eyes at the familiar endearment. "I always loved it when you called me that. And yes, I'd love to see the improvements, my lord. Better late than never," she said, laughing.

He kissed her lips, a lingering embrace that promised so much more to come. "I know," he answered, his voice tinged with desire. "Will you marry me, Madeline?"

Maddie smiled already nodding. "Yes, I will marry you. Again."

William laughed and pulled her into his arms. "I am never going to let you go."

Maddie met his gaze and saw the truth behind his words. She chuckled as he scooped her into his arms. "This is new," she said as her mind started to adjust to the situation. "Is this the medieval William or the twenty-first century William who is carrying his fair lady this day?"

"Both," William replied his face serious.

William carried her out into the bailey and toward the gate. Maddie ignored the startled and curious stares of the people that milled about. "Where are we going?"

"Home," was William's curt reply.

"What about my tour?" she asked.

"That can wait," he said.

Maddie smiled and cuddled into the curve of his shoulder, her arms secure around his neck. She kissed beneath his ear and felt the familiar shiver that ran through him at her touch. "And where would home be exactly?"

"Not far from here. And this time, my lady you will be accompanying me."

Maddie bit her lip, remembering their wedding day in 1102 and William's refusal to allow her to travel with him in his own conveyance. She looked up and watched his profile, couldn't believe her luck in finding him a second time. And it was her William, such memories were not privy to everyone. Her throat closed as emotion swamped her.

"I love you," she said.

William stopped and looked at her, his eyes pools of emotion. "I love you more."

Maddie grinned. "Perhaps some other time, my lord, but today I do not feel like quarrelling with you."

"'Twould seem we are in agreement, ma chère."

Maddie kissed him. "Well, it was bound to happen one day."

"True," William replied. "And it only took nine-hundred years."

Maddie laughed.

Dear Reader,

Thank you for taking the time to read *Defiant Surrender*! I hope you enjoyed my medieval time travel romance.

I'm forever grateful to my readers, and I can't thank you enough for picking up and reading my books. If you're able, I would appreciate an honest review of *Defiant Surrender*. As they say, feed an author, leave a review!

If you'd like to learn about my other time travel romances, may I suggest you start with my Regency time travel, *A Stolen Season*? I have included chapter one for your reading pleasure.

Tamara Gill

A STOLEN SEASON

*One small mistake in the past will change everything about her
future...*

*Archaeologist Sarah Baxter just broke one of the biggest rules of time
travel: leaving a piece of 21st-century equipment in 19th century*

Regency England. Unfortunately, when she goes back to retrieve it, she makes an even bigger mess of things— resulting in the death of an English earl. Now his brother is not only out for revenge, but he also has Sarah's device. Which means an entirely different approach.

It doesn't occur to the new Earl of Earnston that his charming acquaintance is responsible for his brother's death. He is merely swept away by a passion that threatens his very reputation. Yet he gets the distinct impression that Miss Baxter is hiding something from him. Now Sarah must find a way to steal back her device, hide the truth about the earl's brother and—most importantly—to not fall in love...

CHAPTER 1

England 1817 – Kent

S arah shifted in the saddle, the weight of her saturated clothes heavy on her shoulders and hindering her seat. The horse's pounding hooves, as loud as a drum, echoed in her ears. She kicked her mount and urged him over a small hedgerow, her determination not to be caught overriding her common sense.

Rain streamed down her face, but she couldn't stop. The future of TimeArch depended on it. Her father's years of research. The hundreds of hours spent working on man's greatest, most sought-after ability. Sarah slowed her mount to canter through a fast moving ford, the stones causing the horse to stumble, making the short trip across painfully slow. Time was up. She had to get away. Though the horse grappled and slipped up the other side of the muddy bank to continue on, apprehension still threatened to close her throat in panic.

The mount missed a step, and Sarah clutched the saddle, cursing the weather. She flashed a glance over her shoulder and cried out her frustration into the sheeting rain at the sight of the Earl of Earnston not two horse-lengths behind.

His gaze held hers, and with fearless determination, he urged his mount beside, clutching for her reins.

"Let go." Sarah punched his hand and kicked out, trying to push him away. All in vain, as it seemed nothing could deter his resolve.

"What does it do?" he yelled, pulling on her reins.

The horses bumped hard, and Sarah fought for balance. "Let go, Lord Earnston. You'll kill us both."

He released her reins for a moment as a large bush separated them. But, at blistering speed, he drew beside her again.

"What's so important you'd risk your life?" he hollered over the storm.

Sarah shook her head. Why wouldn't he leave her alone? Damn her clumsiness in his library. Had she never knocked over the vase—had she not tripped, for that matter—the Earl would never have investigated the sound. But he had, and he'd found her hands deep in his collection of peculiars, stealing a device not of this time.

"Forget about it. Forget me," she yelled through the deluge. "Go home!"

"No," he said, spurring his horse ahead of hers.

A low-lying tree branch slapped her face. Sarah cringed at the stinging pain. The night was perfect for thievery, but not for escape at breakneck speed. If they kept up the chase, it was only a matter of time before one of them was killed.

"Stop your horse!"

Sarah shook her head and kicked her mount on. No matter the dangers, she couldn't obey him. The future, her father's business, everything she held dear hinged on her getting away. "I won't. My lord, please leave me."

He clasped her reins and jerked hard. Sarah's horse bucked at the aggressive manhandling, and she tipped awkwardly to one side. Feeling herself about to fall, she reached out and clutched at the earl. Her reins slipped from his grasp as his strong arm encircled her waist, struggling to keep her from falling between the two horses. But it was little use. Her horse veered away, and she fell hard against his lordship's mount. Her fingers, cold and wet, slipped for purchase on his saddle, but his horse shied away from her.

"Hold on, I have you." With an oath, the earl tried to pull her up, but gravity was against them.

"I'm slipping. Let me go. I'll bring you down." Sarah's feet dragged on the muddy, stone-strewn road, and she braced herself for a bruising fall. A gentleman to the last, he shook his head and tried to pull up his horse. "Please, let me go." But it was too late. His horse slipped, and they both hit the muddy track with a sickening thud.

Sarah landed on her knees and rolled. Leaf litter and mud entered her mouth, and her leg twisted, shooting a pain into her hip.

Moments later, the wet nose of her horse nuzzled her neck. She dragged herself to a sitting position and wiped mud from her face and eyes with a torn remnant of her shirt. Taking deep breaths, she waited for her body to stop shaking. The only sound was the rain slapping at the leaves through the foliage above.

Then she saw the motionless form on the muddy track. Dread clawed up her spine. Sarah crawled to where the earl lay, his head twisted at an awkward angle. She rolled him over and cursed his vacant, lifeless eyes.

"Don't be dead. Please, don't be dead." She felt along

his stubbled jaw and around to the nape of his neck where a lump protruded from his skin.

Unable to accept what her eyes told her, she bent over his chest and listened for a heartbeat.

Nothing.

Sarah slumped back on her haunches and covered her face. She'd killed him. She'd killed Lord William, the blooming Earl of Earnston! "I'm so sorry," she said, tears mingling with the rain in a muddy pool at her feet. What had she done? The earl wasn't supposed to die, not yet, and certainly not by her hand. Within the space of half an hour, she'd probably wiped out a complete generation of earls. She'd stuffed up history, and she couldn't undo it.

Not even her father could.

A crack of lightning illuminated the dark forest, and Sarah quickly stood when the silhouette of a horse and man loomed from the shadows.

"Halt!"

Ignoring the warning, she grappled to mount her horse as the fired-up mare pranced. "I'm sorry," she said to the cloaked figure as he dismounted and ran to the earl's limp form sprawled on the ground.

He bent, felt for a pulse, and gasped. Her stomach rolled with nausea knowing what she'd done and what he'd discovered. A flicker of silver flashed as he stood.

"Stay where you are or I'll shoot you as dead as my brother."

Sarah turned her head, frantically searching for someone to help. Perhaps Richard, her partner, who'd warned her not to go tonight. He said the weather wasn't good for safe getaways.

And he was right.

It was the flash of lightning outside the earl's library window illuminating a menagerie of severed and stuffed animal heads that had scared the shit out of her, and she'd tripped. The earl heard the commotion, came to investigate, and caught her red handed.

Idiot.

"Please. It was an accident." She watched him cock the pistol and wondered if he'd actually shoot a woman. His voice, trembling with shock and hate, told her he would.

"Get off the horse—now."

"I can't." With shaking fingers, she grabbed the reins. "I'm sorry." She turned her horse and kicked it hard.

"Halt, I say."

She ignored the steely voice that thrummed with warning. Instead, she pushed her mount into a gallop, the horse slipping, unable to move fast enough. And then the shot, followed by searing pain, deafened her and deadened the sound of the thrashing storm to a vague rumble.

Her fingers tingled and warmth seeped along her skin. Sarah looked down, expecting to see her arm missing. He'd shot her! "Get up," she hollered to the horse, ignoring the pain and the curse from behind.

The horse gained its footing, and she peered over her shoulder, the silhouette of the man all she could see. Cold rain set goose bumps over her skin, yet she pushed on, determined to make the inn and London. The second decade of twenty-first century London to be exact.

⚜

WITH A RUNNING NOSE AND AN ARM THAT THROBBED AND ached with every thud of the horse's stride, Sarah sped through the night. At last, she spied the glowing lights of the inn, a welcome beacon on this frightening journey.

Wet and bedraggled, like a beggar woman, she entered

the common room and waited for the innkeeper to acknowledge her.

He walked toward her and eyed her injured arm with suspicion. "Ye have an injury there, lass. Do I need to summon the doctor for ye?"

"No. I'll be fine." She tried to pull what remained of her jacket across her wound, then gave up. She placed her sodden shawl about her shoulders, thankful she had thought to pack it in her saddlebag.

"What can I get ye then, love?" The innkeeper leaned on the counter, his fetid breath making her queasy stomach roll even more.

"Can you direct me to Mr. Alastair Lynch's room please? I believe he has a chamber set aside for a Miss Phoebe Marshall." A knowing twinkle entered his eyes, and Sarah's own narrowed in comprehension.

"Right this way, Miss Marshall."

The smell of wine, beer, and cooking meat permeated the air, making her nose twitch. She needed help and quickly. Summoning a smile, she thanked the innkeeper as he walked her to a door and nodded.

"This is ye're room, Miss. I'll send up a girl when I have one spare if ye wish for a wash."

"Ah, yes, thank you. That would be most kind." Sarah waited for his heavy footfalls to disappear down the stairs before she entered the chamber. The smell of damp wood burning and the flicker of two candles greeted her along with a pair of boots warming before the hearth.

Sarah shut the door and sagged against it. Relief poured through her veins, making her legs shake. The wound thumped, reminding her of the injury, and she pulled her shawl away to look.

Richard jumped from his seat. "Sarah, good God, you've been shot!"

"I have, but that's not the worst part. I also tripped in the Earl of Earnston's library and both brothers came to investigate. I ran." She walked over to the bed, threw her soggy shawl to the floor, and flopped onto the hard mattress. "He caught up with me when I escaped on horseback. How, I have no idea."

Richard came over and pulled her boots from her feet. "Knew the area, I suppose." He checked her wound. "It doesn't appear too bad. Just a graze by the looks of it."

Sarah glanced at the bloodied mess. "Yes. But that's not all. I killed Earnston."

Richard reeled as if slapped. "You killed the Earl... Good God! How? Why?"

She shook her head and gave him a rundown of the night's events. Sarah shut her eyes, not wanting to remember his lifeless gaze staring up at her or the horror of knowing she was the cause of his demise. "His brother came upon us and demanded I stay. Of course I ran. I had to. And...he shot me."

With one hand, she undid the first button at the front of her shirt, stood, and tried to pull the sleeve off her arm.

"Here, let me help you." Richard pulled out a knife. He cut the garment from around her arm and slid it down over the soaked chemise underneath.

Nausea pooled in her throat. "We have to go home. I need this wound seen to and..." "What?" he asked, brow furrowed.

"I don't feel well. It's not very nice being shot."

Richard chuckled, walked over to a bag in the corner of the room, and shuffled the contents. "I should imagine not. I think I have some morphine in here and a tetanus jab, also. Should be enough until we're home tomorrow."

Morphine sounded heavenly at the moment. A knock sounded at the door, and Richard allowed a wide-eyed maid to enter. With steady hands, she placed a steaming bowl of water and linens on a side table.

"Will ye be needing my assistance, Miss?" the servant asked, her eyes stealing to Richard, then back to her.

"No. Thank you. I shall be fine on my own." Sarah smiled and waited for the door to close before walking over to the water. She soaked a small cloth, dabbed it against the wound, and washed the blood from her arm. The injury was surprisingly clean—a flesh wound that wouldn't require stitching. A small mercy this night.

"Does it hurt?" Richard flicked the morphine needle. "Yes, so hurry up and give me the shot; you know I have a low pain threshold."

Within moments, the ache faded, and a warm fuzzy feeling settled over her. Richard fussed with her arm and bandaged it. Then she collapsed before the fire and stared at the flames that produced hardly any heat. What a mess she'd made of things. How was she ever to explain to her father?

"Are you good, then? I'll see you in the morning if so." Sarah nodded. "I'll be fine. The wound's hardly bleeding, and I intend to go to bed before the morphine wears off." She paused, knowing she had one more confession this eve. "Richard, I lost the mapping device."

He frowned. "You don't have it?"

"It was in my pocket, but it must have fallen out when I fell. I have no idea where it would be now."

He came and sat across from her, two fingers pinching the bridge of his nose. "Should we go back tomorrow and try and find it? Do you think the earl's brother knew what you'd stolen?"

"No," she said, standing and walking to the window to look out over the blackness illuminated at intervals by distant lightning. "Not yet at least. And with any luck the mud and rain has hidden the device, and all will be well. Well, at least," she said, turning back to Richard, "until my father finds out what I did and the shit hits the fan."

"Shit's right." Richard paced the room, his footfalls loud in the small space. "This could be a disaster. Now he knows the device is valuable, for whatever reason, and will keep it hidden."

"That's if he finds it." She rubbed the bandage on her arm. "Let's not worry about it now. We'll be home tomorrow, and Father will tell us what to do."

"He certainly will. And let's hope for our sakes he's in a better mood than when he sent us here the first time."

Sarah sighed and pulled back the woolen blankets and coarse linen sheets on her bed. "Don't hold your breath. My father's going to be furious. Not only have I lost a device that could blow the lid off TimeArch and all its secrets, I've changed the history of a family forever."

⚘

ERIC, NOW LORD EARNSTON, CURSED AND THREW HIS flintlock to the ground. Pain seized his chest when he glanced at his elder brother, dead at his feet. His eyes narrowed on the small female figure disappearing into the shadowy forest surrounding his family's estate.

He stumbled to his knees and allowed the rain to wash away tears shed for his closest confidant. A man of honor about to start a new chapter when he married his betrothed.

No longer. Thanks to the woman who'd snatched his future away.

He ran a hand through his hair, wondering why his brother had followed the chit at such breakneck speed.

With trembling fingers, he closed his brother's eyes, sending a prayer to God.

The woman had stolen something. But what?

He whistled for his horse, who, as if sensing death, hung his head lower with every step toward him. Eric lifted his brother, not an easy feat considering his size, and laid him over the saddle.

At the sound of crunching under his boot, Eric bent and frowned at the mud-soaked silver device beneath his feet. He rubbed it against his jacket and stared in amazement at the highly polished silver trinket.

A trinket his sibling had treasured for reasons Eric could never fathom.

With another rolling boom of thunder, he mounted his horse and turned for home to announce the death of his much-loved brother, bury him, and see justice served on the wench who took his life. Then he would find out why the object was so valuable—and why his brother and the woman would risk their lives to possess it.

ALSO BY TAMARA GILL

Royal House of Atharia Series
TO DREAM OF YOU
A ROYAL PROPOSITION
FOREVER MY PRINCESS

League of Unweddable Gentlemen Series
TEMPT ME, YOUR GRACE
HELLION AT HEART
DARE TO BE SCANDALOUS
TO BE WICKED WITH YOU
KISS ME DUKE
THE MARQUESS IS MINE

Kiss the Wallflower series
A MIDSUMMER KISS
A KISS AT MISTLETOE
A KISS IN SPRING
TO FALL FOR A KISS
A DUKE'S WILD KISS
TO KISS A HIGHLAND ROSE
KISS THE WALLFLOWER - BOOKS 1-3 BUNDLE

Lords of London Series
TO BEDEVIL A DUKE

High Seas & High Stakes Series

HIS LADY SMUGGLER

HER GENTLEMAN PIRATE

HIGH SEAS & HIGH STAKES - BOOKS 1-2 BUNDLE

Daughters Of The Gods Series

BANISHED-GUARDIAN-FALLEN

DAUGHTERS OF THE GODS - BOOKS 1-3 BUNDLE

Stand Alone Books

TO SIN WITH SCANDAL

OUTLAWS

ABOUT THE AUTHOR

Tamara is an Australian author who grew up in an old mining town in country South Australia, where her love of history was founded. So much so, she made her darling husband travel to the UK for their honeymoon, where she dragged him from one historical monument and castle to another.

A mother of three, her two little gentlemen in the making, a future lady (she hopes) and a part-time job keep her busy in the real world, but whenever she gets a moment's peace she loves to write romance novels in an array of genres, including regency, medieval and time travel.

www.tamaragill.com
tamaragillauthor@gmail.com

Made in the USA
Middletown, DE
16 January 2024